Praise for Anne Leigh Parrish

"Anne Leigh Parish has written a collection of stories that deserve a place on the shelf next to Raymond Carver, Tom Boyle, Richard Bausch, and other investigators of lives gone wrong. These are potent and artful stories, from a writer who warrants attentive reading."

– C. Michael Curtis, Fiction Editor for *The Atlantic Monthly*

"Parrish is in possession of such precise prose, devilish wit, and big-hearted compassion, that I couldn't help but be drawn into the hijinks and mishaps of the Dugan family. I'd compare these linked stories to those of George Saunders, Elizabeth Strout, or perhaps even Flannery O'Conner, if Parrish's voice weren't so clearly and wonderfully her own."

– Ross McMeekin, Editor, *Spartan*

"Anne Leigh Parrish's fine debut novel is a moving and graceful tale that delves deeply into the histories of two sisters. Parrish, in clear, deft prose, explores the meaning of motherhood, faith, loyalty, and tenderness; effortless, she carries her readers through four generations of one family's checkered history of love."

– Mary Akers, author of *Bones Of An Inland Sea*

"Anne Leigh Parrish's *Women Within* offers a panoramic window into the lives of three remarkable women whose lives intersect at the Lindell Home, where Constance Maynard is an elderly resident and Sam and Eunice serve as her two principal caregivers. Deftly coursing through time in the spirit of Penelope Lively's *Moon Tiger*, and exploring the meaning of romance and motherhood with the depth of Carol Shields' *The Stone Diaries*, *Women Within* negotiates multiple points-of-view to offer a pitch-perfect and strikingly insightful exploration of what it means to be a caregiver, and to be cared for, in modern America. Rich in family secrets and unexpected emotional twists, *Women Within* resonates with truth, beauty and wisdom. Rarely have I been so sad to close the final pages of a book and to say farewell to a world that I relished so much."

— Jacob M. Appel, author of *The Topless Widow of Herkimer Street*

the

amendment

a novel

anne leigh parrish

Published by Unsolicited Press

www.unsolicitedpress.com

Copyright © 2018 Anne Leigh Parrish
All Rights Reserved.

For information, contact the publisher at

info@unsolicitedpress.com

Unsolicited Press Books are distributed to the trade by Ingram.
Printed in the United States of America.
Pre-assigned Control Number: 2017958797
ISBN:978-1-947021-09-9

To John, Bob, and Lauren – forever and always

contents

the

amendment

a novel

anne leigh parrish

chapter one

At first, Lavinia thought Mel was joking. Mel was never not joking. That rubber snake in the freezer last Christmas, during their annual open house. Her husband, Chip, knew he'd put it there. He also knew how Lavinia felt about snakes. She didn't scream or even gasp when she discovered it, flaked with ice, lounging on a bag of frozen peas. She wanted to take it into the living room and toss it into Mel's lap. That would have served the smartass right.

But she couldn't. Mel was Chip's best friend.

She might have understood what Mel was trying to tell her on the telephone if his words hadn't been punctuated by sobs. She'd never known him to be a drinker, but supposed he could have started out of the blue. Some men wept when they hit the bottle, right? Potter, her ex, surely had. That was later, though, near the end of things. Back when he thought he was still secure in her affection, he'd been affable when drunk, sometimes singing as he hauled her to her feet for a quick spin around the kitchen, always when she was paying bills or going over the children's homework. He just couldn't stand to see her working, which was funny because she worked all the time, back then, at least.

She quickly decided that Mel was sober, that the sobs were a put-on to enhance the joke.

"You can cut the crap Mel; I'm hooked. I'm just standing here waiting for the punchline," she said.

She'd taken the call in Chip's study. The enormous windows were crystal clear because they'd just been washed. Lavinia insisted on clean windows when the weather warmed. The winter had been brutal even for upstate New York, full of lake-effect snow, and spring came late and gloriously. Then, all of a sudden, the trees made a wall of green. There seemed to be no glass separating her from the yard, as if she could simply put down the telephone and step over the low wooden sill and escape. But the sky was angry that day, and thunder boomed in the distance. There had been flashes of light, and Lavinia found herself wondering vaguely if Chip was enjoying his golf game despite the threat of rain.

She then understood that Mel was talking about the weather, too, and the storms rolling through. He wasn't making a joke. He was trying to pull himself together in order to deliver his news plainly, so that Lavinia would understand.

Chip was dead. Struck by lightning on the ninth green.

2

Lavinia sat down in the chair by the heavy, solid desk, the chair he'd sat in himself only that morning.

"Are you sure?" she asked.

The police were on their way to her now, Mel said. He called to prepare her, to spare her the shock. He was on his way, too. She needed him. She needed friends and family around her. Would she call her children? Did she want Mel to call them?

"No," she said, and hung up.

She thought of Chip's beautiful son, Ethan, out in Berkeley. And of the two other sons in Texas, whom she'd never met. They would have to be told. Would they come to the funeral? What kind of funeral did Chip want? They'd never talked about it. Chip was—had been—eighteen years older than she. Seventy-one was a good age to think about your final arrangements. Cremation or burial? She wondered how much of him was left after the lightning got him.

"Zap!" Lavinia shouted.

She was alone in the house. Alma, the housekeeper, had gone out. Lavinia was troubled that she didn't remember exactly where. Alma had said. She always said.

Of course, Lavinia's eye fell immediately on the photograph of Chip, just inches from her elbow. It was an old one, taken when he still had most of his hair, when he wasn't jowly, before the bifocals that were always perched on the top of his head. She supposed he kept the picture to remind himself that he'd once had a bit of dash, though it always struck her as odd. Not vain, necessarily, just sort of desperate? She couldn't imagine wanting to see how she used to look. The past was the past. Nothing to cling to, or wish to have back.

She put the photograph face down on the desk.

"You and your goddamn golf," she said.

He'd been obsessive about the game, yet was always over par. They'd talked once about aging, fading passions—his way of apologizing for losing interest in sex—but his love of golf never waned. Now it had killed him.

She covered her face with her hands. The scent of her perfume let her depart the moment. The doorbell ended that calming blankness her mind had found in the floral notes on her wrists.

The police officers looked as young as her own sons—late twenties, early thirties. Their sympathy seemed genuine. When they said what they'd come to say, the shorter one, standing closer to her than the other, extended his hand in case she felt faint, got wobbly, collapsed in a heap. Her footing stayed firm.

CPR had been tried, they said. She wondered by whom. Surely not Mel.

"What about the clubs?" Lavinia asked.

"I'm sorry?"

"His clubs. Will they be returned?"

The officers didn't know. Was there someone they could call for her? Someone who could come over?

Just then, Mel arrived. He entered the circular driveway so fast that his tires chirped. Lavinia and the officers were standing in the open doorway. As Mel hustled his round little self up the brick walk, rain fell. He pushed past the officers.

"Oh, Lavinia, my dear!" he said and embraced her roughly. She allowed his touch only for a moment, then stepped away.

The officers left. Lavinia went into the living room, her favorite room in the house, and sat down on the new white leather sofa. She pressed her palm to the smooth surface. It was untroubled and sleek.

Mel joined her and took her hand.

"A terrible tragedy," he said. His eyes were rimmed with red. He looked awful, all mashed up. But then, he never looked too good. He sobbed. He dabbed his nose with wadded up Kleenex he must have had in his other hand. Lavinia didn't think he'd taken it from his pocket.

"I think we should pray," he said.

"I've got a better idea."

She stood, and for a moment felt as if she might lift off the ground and rise through the ceiling and the rooms above to meet the open air, still alert and roiling with storm. She went to the wooden cart next to the wall of built-in bookcases where many colorful paperweights were displayed. She had bought every one, right there in Dunston, from an old high school acquaintance who'd set up a little atelier after surviving breast cancer. She couldn't remember the woman's name. Her face was clear, though. Long, with a bent nose. She had a cynical manner because her husband had left her during her illness.

Lavinia poured two glasses of single malt scotch. She had acquired a taste for hard liquor over the past few months. She could hold it, too, something Chip had remarked on lovingly more than once.

Mel took the glass she gave him. He drained it. The experience seemed to stun him. Lavinia sipped hers slowly, so that it might approach her softly, gently.

She patted his hand, and he leaned against her desperately, clumsily, the way a scared child does. She put her arm around him without a second thought, the response was that ingrained. But when his lips found hers, tasting of liquor and salt, she pushed him back.

"Get a grip," she said.

Mel sat up, once again in his own space.

"I told him to be careful. We could all see the lightning. The caddy told us to take cover under the tree," he said.

"You're not supposed to stand under a tree in a thunderstorm."

Mel nodded miserably.

"Look, why don't you go home for a little while? Take a shower, get something to eat. I'm okay, really. And Alma will be here any minute."

"It's too sad there, without Sandy."

Sandy was Mel's pet parrot. She'd taken flight the week before. The cleaning lady left the cage door open. Why, Mel couldn't say. She was usually so careful. Maybe she wanted to get back at Mel for something. He'd told this story with his usual mirth, imitating the way the cleaning lady walked, bobbing from side to side, saying he knew Sandy wasn't far, just out exploring the natural world, and would come home when she realized no one had quite the elevated vocabulary Mel did.

"She might be by now. You better go and see," Lavinia said.

"I'd rather stay with you."

She stood up. Mel did, too. He followed her reluctantly to the front door, where he clearly longed for another hug.

Lavinia shook her head at him. She waited until his car left the driveway, then returned to the living room and had more of her drink. She took the half-empty glass to the kitchen. She'd call the children from there. She couldn't stand going back into Chip's study.

The thought came brutally, and with so much force that she had to sit down. The house, and everything in it, was now hers. Chip had made sure of that. She didn't get all his money, though. There were the three sons to consider first. But she'd have enough. She knew the details of the will inside and out. They'd talked it over many times. He'd wanted the discussion, not she. She never saw the need. She was no gold digger. She married him because he came along at a time in her life when she was looking for a way out. Sure, money helped, but it wasn't what drew her to him. She was caught by his calm, steady nature, his genuine kindness, and the clumsy, heart-felt efforts he made with her children. She hadn't made him happy, and she understood later that he hadn't really expected her to. He needed his life to have meaning. She provided it.

She should call Angie first. Angie was thirty-two, her eldest. Angie had grown fond of Chip because, after being an angry teenager and young woman, she'd found a gentle vein of forgiveness for the man who'd replaced her beloved father. She and Potter were still close. Angie had a rare trait. She could see one's flaws, yet overlook them.

Angie would be at work now. She wouldn't mind the interruption, certainly not for such important news. Yet Lavinia suddenly couldn't bear hearing her voice.

She picked up the phone. For a moment, she couldn't remember the number she'd called so often. Then it came. The phone rang five times.

"Hello?" Potter said.

"It's me."

She hadn't called since Christmas. They'd talked a lot the autumn before, when Lavinia was tearing her hair out about Maggie and Marta, their twin girls, who were living the high life in Manhattan and up to no good, Lavinia was sure. Potter's wife wasn't happy about the long and frequent conversations. She suspected, rightly, that their children were not the only subject they discussed.

"Chip died."

"Jesus. When?"

"About an hour ago."

"Heart attack?"

"Lightning strike."

"Holy crap. What are the odds of that?"

"Yeah."

Another pause followed. In the background on Potter's end, there was a loud, mechanical sound.

"Hold on. Mary Beth's sanding drywall. I'll move outside," Potter said. The noise lessened. "Okay. You want me over there?"

"Yes."

"Give me twenty minutes."

"No, it's okay."

"Lavinia."

"Really. I just wanted to let you know."

"You call Angie?"

"Not yet."

"Do it now."

"Okay."

They hung up. Lavinia put the phone in its cradle. She wandered back to the living room. She sat on the creamy sofa.

The tears welled.

Why couldn't you have been like that before?

If Potter had been firm and decisive, acted like a man, not a child, everything would have been different.

chapter two

Life number one had been girlhood. Not a happy time, particularly, not tragic either. Lavinia drove herself hard, even then. She'd wanted to go to college. Instead, she got married. Potter swept her off her feet; he was that good-looking, not to mention incredibly charming and an absolute demon in the sack.

Life number two had been motherhood. Screaming babies, exhaustion, the growing distance between her and Potter that led to her walking out and marrying Chip.

Chip was life number three. This creaky house, money, at first an immense relief, then boredom, restlessness, resentment over her own shallow needs.

Now began life number four: widowhood.

Her new status gave her a position of honor at Chip's funeral. People she'd never met murmured and shook her hand. One old woman kissed her cheek. Mel assured her that these were Chip's business acquaintances, not friends. Lavinia already knew they weren't friends, because she'd never met most of them. The other two players from the doomed golf game didn't show. Mel had asked them to stay away, saying the sight of them would unnerve Lavinia.

The two Texas sons sent their regrets. Mel filled Lavinia in on all that bad blood. They'd been devoted to their late mother, which was why they hadn't attended Chip and Lavinia's wedding. Lavinia knew all that. But there was more. It seemed that Chip had had a number of flings that the mother learned of and suffered deeply over. Lavinia couldn't imagine Chip as a philanderer. The thought almost made her laugh. The mother was deeply depressed for years and years, and the sons thought Chip had ruined any chance she had for happiness. Lavinia thought she sounded like a sap. Your husband does something like that, you give him the boot, not take to your bed.

Ethan came all the way from California. He was the youngest son. Lavinia made sure to give nothing away to remind him of that one visit twelve years before. He remembered her subtle advance, though. She could tell. His eyes held a warm light and something else, maybe a touch of whimsy? That was going too far. She'd done nothing in the least amusing. Pathetic was more like it. She could admit to that.

He sat next to her on one side, with Mel on the other. Lavinia listened to the quick service performed by someone the funeral home had engaged. Chip wasn't a church-goer. Ethan bowed his head. When Lavinia glanced at him to gauge the depth of his sorrow, he was looking at his cell phone. He saw her and smiled. She was done for then. She could feel it starting all over again.

Maybe now that …

She stopped herself. Everything had been on her side only. Yet now, she wasn't so sure, with the way he was looking right down inside her. When the service ended and everyone stood, he put his arms around her and whispered how sorry he was. She returned the embrace. He let go first.

Figures.

Back at the house, Angie took charge. She made sure everyone visited the drinks table, the food table, had a chance to say things about Chip. Angie was in her element, given the age group of the guests. She was a social worker at the Lindell Retirement Home. Timothy, a year younger than Angie, had attended the service, then had to return to work. Her youngest, Foster, was also present. He hadn't liked Chip much, although he was very devoted to Lavinia. He and Mel now had her bracketed on the white leather living room couch. Ethan was somewhere else, maybe wandering around the home he'd grown up in.

He'd asked Lavinia if she planned to sell it. She didn't know. She had no plans, and then one suddenly took shape. She would go on a road trip. Miles of highway. So many places she'd never seen before. What did Ethan think of that? Maybe she could end up in Berkeley sometime next month. Unless, of course, that wouldn't be convenient?

"I'm not sure. I think Laura was thinking of Hawaii around then."

"Laura?"

"My wife."

Well, well. Chip hadn't said anything about Ethan remarrying. Maybe he hadn't known. Clearly, Ethan wanted to keep that part of his life quiet, since he hadn't even brought her along. Had he been worried how Lavinia might react? Did he want to spare her heart? No, that was too much to hope for.

She went into the powder room. She looked at her reflection.

Lavinia Dugan, you are one stupid fool.

Dugan? What the hell happened to Starkhurst? The name you've had for the last fifteen years?

She stood there trying to figure herself out. Someone knocked on the door.

"Mom?"

It was kind, little Foster.

"You okay?" he asked.

Lavinia opened the door. She reached up to smooth down his hair. At twenty-seven, the gesture visibly irked him, but he said nothing. He never did.

"The twins called. They're coming up from the City. They didn't know the funeral was today," Foster said.

"How the hell could they not know? I texted them. You texted them. Angie texted them."

The twins, Maggie and Marta, were twenty-eight and shared an apartment in the Village. Neither worked. Both had artistic aspirations. Maggie thought she might paint. Marta wanted to act. They lived on an allowance Chip had given them. An allowance that was now in jeopardy if Lavinia pulled the plug. The feeling of power was overwhelming, until she summoned the image of their angry, miserable faces.

"I should make up their rooms," Lavinia said.

"They can do that. Or Alma."

"God, poor Alma."

Alma had been with Chip for years. She remembered the first Mrs. Starkhurst, and had had trouble adjusting to the invasion of Lavinia's noisy brood. After they all moved out and it was just Chip and Lavinia, her mood was no sunnier. She spent a lot of time off her feet in the kitchen.

Lavinia returned with Foster to the living room where the group of mourners had thinned. Alma was sunk down in an armchair. The black dress Lavinia had bought for her to wear was too small. The buttons in front looked like there were about to pop open.

Ethan wasn't there. Angie said he'd left, asking her to give Lavinia his very best.

If that was your best, then it's just as well, isn't it?

"You look a little wobbly. Better sit down," Angie said.

"I'm fine."

More people were leaving now, quietly and slowly, out of deference to her grief.

She *was* sad. She would miss Chip. She missed him already, and it had only been three days since he got fried on the green. She missed everything. Potter, her children back when they were nice people—which wasn't fair because Angie and Foster were still nice. The twins, not so much. And Timothy was occasionally warm, though he never came around at all. He seemed root-bound with his roommate/girlfriend in the little house Chip had bought for him the year before. She missed what she might have done with her life besides be a mother and sell manufactured homes, though she'd been very good at the latter and that particular path had led her right to Chip, since he'd owned the company she'd worked for.

anne leigh parrish

Her tears flowed. Angie came to her side, helped her to sit, and gave her a piece of Kleenex.

"Chip wouldn't want you to be sad," she said.

"I've never been to Indiana. Your father had an uncle in Indiana. Did you know that?"

"No."

"He promised to take me, and we never went."

Lavinia wailed and laid her head on Foster's shoulder. Alma leaned forward, in Lavinia's direction, yet remained silent.

"It's okay, Mom. We'll take you to Indiana, won't we?" Foster asked Angie.

"Sure, we will. As soon as you're feeling better."

Lavinia lifted her head up.

"I'm fine. I'll go alone," she said.

"Don't be silly. One of us will go with you. Just give us a little time to plan," Angie said.

Lavinia shook her head. She would wander where the wind took her. Maybe, if she were lucky, it would take her so far she'd never come back. But then, that would leave her five children there without her. They no longer needed her, though. The question was, did she need them?

Lavinia stopped her blubbering. She felt as if some softer air now filled her lungs and that she might just lift off after all.

17

chapter three

Freedom was delayed. She wanted to take Chip's beauty, a 1960 Mercedes, which turned out to have a bum engine. The mechanic turned the key and asked her to listen to that ominous pinging sound. She said it always did that. Plumes of blue smoke belched from the exhaust pipe. Chip seldom used it, and drove a Lexus most of the time. Lavinia hated the Lexus. It reeked of bland. Her own car was a Land Rover, a beast and a gas guzzler. She left the Mercedes with the mechanic and called Mel.

Could he give her a ride home?

He'd be delighted!

The first thing he told Lavinia when she got in the car was that Sandy had returned. She'd picked up some new words, one of which, "douche bag," suggested that she'd spent time in the company of young people. Mel lived across a ravine from a fraternity whose antics could be heard every weekend. He confessed to liking the idea that they'd taken her in, made much of her, and then returned her to freedom.

"Jesus, Mel," Lavinia said.

"Sorry. Didn't mean to talk so much about myself, with poor Chip …"

"Pushing up daisies?"

Mel winced. It had only been nine days since the funeral.

He asked how long the car would take to fix and if she minded postponing her trip until then. She wasn't postponing anything. She just needed a new set of wheels.

"You can take my Jeep," Mel said.

Lavinia hadn't known that Mel had more than one car. The one they were in was a Porsche. It had a stick shift. Mel used it poorly. Lavinia feared for the clutch.

"Old? New?"

"Old. It's a '64."

"Miles?"

"Lots."

"It'll dump me somewhere."

"I wouldn't hand you a lemon."

"That would be bitter, if you did."

Mel fell silent. Lavinia wasn't usually witty. That, along with the yearning for new sights, was something born of Chip's demise. It was as if she stood in the soil fertilized with his own flesh. The idea was loathsome, at first, then made perfect sense.

When they reached her home, Lavinia felt obliged to offer Mel a drink. He said no thanks.

"Really overdid it the other day," he said.

"Understandable, under the circumstances."

"I will come in for a glass of water, if that's okay."

Alma was in the kitchen, perched sloppily on one of the stools at the long stone counter. She was reading a battered paperback. She looked up. She fixed Mel with a stony stare. Lavinia had long thought Alma didn't like Mel. She'd hidden it from Chip all those years, and now there was no need.

Opens the door for all of us, doesn't it?

Lavinia poured Mel his water, then went through the dining room to Chip's study. Mel followed.

"What's all this?" he asked, meaning the pile of roadmaps on Chip's desk.

"I need some idea where I'm going, don't I?"

"Sure."

Lavinia sat in Chip's chair. She pressed one of the maps flat.

"I'm going north first. Maybe to Maine," she said.

"Not a lot in Maine."

"You've been?"

"Once."

Lavinia didn't know much about Mel, only that he'd once worked with Chip in some capacity before her time, then retired. He'd been married once, years before. He had no children.

20

Mel helped himself to the easy chair on the other side of the desk. It was large and deep and made him look like a little boy. A bald little boy with a white mustache.

"He had a friend with a cabin. We went one fall. Hunting season," he said.

"Chip hunted?"

"Well, none of us actually did, but that was the plan."

The friend, Rob, was someone Chip had been at school with.

"Yale," Lavinia said.

"That's right."

At the time—and this was years before, shortly after Chip lost his first wife—Rob had his own set of problems. For one, his wife was divorcing him. Seemed she'd fallen for her tennis instructor, which Mel thought was funny, hence several jokes about powerful serves, but then he realized that Chip didn't care so much for the off-color remarks, even though they were made in Rob's absence. In fact, at that point, Mel hadn't even met Rob. Then Rob invited Chip to come bag a moose. Chip had hunted as a boy. He thought the change would lift them both out of the doldrums. Mel was brought along for comic relief—if the jokes wouldn't hit too close to home.

Mel knew nothing about guns. Not a damn thing. Chip knew about shotguns. Rob carried a pistol, though per the

21

Department of Game and Wildlife, they were not to be used in the killing of animals. Rob's cabin was lavish. That was the only word for it, really. It had a high-end kitchen, propane stove, a huge stone fireplace, and three bedrooms, which meant no one had to bunk together. A girl from the village came around to clean up after them, which was convenient as all get-out, except that she was an early bird and woke them all up just as the sun was rising.

They set off with their gear, following a trail Rob said moose were routinely spotted along. They came to a blind, built years before by Rob's father. The place depressed him. Everything depressed him at that point because of the fickle wife. The talk turned from the matter at hand to how to cheer him up. Mel tried a few harmless jokes, all leaving infidelity far off to one side as a subject, the best of which was this one: "Three bear hunters drove out into the woods. They came to a sign that said Bear Left, so they turned around and went home."

Even Chip worked on him by saying sometimes these things were all for the best. It was common knowledge that the marriage hadn't been happy. Then Chip and Mel said they should turn their attention to bringing down that moose. Chip was on station, shotgun loaded, closely watching the trail scattered, Mel remembered, with the most gorgeous fall leaves. In fact, Rob commented on the foliage more than once, saying that such beauty was always a shame because it never lasted. In fact, nothing ever lasted, and one had to accept that all good things were doomed. "Oh, for God's sake, Rob," Chip had said. "Lighten up, will you?" Mel recalled Rob laughing, or at least smiling, seeming to accept how silly he sounded. Mel went to the viewpoint, crammed up next to Chip, longing for a moose to come along and save what was becoming a very bleak day.

At first, they both thought the shot came from in front of them, another hunter too far down the trail to be seen. Chip was furious. "What's that damn fool trying to do, scare off any four-legged creature out there?" But quickly both he and Mel realized that the shot they'd heard had come from Rob's pistol. His hand had shaken so badly that the bullet missed his head completely and tore a hole through the thin plywood of the blind. Chip yanked the pistol out of his hand, emptied the chamber, and tossed the bullets out the window into the brush. What happened next came as a shock to Mel—even more shocking than Rob's having tried to kill himself. Rather than offer support or sympathy, Chip was enraged. He told Rob he was a coward, a weakling, a whining baby who needed to grow up and face the situation like a man. Okay, he was miserable, but misery passed. Had he considered his daughter, then only eleven years old? What would her life have been like, knowing that her father hadn't loved her enough to stay alive? Chip told Rob to stand up—he'd made the failed suicide attempt sitting with his back to the wall—and account for himself. At that point, Rob was weeping, and Mel found himself quite unnerved. Chip hauled Rob to his feet and smacked him hard, right across the face. Mel had never thought Chip capable of violence. Had Lavinia?

She thought about it. Once, he'd been upset at one of his sons for wanting money to invest in what later became his plumbing business. It was soon after she and Chip married; the memory of how he and his brother—not Ethan—had boycotted their wedding was still raw. There'd been a long and difficult phone call, right there in that den, Chip sitting where Lavinia now sat. Lavinia listened just beyond the closed door. Chip's voice rose and fell, then became quite loud as he said, "You're one sorry bastard!" Then the phone hit the cradle hard. Something landed on the floor with a heavy thud. Clearly, Chip had thrown something. Then all was quiet within, and Lavinia tiptoed away. Chip emerged some time later looking hollow. He smelled of liquor. Lavinia had him sit while she stood behind him, rubbing his shoulders. He never shared exactly what had been said between father and son, although she knew the money was eventually sent.

24

"What happened to Rob?" Lavinia asked.

"He went back to his life. Got divorced, and then married again."

"That always seems to be the outcome, doesn't it?

"People shouldn't live alone."

Lavinia realized from the way Mel was looking at her that she'd unwittingly broached a dangerous subject.

"Well, I've spent most of my life married, and I'm looking forward to being single," she said.

"You wish Chip hadn't died, though."

"Of course."

"Are you sad?"

"Honestly, I don't know."

Mel looked out the window in a state of what Lavinia assumed was either disappointment or disgust.

"That sounds bad. I just can't feel much of anything right now," she said.

"You cried at the funeral."

"Did I?"

"Profusely."

"Isn't that what one does? Cry at funerals?"

"And at weddings."

Lavinia never cried at weddings. The last one she'd attended had been for Potter's sister, Patty, and her long-time boyfriend, Murph. They held the ceremony right there in Chip's house. They both looked completely crazy about each other as they stood there before the judge, gazing into each other's eyes. Lavinia sat with Chip, held his hand, remembered when it had been their turn only a few years earlier, before another judge, with two witnesses provided by the Courthouse staff.

She'd felt such gratitude! And a warm sense of safety. Her worries were over. Her children would have enough to eat, new clothes, higher education, because Chip had made it clear he wanted to make all of that possible. It seemed to please him a great deal to put before her everything he intended to provide. At the time, in their earliest days, Lavinia thought he'd been taken for granted much of his life. He was a generous person, and fundamentally a kind one. Dark moods, when they came, were random. Lavinia had asked about them. He didn't speak on subjects that were hard to pin down.

"I'm just trying to sort things out," Lavinia said.

"You need help with the estate? Didn't Caruthers say he had it all in hand?"

Caruthers was the lawyer, a tall, ancient man who'd spoken so quietly to Lavinia at the funeral she'd had to lean in close enough to pick up the spicy scent of his aftershave.

"The estate's fine. I'm just getting ready for this trip."

26

"How long will you be gone?"

"I don't know. A few weeks, maybe more."

"Just driving?"

"Not all the time, no. I'll stop here and there."

"Sounds pretty vague to me."

Lavinia stood up. Mel was boring her now.

"You'll tell me where you're going. I mean, you'll check in, won't you?" Mel asked. He also got to his feet.

"Sure."

"And if I want to reach you?"

"Then call me. What's so hard?"

"What if you're driving and don't want to pick up?"

"Jesus, Mel! Then call Angie. She'll pass the message along."

"I don't believe I've got her number."

"She works at Lindell."

"Oh, that's right. You know, I looked that place over not too long ago. Sort of planning ahead, I guess you'd say. Didn't strike me as terrible. They seem to have lots going on."

The finer points of their local retirement community weren't of much interest to Lavinia. She'd assumed that as Chip got older, she and Alma would take care of him. Well, mostly Alma, to be honest. Lavinia had done her share of caregiving. Alma, with no husband and no children, hadn't.

After Mel left, Lavinia sat awhile longer with her maps. The idea of the open road began to scare her, as if something might swoop down from above and carry her off. Then she realized she was replaying Chip's death, recasting it into a private nightmare of her own. She felt haunted, not by Chip's ghost, but by her own cruelty.

That last morning, they'd quarreled over breakfast about her wanting to repaper their bedroom. They'd had it done only the year before, but she'd no longer cared for the pattern of bamboo leaves. Chip, for once, thought she was being silly. He'd indulged her for years, then suddenly refused to, and she was dismayed. Dismay turned to smoldering rage, which brought steel to her words.

"Why on earth do you care what's on the walls? You never notice anything."

He was taken aback. He said he noticed everything she did in the house, and everything about her, as well. He noticed, for instance, that she was letting her hair grow long, that she'd had her nails done two days before, and that she'd served French wine for dinner all that week.

She made no reply. Mel called to say perhaps they should call off the game because the weather looked iffy. Chip told him to meet him at the club in an hour. Then he was gone.

A last look at the maps told her she wouldn't go to Maine.

28

She'd have to head west, unless she wanted to go south, and that idea sat poorly.

She'd been to Kentucky once, as a teenager, with her father. He'd been a farrier at the Dunston University stables. Someone had requested his services out of state. The drive had been lovely, the time away from home and routine both welcome and exotic. The farm they'd gone to wasn't a farm at all, but a lavish estate on rolling acreage. The real purpose of the mission, Lavinia then learned, was for her father to take a bribe. The owner of the thoroughbred wanted some certification from a prominent vet at the university. There'd been an accusation of performance-enhancing drugs, which the owner sought to disprove. No one local could be enlisted, apparently. How the two men knew each other, Lavinia had no idea, until it was mentioned that he'd been a student at the university years before, rode a great deal, and made the acquaintance of Lavinia's father, then just starting out himself. Money changed hands. Lavinia's father promised to put in a good word with the vet, even offered to share the generous gift of cash. Lavinia didn't see how either of them could be sure it would be that easy.

"What if he doesn't bite?" she'd asked.

Neither man seemed to have recalled that their conversation was taking place right in front of her. Her question caused her father's eyes to fill with anger. The horse owner, too, looked on edge. Her father was quick to speak.

"You have no idea what you're talking about. I should have left you at home with your mother!"

They drove home in silence. The matter was never raised after that. Lavinia didn't know what happened to the money, the horse, or his owner. Her father went back to treating her as he had before, generally uninterested, occasionally annoyed.

Why had he included her, then? To enlist her as an ally? To show her that you could get ahead if you overlooked legalities? Or to share some side of himself others didn't see, to prove that contrary to her mother's opinion of him, he was cunning and capable?

That disappointment, the belief that she'd ruined the chance to know him better, made her want a man she could penetrate and control.

With Potter, that was easy. He'd been so keen to please her! And she was easy to please then because she adored him, though he tended to be feckless, had trouble holding a job, and drank too much. She adored him still. There was no point in denying it.

Had Chip known that? He wasn't a stupid man. He was shrewd in business. He read people well. When she first started working for him, he saw right off that she was miserable at home though she never spoke of her private life. He wanted her from the beginning, which she used to her advantage the moment his desire became clear.

Yet she had genuinely cared for him. Her affection might have touched on love. At times, she justified her lack of passion on the grounds that he'd loved his first wife completely and that she, Lavinia, was guaranteed nothing more than a second-place spot in his heart. Wasn't that how it worked? First love was always the truest. That's why she didn't feel guilty about still loving Potter.

But Chip's first marriage hadn't been entirely happy, as evinced by his affairs. It was possible that he'd felt for Lavinia what he couldn't feel for his first wife. Perhaps, therefore, Lavinia had been Chip's one and only love.

The thought was too much to bear.

She shoved the road maps in a drawer and wept.

chapter four

Angie wasn't letting up. She was on her soapbox, urging Lavinia to reconsider. Lavinia had no use for grief counseling, or any other kind of counseling either. Angie could be such a nuisance when she got a notion. Last year, she'd pressed Lavinia to take a yoga class so she could relax and meet people. Chip had liked the thought of Lavinia in spandex, dripping sweat, chatting with all the friends she was sure to make. He bought her a pink mat and a bright green Pilates ball to get her started. Both the mat and the ball were in the laundry room, taking up space, as Alma often reminded her. Lavinia intended to purge the house of every useless thing when she got back from her trip. If Angie really wanted to do something for her, she could pitch and toss with her.

Then Karen called. They'd recently resumed their interrupted friendship. Karen had been the bookkeeper at Starkhurst Manufactured Homes until five years before when Chip sold the business to a competitor who had his own staff. Her husband taught math at the high school. They seemed to live an active life. They went camping or hiking or cross-country skiing. They stayed in cheap motels. Their only child, a daughter, lived in Brooklyn, and they visited her often, too.

Their excursions were curtailed when Karen got laid off. She and Lavinia had spent a lot of time together then. Lavinia took her to lunch, out for drinks, a nice dinner once in a while. At first, Karen protested, saying Lavinia mustn't spend money on her. Then one day at a nice French place she said, "I guess it's only fair."

Clearly, she blamed Chip for her financial woes. She'd still be working if he hadn't sold out. Couldn't she get another job, though? Lavinia had to think that there were a lot of places that needed a bookkeeper. She didn't know how to interpret Karen's silence. Had she tried and failed to find a new position? Lavinia asked her this directly. Karen said no one was hiring. Lavinia let the matter go.

Then it seemed that Karen never had time for her. It was hard for Lavinia to admit she was hurt. She wondered if she should demand an explanation. She asked Angie her opinion. Angie said it was a question of how much she valued the friendship. Sometimes relationships had a natural life cycle, and maybe this one had reached its end. Lavinia thought that what Angie was trying to say was that it hadn't been a real friendship, more of a convenience for both women, a way to pass time. Perhaps she was right. Lavinia didn't reach out.

Karen and her husband came to the funeral. They'd read about Chip in the paper. Karen was warm. She apologized for not being in touch sooner. They hadn't seen each other for a couple of years at that point. Karen had gained weight. Lavinia hadn't. Karen said it had been too long. Lavinia agreed, though she hadn't forgotten that it had been Karen who withdrew. She decided it no longer mattered. Now was the time for a fresh start.

That afternoon on the phone, as they chatted about unimportant things, like the health of Karen's tomato plants, Lavinia mentioned that Angie had been urging her to do grief counseling.

"I think it's a good idea," Karen said. In the background was the sound of music, upbeat jazz, as far as Lavinia could make out. It filled her with sudden longing. She was anxious to get off the phone.

"I can't see the use. A bunch of people spilling their guts," she said.

"Sharing is helpful."

"Oh, I don't know. Listen, I'm running late for my hair appointment. Can I call you back?"

"Of course! Have a beautiful day."

A beautiful day? Jesus.

Lavinia wasn't getting her hair done. She was shopping for a suitcase. She didn't like her luggage. She couldn't see hauling Louis Vuitton around in Mel's Jeep. He'd delivered it to her the other day, and she took it around town to get the feel. Like his Porsche, it had a clutch. She'd learned to drive stick shift years before, in her father's Chevy pickup truck. It all came back easily enough. The steering was a little loose. She didn't think it would be a problem, rolling down the highway. The brakes were tight. The tires seemed good. The odometer read over 120,000 miles.

There were two high-end leather shops in Dunston. Lavinia avoided them and made for the mall, where a travel goods store had just moved in. The ad in the paper showed a young couple with a pair of wheeled suitcases smiling their way through a crowded airport. Lavinia could see herself gliding across the parking lot of some humble Midwestern motel. She had always admired efficiency.

The store was brightly lit, with quiet classical music oozing from the speakers overhead. Athletic clothing hung on a series of circular racks, men's to the right and women's to the left. One wall was covered with pegboard, and on the hooks were an astonishing number of backpacks. Lavinia gazed at them, remembering the backpacks her children had all carried during their school days. Most were in sober colors: dark red, navy, green, and black. One was lavender with small flowers stitched in dark purple. A sales clerk appeared at her elbow. Did she care to look at it more closely?

The guy had about eight inches on her and was one hairy creature. The beard alone could house a small rodent. The forearms were shaggy and strong. His teeth were huge, white, and even. Lavinia envied those teeth. She'd never gotten hers straightened. Chip said he found the way the front one crossed over its neighbor rather charming.

"It's too young for me, don't you think?" Lavinia asked.

"Which? The purple? No, not really. I mean, a backpack's a backpack, right?"

He went away and returned with a long metal pole, hooked on the end, with which he removed the backpack. Up close it was larger than she'd first thought. It was a miracle of zippers and straps. Pockets, too, some hidden inside. There was a little cave for her cellphone, a plastic ring she could attach her keys to. One slot she couldn't figure out. The insignia on the outside was unfamiliar. She asked the clerk.

"Your mouse."

"I see."

His nametag said Brian.

"You a student?" he asked her.

"Me? No. Just getting ready for a trip. Don't care for the suitcase I have."

"Huh. Well, if you're going for a long time, you might want something bigger. Course, this one can really hold a lot. You gonna do any hiking?"

Lavinia hadn't thought about that. She used to hike a little, in the woods around Dunston. Sometimes over in the Adirondacks with Potter when they were first married. They took Angie once, when Lavinia was pregnant with Timothy. Potter had just lost another job. He said time away would help him think. It was late-season and turning cold. The campsite was empty. The plan was to hike only a little, just enough to get the real taste of it. Potter would tote Angie in a baby backpack. Lavinia was too clumsy with her big belly to safely navigate the trail. Potter said that was fine, he was glad just to hang out in the woods and sip his bourbon. But then he went off alone, leaving infant Angie and sow Lavinia by themselves in the tent. He needed that hike after all. Angie cried, Timothy kicked her stomach, and Lavinia wondered how the world could be so beautiful, with all those golden leaves on the ground and the softest blue sky overhead, while the human heart was wretched, miserable, and cruel.

"Maybe. Yeah, I probably will," she said.

Brian said he'd show her the larger packs, if she wanted. Lavinia said the smaller one would be fine both for travel in general and day hiking. She wouldn't camp out, because she didn't want to buy a tent. Brian said she could rent a tent.

"Really?"

"Sure. People do it all the time."

"They're tricky to set up by yourself, though. Not that I couldn't figure it out, of course."

Brian gave her a close look.

"I always like to see a lady who's not afraid to tackle things on her own."

Good for you.

She held the pack in her arms, the way a child does a teddy bear, and looked around the rest of the store. It was a highly practical place, she decided. There must be a lot of things that would help one stay organized. Though for the moment, she couldn't think what they might be.

"Where you headed?" Brian asked.

"What?"

"On your trip."

"Oh, west."

"When you going?'

She thought for a moment, and then decided.

"Monday."

"Cool. Well, if you're ready, I can ring that up for you."

"Shit! I can't. Monday's my son's birthday!"

Timothy would be thirty-one. How the hell could she have forgotten that? Usually the twins set something up for him. They often enlisted Foster. No one had said anything to her. They were all giving her space, in deference to her grief. The grief she didn't feel.

She called Timothy from the car and demanded to know what plans had been made for him, and by whom. He said they weren't really doing anything, given that, well, given what had happened.

"Nonsense. You need your birthday," Lavinia said. Driving was difficult with the phone to her ear. Mel's Jeep had no accommodation for hands-free talking. She'd have to take care of that before she left.

"Why don't you come for dinner? I'll ask Alma to make roast beef. That's still your favorite, right?" Lavinia asked.

Timothy reminded her that he'd become a vegetarian five years before.

"Well, then maybe a nice quiche. What time should we make it for? Can the twins come up from the City? You've talked to them, haven't you?"

"Mom, listen. I'm just having dinner at home with Sam."

"Who the hell is Sam?"

"My roommate. I told you."

"You said it was a girl."

39

"Short for Samantha."

"Isn't Foster coming, too?"

"He said he had plans, but he'd come if I wanted him to."

"Angie?"

"She'll be there."

"And you didn't invite me?"

"Of course, you can come if you like. I just thought you were spending a lot of time with Mel."

"What the hell gave you that idea?"

The connection thinned, then failed.

A few minutes later, the phone rang. It was Maggie.

"Are you okay? Timothy says you sound weird," she said.

"How are you, dear?"

"I'm fine. Are you fine?"

"I'm ducky."

The car in front of her slowed suddenly. Lavinia honked. She dropped the phone.

"Let me call you back!" she said.

When she got home, the kitchen was full of flowers. Three vases choked with stargazer lilies, her favorite. Alma was working on a crossword puzzle. Her fingernails were dirty, and her curly gray hair looked greasy.

Everyone grieves in a different way.

"What's all this?" Lavinia asked, and put the new backpack on the counter by the coffee maker.

"Mel. Wants to wish you a good trip."

"You don't send flowers when someone's about to leave, do you? Unless you're setting sail, standing up on the deck as you pull away from all those tiny waving people below."

Alma looked up over her bifocals. Her eyes were rimmed with red.

"Maggie called. So did Timothy," she said.

"They're worried about me."

"They should be."

"Because?"

"You're acting like a loon. If you'll forgive the expression."

"Dear Alma."

Lavinia poured them both a glass of wine.

Alma looked at the clock on the wall. It was seventeen minutes past three. She seemed to decide that although the hour was early, a drink would do her no harm.

Lavinia sat on the stool next to hers. Alma sighed. She wiped her eyes with a tissue from the box by her elbow.

"I won't be gone all that long," Lavinia said.

"The place is so big and quiet; I just can't stand it."

"Can't you ask your sister to come and stay? Or she might put you up at her place?"

Alma didn't like her sister, because she thought Alma could have done more with her life than keep house for other people.

"Or your niece, what's her name?" Lavinia asked.

"Becky."

"She's in college now, right?"

"She graduated. Took a job in Iowa."

Lavinia poured Alma more wine, though she hadn't had much of her first round.

"I'll be all right. Don't worry. It'll give me a chance to think about what comes next," Alma said.

"You know you always have a home here."

"*He* needed me. You don't."

"That's not true. I do need you."

"Someone else would do just as well."

"They wouldn't know how I like things done. You know me inside and out."

Alma gave Lavinia a skeptical glance.

"Then for old times' sake, say you'll stay," Lavinia said.

Alma studied her puzzle.

Lavinia took her drink into the living room and sat down on her gorgeous white leather couch.

The telephone on the end table rang. Lavinia didn't move. Alma answered in the kitchen. A moment later, she appeared.

"Timothy again," she said.

Lavinia reached over and lifted the phone.

"Why didn't you answer your cell?" he asked.

"Oh, I must have left it in the car."

"Jesus. I thought you had a wreck or something. Maggie said you were talking and the line went dead."

"I dropped the phone."

"Your Lexus dials through the console, so how …?"

"I'm driving Mel's Jeep these days."

"Really? Why?"

"Oh, for Christ's sake! What difference does it make?"

"Mom."

"I'm sorry. I wish you'd stop worrying about me. I'm fine."

An uneasy silence fell.

"Angie really thinks you should do that grief group, or whatever it is," Timothy said.

"Oh, all right. If it means I'll get some peace. But I'm leaving Monday. No, Tuesday."

"There's a meeting tomorrow."

"On a Saturday?"

"Easier for working people, I guess."

They spoke a few minutes longer. Timothy was at work and said he needed to get back to the floor. He sold clothes at the GAP store in the mall, not far from where Lavinia had bought her backpack. She could have dropped in to see him. It simply hadn't occurred to her.

chapter five

On Saturday morning, Lavinia headed out to dutifully attend the grief group at Lindell Retirement home and discovered that the Jeep had a flat tire.

"Wouldn't hand you a lemon, my foot," she said.

She dug around for her cell phone, which had been in the car since it flew from her hand. It was wedged between the passenger seat and the door. Of course the battery was dead.

She returned to the house and asked Alma to call a tow truck.

The lemon-scented air freshener in the Lexus was overpowering. The car hadn't been driven since Mel brought it back from the country club. He'd had to come and get the spare key from Lavinia. Chip's keys had been found on him and returned days later, along with his wallet and wristwatch. Lavinia had asked Alma to put everything in a large envelope, then put the envelope on his desk. She hadn't looked at the contents. She couldn't bear to. She removed the air freshener and threw it in the blue plastic bin at the back of the garage. The bin was stuffed and redolent. Lavinia realized that Chip was always the one to wheel it down the long driveway to the curb and back. She'd assumed Alma would take over that chore. She hadn't. They hadn't even really talked about the running of the house. Bills were collecting daily on Chip's desk. Lavinia would see to them. She was perfectly capable of managing money, but there were things she simply didn't know, like how to contact the gardener or the man who cleaned out their gutters. Chip had kept all that information in his head.

All this should have crossed her mind before today. Chip had been in the ground for two weeks. She'd accomplished very little. She wasn't even ready for this trip. There was a time when she'd juggled the schedules of seven people—her whole family, including Potter, though he usually didn't have much going on. While she'd had a job, no less. Now she couldn't even take out the damn trash!

She wept just as lustily just as she had at the funeral. Her shoulders heaved painfully. Snot flowed. Wiping her face slicked her hands. They felt greasy. Dirty. Ugly.

Before Chip swallowed the thunder bolt, she seldom cried. In fact, she couldn't recall the last time. Probably when she found out Potter was marrying Mary Beth. Like Lavinia, she was highly capable. She was a contractor, now using her skills to remodel Potter's house. Their house. Potter liked—needed—energetic women, women good with their hands. When she made that connection—or assumption,

46

whichever—that Potter was marrying a Lavinia clone, she went to pieces. She took to her bed for one whole afternoon. Chip was out of town at a conference, so he never knew of her collapse. Alma knew, though. Bless Alma for keeping quiet.

She dabbed her eyes with her fingertips. Her shadow was no doubt smudged. She wore her favorite shade, lavender. And a new blue silk blouse, her best leather jacket, and designer jeans. She got up that morning determined to be who she was, capable, dignified, and serene.

And now look at yourself!

She plugged her cell phone into the charger Chip kept in there just for her, and started the engine. She called Mel. When he answered, she told him about the Jeep's tire and how little she appreciated having to deal with it.

"You call a tow truck?" he asked.

"Alma's doing that."

"I'll pay for a new tire."

"I thought you said that thing was in good shape."

"You must have run over a nail."

"When was the last time you had it serviced?"

"Why?"

"What if something else is wrong with it?"

"Does it drive as if there's anything else wrong with it?"

"No. But you know I hate surprises."

"I'll call my mechanic, see what his schedule looks like."

"Jesus, Mel! I'm supposed to leave on Monday. Tuesday, I mean." She'd promised to have lunch with Karen that day, and would leave immediately after. She hadn't wanted to agree, but Karen pressed. Karen had adopted the same helicopter vigilance everyone else had. God, if she could just get on the road!

"I'll call him right now," Mel said.

"You know what? Forget it. I'll take Chip's car. The one that just had an oil change and a new set of tires, and has about half the miles that piece of crap has."

"Lavinia, are you all right?"

"Why wouldn't I be all right, Mel?

"You don't sound like yourself."

"Yeah? Then who the hell do I sound like?"

She hung up.

She backed down the driveway far enough for a K-turn. Then as she pulled forward, something thumped under the wheels. She set the brake and got out. She'd run over the garden hose. Alma must have used it to fill the birdbath. She obsessed about that birdbath, although its only visitors were crows moistening bits of stolen food. Lavinia had seen a lot of moldy clumps in there recently. Why hadn't Alma wound the hose back up? For the same reason Lavinia had forgotten all about the trash.

Finally, she left the long driveway and joined the main road. She was immediately blocked by a garbage truck, which made her recall the stinking bin she'd just left at home. She honked—a long, piercing howl. The truck continued to crawl. It stopped at the next driveway, and a thickset man plopped out of the passenger side and ambled toward the waiting container. Lavinia honked again, and the driver's arm appeared from the other side of the truck, motioning her forward. She couldn't see past it. Was she just supposed to trust this clown to guide her through?

She got up her nerve and pulled sharply left. As she passed the driver, she gave him the finger. Since the windows of the Lexus were tinted, he probably hadn't seen. That was a shame. She hadn't flipped anyone off for quite a while. She hated wasting a well-delivered gesture.

Somehow, with all the delays, she managed to arrive ten minutes early. She parked, flipped down the sun visor, and gave herself a good hard look in the lighted mirror on its back. Her shadow had survived her weeping fit. Her hair was another story. She removed the clip, brushed it hard, pulled it into a severe knot, and reclipped it.

Angie was waiting for her by the reception desk. As always, she looked calm and business-like in her matching navy jacket and slacks. She gave Lavinia a cautious smile. Lavinia knew that look. As a teenager, Angie was hell on wheels. When her report card had been mailed home, she hid it until Lavinia demanded that she produce it. The performance never changed: resistance, denial, pulling the document from a back pocket, and handing it over with those same pleading eyes.

Which meant this meeting would be a dud, and Lavinia shouldn't mind too much. Angie probably just wanted to get her out of the house and couldn't think of a better ploy.

"You look so nice!" Angie said.

"Surprised?"

"Not at all. You're always a snappy dresser."

A middle-aged woman pushed a very old woman along in a wheelchair. Lavinia shivered. How the hell did Angie stand working in God's waiting room? But Angie wouldn't think of anyone's age. She'd think of their mental acuity, their quality of life. Those were good things, weren't they? Helpful things?

"Would you like some coffee?" Angie asked. She was leading Lavinia along a pleasant hallway lined with stunning black and white photographs, all of trees.

"Do I look like I need it?"

"Please stop being defensive."

"Sorry. No, I'm fine, coffee-wise."

They entered a large room where chairs had been arranged in a circle. Lavinia was back in kindergarten then, seated cross-legged on the floor, taking her turn to read aloud in a high, clear voice.

"What's the matter?" Angie asked. Lavinia had stopped walking just beyond the doorway.

"Nothing."

"It won't be that bad, I promise. You don't have to talk if you don't want to. Just listen."

"Who's coming, anyway?"

"People who've lost a loved one. I told you that."

"I know. But *who?*"

"You'll find out in just a minute. Why don't you take a seat?"

Lavinia positioned herself on the circle directly across from the doorway. The seat of the metal chair was uncomfortable. Honestly, how could anyone unburden himself on a chair like that? You'd want to talk fast, that's for sure.

People filed in. They were all middle-aged except for one woman who looked younger than Angie. There were no men.

Didn't men lose people anymore? Lavinia counted seven souls, none dressed as nicely as she, none as slim.

She searched each face for grief. She saw only fatigue, sometimes exhaustion.

But no, sorrow was there in their slumped shoulders and dark eyes.

Angie sat. She said how glad she was everyone could come. This was an open group. Anyone could speak. The only ground rule was to listen. She gave them all another moment to get settled. Then she turned to the woman across from Lavinia.

"Clara, you lost your mother only a few weeks ago, am I right?" she asked.

A large Scandinavian woman with short iron gray hair nodded.

"Clara's mother was a resident here," Angie said to Lavinia. Obviously, everyone else must already have known that.

"You spoke last time of a sense of guilt where your mother was concerned. Is there anything you care to add at this time?"

Clara sat like a hen in a turtleneck sweater. Her hands were folded in her lap. Lavinia could see how fat her fingers were. A gold wedding ring cut into one. Lavinia looked at her own hands. She still wore Chip's ring. Why hadn't she taken it off? When your husband dies, you aren't married anymore, right? Being single meant you didn't wear a wedding ring. But this was no ordinary band, like clucky Clara's. This one had a two and a half carat diamond, top notch. It was a thing of beauty. Lavinia loved having it on her hand, loved how it turned a beam of sunlight into bright points of red, green, and blue. She'd gone with Chip to choose it. She quickly surmised, from the ties he wore and the cufflinks that were mini golf balls, that the poor man had no taste. Had she left it to him, God knows what he'd have presented her with. He gave her jewelry for her birthday, Valentine's Day, Mother's Day, their anniversary, and Christmas. Her box was full of expensive and hideous, overdone pieces, often in the shape of some animal. Chip had been particularly fond of bumblebees.

Clara droned on.

"She was hard on me and my sister, that's a fact. My sister lit out first chance she got, but I stayed," she said.

"You felt you were doing the right thing," Angie said.

"That's what I told myself, but the truth, well the truth was that I stayed to make her as miserable as she made me."

Jesus Christ!

"I'm sure you didn't make her miserable," Angie said. Her tone had gotten soothing, as if she were addressing a cranky child.

"I did, though. I wouldn't come by when I said I would, I wouldn't call her back, and when I did come, I told her she looked like shit."

Heads lifted. Expressions turned curious.

"She knew you didn't mean it," Angie said.

"Well, that's what she always said. But she was afraid I really did."

Clara's face crumpled. She cried. Angie passed a box of Kleenex to the woman next to her. The box made its way around the circle to Clara.

"Then she died. Just like that. No sign, no warning," Clara said, haltingly.

"I'm afraid that happens sometimes."

Lavinia shrank inside. Chip's gait had been vigorous as he walked to the garage that morning, his golf bag over one shoulder. And what had she thought, watching him for the last time? That he had a fat ass.

"I'd been easing off those last few weeks. I think I got to a point where I realized there's just no rhyme or reason to make someone pay for doing what they thought was right. It was her nature to be strict. She didn't think of herself as cruel or mean. She just figured children need direction. They need to be told what's right, and what's not," Clara said.

Lavinia had raised her own kids that way. Did they think she'd been cruel? At one time or another, each had said exactly that. If, later on, their opinion of her changed—if her behavior had indeed changed—it was all because of Chip and what he gave her. Money. The end of worry. Replaced with boredom and resentment at being bored, resentment that he wasn't more exciting, the way Potter had been, even when he was three sheets to the wind. So, being bored and resentful, she picked on him, Chip, who never fought back.

Clara wiped her eyes. A calmer attitude took hold. The woman next to her (Laura, Laurie?) talked about having trouble realizing her father was gone. She kept going to the phone to dial his number. The one time she didn't catch herself, she got his voicemail, which hadn't yet been disabled, probably because the number hadn't been reassigned, and she just stood there, listening to him say he wasn't home and to leave a message. She wished she could do just that. She didn't believe in the afterlife or that spirits visited the living. But she did think that if she could concentrate her thoughts, somehow, he would know them.

"Uh, huh," Lavinia said.

Angie glanced sternly at her.

"I think it's normal to want to reconnect, even when we know we can't," a woman named Dina said. She was the youngest. Lavinia wondered whom she'd lost.

No one spoke.

"It's natural to question the relationships we had with the departed," Angie said.

The silence continued. Lavinia studied the shoes the other women were wearing. Shoes said it all. Clara's were running shoes, though clearly even a brisk walk would tax her. Laura/Laurie's were flip-flops. Her nails were painted silver. Lavinia was on the fence. Silver polish could be a nice touch, but the flip-flops were tacky. Dina had on high-heeled sandals. There was also a pair of hiking boots; low-heeled pumps that made no sense with the rest of that woman's outfit—jeans and a tank top; a pair of loafers not as nice as Lavinia's hand-stitched ones; and more flip-flops.

"Now might be a good time to ask our new member to introduce herself," Angie said.

Lavinia took a moment to realize she was up.

She gave her name. Then she said she was Angie's mother and that she didn't know if she'd be coming to any more meetings because she was going out of town.

"It wasn't your father, was it?" Dina asked Angie.

"Who passed? Oh, no. It was my stepfather."

"My second husband," Lavinia said.

Sympathetic murmurs were voiced.

"Had he been ill?" tank top lady asked.

"No. He got hit by lighting on the golf course."

"I read about that! Said it was an incredibly rare event."

"He was pretty rare, himself. Now, of course, he's well-done."

Angie shifted restlessly in her seat.

"Yeah, so anyhow, he died, and now I'm going on a trip. If I can pin down all the details. Things keep coming up. This morning the car I want to take had a flat tire. Then this friend of mine just has to have lunch with me next week—on the day I'm leaving. And oh, my son's birthday is Monday, which I forgot for some reason, probably because I'm so distracted with everything else. Makes you realize how inconvenient a thing death is. I mean, it's a major speedbump, you know?"

Everyone was watching her now.

"Can you tell us how you're processing your loss?" Angie asked.

"Processing? I don't know that I'm processing anything. I mean, I'm thinking about it obviously. How can you *not* think about it? I feel bad. I'm sorry he's dead. I probably should have been nicer to him when he was alive. Not that I was a bitch. Well, okay sometimes I probably was. I'm sure he thought so, though he never said a word. He was like that. Long-suffering."

Angie nodded. Whether she remembered this about Chip or was simply validating Lavinia and encouraging her to continue, Lavinia couldn't tell.

Another woman joined the group. She was quite a bit older than the others, very nicely dressed, with a steely, distant look to her. Angie introduced her as Meredith Maynard. Her mother had recently died.

Meredith apologized for arriving late. She mentioned someone named Eunice as the cause, and some project they were both involved in.

When Meredith was settled, Angie asked Lavinia if she cared to continue.

Lavinia said she understood that guilt and grief could get mixed up. That if she felt less guilty, maybe she'd feel less sad, or something like that. The funeral sort of brought the whole thing home because Chip's son—one of three, never mind about the other two—had been there. It hadn't helped her take on her whole marriage—her years with Chip—to remember that she'd once had quite a thing for the son. Truth be told, if he'd shown the slightest interest years ago, she might not be sitting there now. Anyhow, there he was, just as gorgeous as ever, and she put out a feeler, if you will. And guess what?

Turned out he'd gotten married again. Never said a word. Would have been damn helpful if he had, because in matters of love, who likes wasting time?

She had the close attention of everyone in the room. Some looked cross, some keen to hear more. Meredith seemed amused. Angie, terrified. That's when Lavinia realized her coming there had been a mistake. How could she be expected to spill her guts in front of her own daughter?

She excused herself. Angie followed her out of the room.

"Mom, wait."

"Didn't think your old mother had it in her, did you? That I was old and dried up and just as dead as Chip."

"I don't think that at all."

"Then maybe you should get that look of shock off your face."

Angie took her by the arm and led her down another hall into a small, brightly lit sitting area, at present unoccupied.

"I'm not shocked. I knew about Ethan. Everyone did," she said.

"Chip didn't."

"I'm sure he did."

Lavinia felt like the air was thickening all around her. She wanted to sit down and didn't. She might not get up again for a while.

"You need to sort out your feelings," Angie said.

"I just did."

Angie withdrew her hand from Lavinia's arm.

"Find someone to talk to. I'll give you some names," she said.

"Honey, you wanted me to come; I came. You wanted me to share; I shared. That's all I got for now."

Angie nodded. She said she had to get back.

"You can go out this way. It's closer to the parking lot," Angie said.

"See you at Timothy's party."

"Yeah, okay."

Lavinia came out into warmth and sunshine. As she got into her car and drove slowly down the wide, flat road ringing the retirement home, she wondered why her children never approved of anything she did.

Forget it! What the hell do they know, anyway?

chapter six

Lavinia unburdened herself to Alma about the grief meeting, calling it a fucking fiasco. Alma sighed, shook her head, and said, "Damned if you do; damned if you don't," which Lavinia couldn't make sense of.

Mel called to ask if she could get the Jeep to the mechanic on Monday, or if it would be easier if he took care of it for her. Lavinia reminded him that she wasn't taking it. In fact, he could come collect it anytime he liked. Then she realized that her tone was steely, so she softened.

"We'll have dinner. On me," she said.

"That sounds lovely! Shall you pick a place, or I?"

"I will. How about L'Auberge?"

"Perfect."

The restaurant didn't have an open table until eight-thirty that evening. She called Mel back and told him to come by an hour beforehand. She'd have some hors d'oeuvres ready.

"Deviled eggs?" he asked.

"Sure, if you like."

"Tell Alma not to poison them. I know I'm not her favorite child in the world."

Child?

"She's got nothing against you, Mel. She's just sad," Lavinia said. She was in her room, on the bed. She was overcome with fatigue and lay back against the quilted headboard. There were no pillows. She'd removed them when Chip died. She'd always preferred to sleep without them, though Chip told her doing so was bad for her neck.

They hung up.

Lavinia's moment of exhaustion was immediately replaced with nervous energy, as if something were crackling across her skin. She took off her fancy jacket and went into the deep walk-in closet to find a hanger for it. There, on the left side where they'd always been, were Chip's clothes. Below the jackets, shirts, and slacks were several rows of shoes: wingtips, loafers, and a pair of cowboy boots Lavinia had never seen him wear. The built-in drawers still held his boxers, socks, and carefully folded ties. The leather jewelry box was full of his silly cufflinks. Along with the mini golf balls were a pair of shamrocks, smiley faces, riding crops, and jockey caps. They'd all been gifts from his first wife and people who worked for him over the years. Nothing in there had come from Lavinia. When she gave him a gift, it was usually a good bottle of whiskey or another paperweight, and once a very expensive fountain pen he said tended to leak.

Lavinia went into the hall, leaned over the railing of the curved stairway, and hollered for Alma. After a moment, Alma appeared below, standing solidly on the black and white tile floor Lavinia had always hated. She looked up crossly. Lavinia asked her to come upstairs for a moment. Alma ascended, puffing audibly.

Lavinia said the time had come to get rid of Chip's clothes. Alma nodded. There were some cardboard boxes in Timothy's old room down the hall. He'd taken a lot from the grocery store, thinking he'd need them to move his things to the cottage Chip bought for him to live in. That was now Lavinia's, too. She wondered if she should ask him to pay rent, then decided that would be cold, especially when she didn't need the money. She didn't know if his roommate lived there for free or not. Samantha. Odd creature, from the sound of her. Alma returned with two large boxes, then went for two more. Lavinia began removing the jackets and shirts. At first, she took time to fold everything carefully, but quickly became frustrated and tossed the garments down any old way. Alma said they should go through the pockets; they might find some money. Lavinia didn't think so. Chip seldom carried any cash, but she looked anyway, to please Alma.

Pocket after pocket yielded only gum wrappers, rubber bands, a paperclip or two, and loose change. Things he hadn't worn for years still had bits of trash. Why hadn't the dry cleaner been more thorough? You paid good money for bad service, that's what Lavinia thought. She asked Alma if she didn't agree. Alma said nothing. She was unfolding a piece of paper she'd found. It had been torn from a legal pad, the kind Chip kept for doodling in his office. This didn't contain doodles, but a list of items to buy for Christmas.

Lavinia looked it over.

Timothy – new roller skates. Check with L. May not approve.

Angie – butterfly hair clips she saw at the mall

Foster – Lord of the Rings video

Marta & Maggie – cash

Lavinia – peacock brooch

Alma – cashmere socks

Mel – mystery novel or French cookbook

Lavinia remembered those gifts—it had been their second Christmas as a family. The Douglas fir had been nine and a half feet tall. Foster had been sick, so had Maggie, and both spent all day in their pjs and bathrobes. Chip drank too much and sang off key until Lavinia begged him to stop. Then, when he wouldn't, she summoned Alma who guided him down to the finished basement they'd turned into a rec room for the kids. There he shot a few wobbly games of pool until he sobered up just enough to manage a formal dinner at the antique table that had belonged to his mother. The memory was unexpectedly sad.

Alma slumped down on the embroidered bench Chip had used for putting on his shoes. She cried noisily. Lavinia felt like pressing her hand to her mouth to make her stop.

Take it easy. Just breathe.

"I know, I know," she said.

"I told him I didn't like those socks. They scratched."

"These socks? On the list?"

"I couldn't for the life of me figure why he'd gotten them for me in the first place. Then I remembered liking that cashmere sweater of yours—you know, the red one, sort of a berry shade—and thinking how nice it would be to have something warm like that, so I said, 'Wonder what a pair of socks made outta that would feel like.' I didn't think he'd heard me, or maybe he didn't and one of the kids told him, I don't know. Of course, it was a darn generous thing to do, and I'm sure lots of people enjoy wearing cashmere socks, but when I put them on, my feet itched like crazy. I wasn't going to say anything to him. I didn't want to hurt his feelings or make him feel that I was some stuck-up ingrate, but then he asked me how I liked them and I had to tell him the truth."

Alma wiped her nose on the sleeve of her plaid shirt, leaving a smear of snot. Lavinia swallowed hard.

"What good is it if you can't tell someone the truth, right? I mean, I'd worked for him for years by then, and I just couldn't lie. I tried to be as soft about it as possible, but I could see it in his eyes that I'd disappointed him."

"Alma, I'm sure you're exaggerating. Chip probably didn't care all that much. It was just a pair of socks."

At that, Alma wailed. Lavinia turned away. She said it was time to get back to work. Alma didn't move. She said she was going to sit there awhile and do some hard thinking, if Lavinia didn't mind.

"All right, dear. All right."

Lavinia trotted downstairs into the kitchen. She splashed water on her face. Her hand shook. Was she really that mad at Alma? Or just generally freaked out? She told herself to calm down. If Alma wanted to sit in the closet, let her. Sooner or later she'd have to answer the call of nature, if nothing else, and she'd come out.

She returned upstairs, went to her side of the closet, and pulled several light-weight blouses from their hangers. One by one she crushed them into cylinders and stacked them on the bed. What was she going to use for a suitcase? She hadn't even decided yet. The cute backpack she'd bought wasn't nearly large enough.

"Alma, is that backpack of Foster's still here? The one he took around Europe last summer?" she asked.

"Don't know."

"I don't suppose you could rouse yourself long enough to go and check?"

"Not now."

"Dear Alma."

"Fire me if you want."

"Jesus Christ."

Lavinia marched down the hall to Foster's former bedroom. Sure enough, in the closet was a large, silver-gray backpack—not exactly what you'd call stylish.

She brought it back to the bedroom. She dug through all the compartments and pockets. She found a crumpled train ticket in a foreign language, Spanish probably, also a squeezed-out tube of toothpaste. Foster's trip had been a graduation gift. He'd finished college at the top of his class. Lavinia had worried about him every minute, over there on his own. Chip said she was being an old mother hen. That wasn't true. Lavinia just had never had any of her children on another continent before. None of the others had had the same interest in going abroad. The furthest Angie had ever gone was to Maine one summer with a friend. Timothy had spent a little time in Florida, trying to sort himself out after college. He'd wanted to write a novel and thought being down in the Keys, where Hemingway had hung out, would inspire him. It didn't. Marta and Maggie liked to fly off to L.A. sometimes.

Lavinia put the clothes she'd rolled into Foster's backpack. They barely took up any room at all. Next, she added shoes. The most casual pair she had were canvas slip-ons. She figured they'd be comfortable to drive in. If she got out and wanted to walk around in some brand-new city or town, she could buy something sturdier, like hiking boots.

The big pack would be for clothes, the smaller one for personal items like perfume and jewelry. Should she bring a purse? If so, maybe the purse could go inside the small backpack?

If she'd ever taken a trip by herself, she wouldn't have so many questions. When she traveled with Chip, Alma had done their packing. She was good at it, too. Lavinia wished she'd stop sniffing in there and come make herself useful. Another look at her, hunched over on the bench, said that wouldn't happen anytime soon.

She made another trip to the kitchen. From the refrigerator, she removed a bottle of white wine that was about two-thirds full. With that in one hand and two glasses in the other, she returned to her bedroom to be met by the soft sound of Alma crying.

Lavinia poured them both a glass of wine. She gave Alma hers, then sat down on the thick carpet underneath the now vacant metal rack where Chip's things had been.

Alma sipped her drink, snorting a little.

"Charity, you think?" Lavinia asked. She meant the clothes.

"Sure. Or you could pedal them to Value Village."

"I used to buy the kids' clothes there. Pretty good bargains."

Alma nodded.

"I wonder who they'll be," Lavinia said.

"Who?"

"The guys who end up wearing Chip's clothes."

"Guys trying to get a leg up."

"With the help of a pretty fancy wardrobe."

Chip used to give money to charity every year. Some boys and girls club; a scholarship through the Rotary; the animal shelter. He always asked Lavinia if there were any place in particular she'd like him to donate to on her behalf.

"AA," she'd once said bitterly, thinking of the time Potter fell off the wagon and didn't see the kids for a while, though their divorce settlement stipulated that he could every other weekend. Lavinia was glad that he made himself scarce, but the kids suffered, particularly Angie.

They heard the telephone. Neither made a move.

"Have you noticed how much more that damn thing rings, now that Chip's dead?" Lavinia asked.

"Yup."

They drank in silence.

Alma let out a little giggle.

"What?" Lavinia said.

"The way he used to walk around with his glasses on his head saying he couldn't find them."

"Yeah."

"And the time Mel put that cushion on his chair at dinner."

"What cushion?"

"The one that sounds like a fart when you sit on it."

"Right."

"And Chip said, 'Oh, I beg your pardon.' I think he really thought he'd done it, himself."

Alma paused for another sip.

"Mel's such a jerk," she said.

"Sometimes."

"He should have manned up."

"What do you mean?"

"Letting Chip go on playing once the storm came up."

"I'm sure he told him to get off the green."

"And where was he?"

"Under a tree."

"Coward."

"Dear Alma. Would you stand out in a lightning storm?

"To save a friend, I would."

The doorbell rang.

"Oh, who the hell is that?" Lavinia asked.

"Let's go see."

They left the closet, glasses in hand, and went down. It was a young guy bringing back Chip's golf bag from the country club. He apologized for the delay. They'd been stowed in the manager's office, and he just that afternoon had remembered them. Lavinia stared at the clubs in the bag. Which had been in his hand when he got fried? She couldn't think about that, couldn't have the damn things in her house. She told the guy to keep them for himself. He said he couldn't possibly.

"Donate them. Use them to start a golf scholarship for needy children," she said.

He sized them both up, and the glasses they held. He told them to have a good day, and left, the bag over his shoulder.

"Nicely done," Alma said.

Lavinia asked if she could make those deviled eggs Mel was so fond off.

"Must I?" she asked.

"I'm afraid so. I'll help you."

"Don't bother. I can make the devil his eggs on my own."

chapter seven

Too much mustard, Mel said. The eggs weren't sitting all that well. Lavinia asked if they should cancel dinner and go home where she could set him up with a bottle of Tums. He told her not to be silly. He'd be just fine as soon as he got a glass of sparkling water down. Then he said she was looking particularly lovely this evening. That green dress had always been one of his favorites.

The wine she'd had earlier with Alma had given her a headache, probably because she hadn't eaten anything to soften the blow. She'd served crackers and cheese along with the eggs, and watched Mel help himself to everything with gusto, even as her own appetite shriveled away. Now, though, with the gilded menu in her hand, the thought of lamb made her stomach stir happily. A good Bordeaux was being poured by a sullen young woman with a delicate nose ring. She asked Mel if he'd care to taste it.

"He's not the one who ordered it. I did," Lavinia said.

The server poured her a small amount. Lavinia swirled it around and around, then brought the glass to her nose. She sipped. She nodded. The server filled their glasses half-way and departed.

"Such a firebrand, Lavinia," Mel said.

The candlelight had mellowed his usual ruddiness. She hoped it was improving her, too. Since Chip died, every time she looked in the mirror the feral eyes of a stranger stared back at her.

They looked at their menus. Soft classical violin music played on the sound system. The atmosphere was warm, full of gentle voices. The last time she'd dined there with Chip the air had felt harsh because she was upset about something she couldn't now recall. What was it? Something to do with the house, no doubt. For the past several months, Lavinia had become increasingly frustrated with it. She'd mentioned selling and moving into a new build. Chip said he felt too old to move. And that was it, wasn't it? The difference in their ages finally hitting home in a way it hadn't before.

"You know I'm going to try to talk you out of going," Mel said.

"Don't bother."

"All right. Have you thought about what you're going to do afterward?"

"Sorry?"

"When you come back."

"I have no idea."

"I'm a great believer in making plans."

"My whole life has been one long plan. Now the only thing I want to do is get out of here."

The server returned and told them about the special, a mushroom risotto with herbed parmesan. Mel wrinkled his nose. Lavinia said she'd have the lamb; Mel chose the veal. Neither wanted a salad to start.

Mel apologized again for the Jeep's tire. She told him to forget it. He asked her about the grief meeting.

"Basically a waste of time," Lavinia said.

"Too much misery?"

"I just don't have anything in common with those women."

"Someone close to you died. You have that in common."

"That's not what I mean."

Mel sensed her reluctance to discuss it further. Lavinia's headache intensified. She drank some water and spread butter on a piece of warm bread from the basket the server had tossed abruptly on the table a few moments before.

Potter said her name. He was standing at their table with a woman—no doubt the wife. He was dressed in jeans, a button-down shirt, and a jacket. The wife—Mary Beth—was tall and lean, in an ankle-length black dress with a heavy silver choker, not at all what Lavinia had imagined. Her high-pitched voice on the telephone always suggested someone short and wispy.

"Fancy seeing you here," Lavinia said.

"It's our anniversary," Potter said.

"Congratulations."

"Would you care to join us?" Mel asked.

"Don't be stupid, Mel. They want to be alone," Lavinia said.

"We're always alone. Company would be nice," Mary Beth said.

"Are you sure, honey?" Potter asked her.

"Absolutely."

Potter pulled over a chair for Mary Beth. She slid quickly into it. She wore a charm bracelet on one wrist. Lavinia could make out a hammer, saw, and screwdriver.

Contractor charms! Who knew?

Potter put his napkin in his lap.

"This is awfully nice of you," he said.

"Mel Gains," Mel said, shaking hands.

"Potter Dugan, and my wife, Mary Beth," Potter said. A slow light of understanding came into Mel's eyes. Lavinia realized that Mel hadn't known who Potter was when he asked them to sit down.

"Mel was Chip's best friend," Lavinia said.

"Ah, poor Chip," Potter said.

"We heard about that! We're so sorry!" Mary Beth said.

We. We're.

The classical music in the background changed to something keening and high—a movie theme song, maybe—bringing an image of shipwrecks and lost souls.

"Well, an anniversary, how about that?" Mel asked.

No one spoke.

"How many years?" he asked.

"Six," Potter, Lavinia, and Mary Beth said in unison.

Mel looked at Lavinia.

"Did you hear the one about the couple who'd celebrated their twenty-fifth? When the husband was asked what he'd learned over the years, he said, 'Marriage is the best teacher of all. It teaches you loyalty, forbearance, meekness, self-restraint, forgiveness, and a great many other qualities you wouldn't have needed if you'd stayed single,'" Mel said.

Lavinia spread even more butter on her bread.

"Good one," Mary Beth said.

"A man puts an ad in the paper, saying he's looking for a wife. In one day, he gets over a hundred responses. 'You can have mine.'"

"Mel," Lavinia said.

Mel tried to catch the server's eye. When he did, he motioned her forward. She appeared and glared at Potter and Mary Beth. Mel asked for two more place settings and two menus. She was slow bringing everything.

"Would either of you care for a cocktail?" the server asked.

"Margarita for me," Mary Beth said.

"I'll take a beer. Anything you have on draft is good," Potter said. The server listed the options. He chose an Amber Ale from Washington State.

The server left. Lavinia put her heavily buttered roll on her plate. She lifted the basket and offered it to Potter. He declined. Lavinia offered it to Mary Beth. She helped herself to a roll. She gave the basket to Mel, who peered into it suspiciously, then put it back in the center of the table.

Mary Beth studied Lavinia. Lavinia poured herself more wine. She didn't offer any to Mel, who was sizing up Mary Beth.

"I got Timothy a new DVD player for his birthday," Potter told Lavinia.

"You mean *I* got it for him," Mary Beth said.

"Well, I picked it out. You just brought it home."

"I haven't gotten him anything yet. I totally forgot all about it, in fact. I was in that new travel store when I remembered," Lavinia said.

Potter leaned ever so slightly in Lavinia's direction. Mary Beth watched them both.

"Taking a trip?" Potter asked.

"Next week."

"Oh, where?" Mary Beth asked.

"She doesn't know," Mel said.

"I do, too. West. I'm heading west."

"Seeing Patty and Murph?" Potter asked.

"Maybe. I don't know. I hadn't thought about it."

"They'd be glad. Especially now that …"

"I'm all alone, footloose and fancy free?"

"Lavinia," Mel said.

The server brought drinks for Mary Beth and Potter. She asked if they were ready to order. Potter would have steak. Mary Beth, the special risotto. The server collected the menus and left. Potter drank half his beer in one go. He relaxed and leaned back in the chair. Mary Beth observed him closely. Her cell phone buzzed. She picked it up with one hand, her drink in the other.

"Sorry. Business," she said, and put the phone face down on the table.

"George again?" Potter asked.

Mary Beth nodded. She explained that George was the plumber she'd hired for a job out in Lansing. An entire house was getting new copper piping. George was a good worker, when he showed up and stayed longer than two hours. The homeowner was making noise about firing Mary Beth and going with his brother-in-law, a man Mary Beth knew and had once worked for herself when she was learning the business.

"He'll be sorry if he does that. Guy's an idiot," she said.

"A real drip?" Mel asked, then laughed heartily. Several heads around the room turned in his direction. Lavinia ate her roll. Potter finished his beer.

He told Lavinia he'd heard from the twins. He hated to mention it, but they were worried about their allowance. They hadn't seen a check for a few weeks. He'd sent them one to tide them over.

Lavinia put her palm on her forehead. She described the stack of items on Chip's desk she had to take care of before she left, though their allowance wasn't in that pile, of course, because it wasn't a regular bill, just a recurring expense that wasn't listed anywhere. Chip had had many of those, and he remembered them all, somehow. Lavinia didn't know how he did it, really. He must have had a system, but God forbid he should ever share it with her. The man must have thought he was going to live forever, right?

Mel shook his head. Mary Beth scrolled through the text messages on her phone. Potter stared into his empty glass.

"Maybe I should just give them a big lump sum so I won't have to think about it for a while," Lavinia said.

"Not a good idea. They'd go through it in no time," Potter said.

"True. They do love to shop, don't they?"

"Have you seen their closet?"

"That third bedroom they converted? It's jammed."

"How many shoes do two women need?"

Lavinia asked if they were always like that—greedy. Potter wasn't sure they were greedy so much as needing an outlet for all their energy.

Wasn't that what acting and painting were for?

Yes, but those were hard. Shopping was easy. And, it seemed to give them a sense of power—the simple act of spending, that is.

"You're saying it's my fault," Lavinia said.

"What? No!"

"Because I bitched so much about money when they were growing up."

"Come on."

Mary Beth and Mel, who'd been talking together, stopped.

Mary Beth's phone vibrated insistently. She lifted it, turned it over, and stared at the screen.

"I need to take this. Be right back," she said, and stood up.

"Hard worker," Mel said.

Potter went on watching Lavinia. Mel did, too.

"I'm sorry. I didn't mean that," she told Potter.

"It's okay. I know you're upset about losing Chip. It hasn't been that long since he died. You have to take time to adjust," he said.

"Jesus, Potter! When was the last time you lost someone?"

"The day you walked out."

"Potter, looks like you could use another round," Mel said and waved furiously for the server.

Lavinia chugged her wine. Potter helped himself to a lot of bread, emptying the basket.

A woman at a table behind them laughed raucously, then clapped her hands together twice. Lavinia turned. The woman's hair was so short it seemed like she might have been bald only a few months before. Cancer patient? Blazing her own riotous trail? The man opposite her looked giddy, as if he'd had one too many, yet his face showed genuine joy, more than booze alone could account for.

The server brought their plates. Potter asked for another beer. Lavinia said she'd like to order up a second bottle of wine. Mel asked if she were sure she wanted to, since they hadn't yet finished the first one. Lavinia didn't answer him. The server said she'd be right back with the beer and the wine. Mary Beth returned to the table and looked at her food.

"*That's* risotto?" she asked.

"Yes," Lavinia said.

"Huh."

"Huh, what?" Potter asked.

"Nothing. I just thought it would be different."

"Who was on the phone?" Potter asked.

"Nina."

"Oh, God."

Nina was an old friend, Mary Beth said. She had family trouble—well, who didn't, right? But hers were sort of worse. Not only was she divorced, but her twenty-something son had recently decided she was evil and refused to have anything to do with her. He moved out and wouldn't tell her where he was living. The ex knew but wouldn't say. Nina was thinking about hiring a detective to track him down.

"I say let the little son of a bitch go, if that's his attitude," Lavinia said as she helped herself to another glass of wine.

Potter carved his steak enthusiastically. Mel nudged his veal around on his plate. Mary Beth was about to shovel in another forkful of risotto, and stopped.

"Well, that's one option, but I think she'd really like to find him," she said, and put the fork in her mouth.

Lavinia shrugged and had some of her lamb. It wasn't bad. The vegetables were better.

Nina had just learned that her son wasn't living in Dunston anymore and had gone out west somewhere. California, she thought, because he had a college friend there he was close to.

"California's a big place," Mel said.

"The friend's in Santa Barbara," Mary Beth said.

"So, what does this pukey little ingrate think his mother is guilty of, exactly?" Lavinia asked. She polished off the creamed spinach on her plate.

"Lavinia, you don't even know the guy," Potter said.

"She was hard on him when he was young," Mary Beth said.

"Probably deserved it."

"I wouldn't say that."

"You have kids?"

"No, but ..."

"Then you have no idea."

84

Potter kicked Lavinia under the table. Liquid swayed in glasses. The flame in the small glass holder flickered.

Mary Beth's phone vibrated again. She rolled her eyes, stood, and went off with it. Lavinia saw that she'd almost finished her plate. She must have suspected there would be more interruptions.

"She's a good friend," Mel said.

Potter nodded.

"She a good wife, too?" Lavinia asked.

"I'd say so."

"Would you?"

"Yes, Lavinia, I would. And no, I don't compare the two of you and think she's better and you're worse."

Mary Beth could be clearly seen standing out by the hostess desk, the phone to her ear, the other hand gesturing.

The server appeared with the wine and Potter's second beer. She opened the wine and poured for Lavinia. She asked if she should clear their plates and if they'd like to think about dessert. Mel asked her to check back in a few minutes, but the plates could go, if Lavinia and Potter were finished. They were. The server took the plates away.

Potter didn't touch his beer. His expression was unmistakably sad, and for a moment Lavinia's heart went out to him. She regretted her words, her attitude, the inner workings of her mind, the very fabric and fiber of her soul.

"I'm sorry," she said, so softly neither Mel nor Potter heard.

"I better go see if I can get Mary Beth off that phone. Once Nina latches on, it can take a while."

"Tell her we're waiting to decide about dessert," Mel said.

"Nah, I think we better get going. Thanks, though."

Potter rose from his chair, removed sixty dollars from his wallet, and put them on the table by his full glass of beer. Then he bent and kissed Lavinia on the cheek. He shook Mel's hand, thanked him, and went on his way.

It took Mel a few minutes to get the server to bring their bill and pay it, by which time Lavinia was in the parking lot, leaning against her car, crying as if she'd never stop.

chapter eight

Sundays had always been bad. As a girl, that was the day her mother aggressively cleaned and scrubbed, right when her father wanted to sit with his feet up and watch the game. Her parents routinely quarreled, and their harsh voices could still haunt. How Lavinia had longed for a sibling, someone to keep her company! She supposed, later, that was why she had had so many children, herself. As Potter's wife, Sundays meant the low point in his week. Any job he had, he hated. When he wasn't working, the thought of the new week ahead, when he would be unwillingly idle, made him retreat into liquor. As Chip's wife, they meant time alone while Chip golfed, which she didn't really mind at first. Then, she did.

And now, as Chip's widow? Based on the small sample of Sundays since his death, it seemed as if the trend would be poor.

Her head pounded. After Mel had gone home, she had more wine with Alma. She told her all about seeing Potter and what a dope Mel had been to invite them to their table.

"They could have said no, right?" Alma had asked.

"It was the wife's doing. Potter looked like he wanted to run for his life."

They'd gone to bed late.

Now the daylight was leaning in hard because she'd neglected to pull the drapes.

Alma knocked on the bedroom door. Lavinia said to come in.

"Thought you could use this," Alma said. She held a mug of coffee in her hand.

"Dear Alma."

Alma put the coffee on the table by the bed. Then she went into the connecting bathroom and brought Lavinia a bottle of aspirin and a full glass of water. Lavinia had used that glass to rinse after brushing, and it had a distinctly minty flavor.

"What time is it?" Lavinia asked. Alma pointed to the porcelain clock on the table by the coffee mug. Its hands said it was almost eleven-thirty.

"Jesus!"

"Angie's downstairs."

"Why?"

"She wants to take you to brunch."

"I couldn't eat a damn thing."

"Then just go and be nice."

Alma energetically tossed the dirty clothes Lavinia had left on the floor into the laundry basket.

"How can you be so chipper after so much wine?" Lavinia asked.

"I got a lot more fat on me than you do. I can take it, I guess."

Lavinia massaged her forehead. Her skin felt oily.

"I thought hard liquor was the only thing that could give you a hangover like this," she said.

"Live and learn."

Lavinia gestured that Alma should leave. When she was alone, she took a long, hot shower. The shampoo Chip liked was still in the stall. She opened the glass door and tossed it into the sink, where it bounced up onto the counter. His side of the vanity still held his shaving things. Those would go that very day. And his prescription vials that lined the marble shelf. She scolded herself for not doing so before.

Grief, my eye! You're just a lazy bum.

Nearly forty-five minutes later Lavinia descended the curving staircase in her most elegant silk pantsuit. Her sandals were new. The straps were decorated with small, red stones. Her hot pink toenails had been painted a couple of weeks before and were still shiny.

Angie was lying on the white leather couch reading a book.

"Glasses?" Lavinia asked.

Angie sat up and removed them.

"Yeah. Need them to read."

"At your age?"

Angie shrugged. She took in Lavinia from head to toe.

"How are you feeling?" she asked.

"Fabulous."

"Alma said you had quite the evening."

"Yup."

Lavinia sat down. Her headache was better but still nagged.

"Dad called," Angie said.

"Not surprised. Let me guess. He told you to come spy on me."

"Is that what you think I'm doing?"

"More or less."

Angie closed her book and put it on the coffee table.

She said she hoped Lavinia understood that she—everyone—was naturally concerned. Sudden death was very hard to handle. It could make people unpredictable, sometimes even out of control. Lavinia held up a hand to silence her.

She wasn't out of control, she was just ... a little *emotional*. That was her right, wasn't it? To express herself however she wanted? Who was getting harmed by it, anyway?

"You are," Angie said.

"I drank too much last night; I own that."

Angie's gray eyes were Potter's, trying to see inside.

"Is this about what I said at the grief meeting yesterday? About Ethan?" Lavinia asked.

"I already explained that everyone knew you were attracted to him."

"It was more than an attraction."

Angie told her to go on. Lavinia had the sensation she'd had when she first learned of Chip's death—of rising up and away.

She didn't know it at the time, she said, but she saw in Ethan a way out. Yes, he was dashing and brilliant and built like a stallion. All of that was perfectly understandable. What was harder to understand was how trapped she felt by marrying Chip. She'd left Potter because she needed a reliable partner, which Chip was, but all that safety and security weren't very interesting, at the end of the day. She needed to remember that she was still young, and she supposed in some very pathetic, even desperate way, she hoped Ethan might help her there. She'd never really seen before that love—or what one called love—was only a little about physical attraction and a lot about the way someone made you feel. She wasn't talking about happiness, really, but a sense of possibility that went beyond companionship. What she meant, what she trying to say, was that you fell in love with someone when they opened a door inside you that you didn't know was there.

"Was that how you felt when you married Dad?" Angie asked.

"I don't remember."

"Try."

Lavinia dropped back. Potter had made her feel more alive than Chip ever had, yet he leaned on her and looked to her for strength.

"I guess I saw myself as a good person, a responsible person. And believed that I could make him one, too."

"You must have felt very powerful."

"Until I realized he'd never change."

Angie looked at her watch. She asked Lavinia where they should eat. Lavinia said maybe that new place, out on the lake. The fresh air would perk her up. Afterward she absolutely had to find a birthday gift for Timothy.

They took Angie's car, a sensible station wagon. Angie was dressed in a dull pantsuit she'd spiced up with a long necklace of blue beads. Her hair, Lavinia noticed then, had a few gray streaks. It was as if she'd gone from being a wild teenager directly into middle age. Maybe she would never marry and never have children. She lived alone. She seemed contented with her life. A lot more so than Lavinia was with her own.

"When I was your age," Lavinia said.

"Yes?"

"Just thinking aloud."

"You were married with five bratty kids."

"You weren't bratty."

"The hell we weren't!"

Lavinia laughed, for the first time in weeks.

They passed through downtown, crossed the railroad tracks, and headed up the west side of the lake. Several months before, on that same road, Chip announced that he wanted to buy a boat and learn how to sail. Lavinia wanted a motor boat, something that could really clip along and go fast enough that you weren't able to think about anything else out there on the water, the wind so fierce your eyes ran and your cheeks numbed.

"I can see you, racing along," he said.

"With you by my side."

She'd meant it. His expression said he wasn't entirely convinced. That he'd lived with silent doubts gnawed at her.

In the road ahead lay the smashed remains of a fairly large animal, maybe a deer. Crows picked at the carcass, and lifted as Angie steered around it.

"It was interesting, what you said before, about love. Just the other day a lady at Lindell was talking about being a young pianist, and how hard it was to deal with the other students at her college because she couldn't stand that they loved the same thing she did," Angie said.

"Huh."

"She could accept that they were eager, wanting to learn, achieve, succeed, but that was just career parameters. It was the passion they had for the keyboard that she just couldn't bear."

"Why?"

"Seeing all that devotion sort of lessened hers, or made hers seem insignificant."

"That's bull."

"Hey, I'm just saying what she said."

Lavinia said it sounded like a very strange conversation. Why was this old lady even talking about something that happened decades ago? Angie explained that her granddaughter was applying to music schools, and the memory presented itself.

"Loving a career and loving a person are two different things," Lavinia said.

Angie conceded the point. She turned into a gravel driveway that led to a one-story home that had been made into a restaurant.

Since they didn't have a reservation, the wait would be half an hour, at least. Did Lavinia mind? Not if they could wait on that nice shaded corner of the patio. Would it be possible to have a drink before their table was ready?

Angie's face was perfectly calm, inscrutable really, which meant she wished Lavinia would confine herself to an iced tea. She asked for a gin and tonic. Angie wanted a Virgin Mary.

They sat. The lawn below sloped to the water's edge. A wooden dock extended about twenty feet over the surface of the lake, and there a man and a woman stood together, facing each other, yelling. The woman's arm went up and down in a slicing motion. The man stood, arms crossed, looking down. When the woman fell silent, he yelled, "Bullshit!"

Lavinia thought how easy it would be to write their entire script:

I never said that.

Yes, you did! More than once!

You're a liar. You've always been a liar!

Yeah? How about the time you said you were working late/having lunch with Jill when you were really seeing what's his name?

But then strife needn't stem from infidelity.

"What happened to the school clothes you were going to buy for the kids?"

"They didn't find anything they liked."

"Where'd those three bottles of Bourbon come from?"

"Left over from a party my boss had out at his place. Said he never touches the stuff, didn't mind if I helped myself. I wasn't the only one. The other guys got some, too."

"Funny, he didn't mention it when he called."

"He called?"

"On account of you not coming to work for the last four days. And guess what? You're fired."

Oh, but that was her own personal teleplay, wasn't it?

Did Potter reminisce, too? Did her steely silences, slammed doors, and sudden departures in the car when she couldn't take it anymore sneak into whatever else he'd been thinking about, demanding another look, another kick in the gut?

As she sipped her gin and tonic gratefully, knowing it would ease the stupid hangover she'd inflicted on herself, she thought about the liability of an intact memory.

"Let me ask you something. When they go off the rails— the old folks, I mean—and can't remember anything, are they happier?" she asked Angie.

"Almost never. They're usually anxious and depressed. Why?"

"Just thinking how nice it would be not to have to remember anything."

"What about the good things, though? They get lost along with everything else."

That was a problem, to be sure, Lavinia thought. If only you could choose what stayed alive in your soul, and what died. You didn't get that kind of power. When it came right down to it, you didn't get any power at all. Things happened, you picked a way forward, a solution, some sort of fix, and when it worked, great. When it didn't, you were screwed.

Lavinia's cell phone buzzed inside her purse. She removed it. Mel's number was displayed.

"Oh, not now," she said and rejected the call.

"Mel?"

"Who else?"

"He's very devoted."

"He's a damn nuisance."

"He wants to marry you, you know."

"Oh, go on."

"He said so. Just this morning, in fact."

"You saw him?"

"He called."

97

"Is that why you came by? To break his news?"

"No. I came by to take you to brunch."

Lavinia had long known that Mel had feelings for her. He never hid them. Chip knew, too, and thought it was cute. "Like a big puppy," he said. But calling Angie?

"What did you tell him?" Lavinia asked.

"That he had to wait for your grieving period to end before he could raise the matter."

"And now you've already raised it."

"I didn't promise to keep quiet, and he didn't ask me to."

That was probably the way Mel wanted it. He knew Angie would talk about it, and that way Lavinia wouldn't be caught off guard. Did he think that giving her time to consider in advance of the actual words would help his case? Or did he think that on the spur of the moment, out of fear or loneliness or some unshakeable misery at her solitary state she'd jump at the chance?

She hadn't thought Mel was capable of such cunning and logic.

"I suppose it's what you all want, isn't it?" she said.

"I wouldn't say that. We just want you to be happy, is all."

Angie combed her hair with her fingers, just as she had as a little girl. Then she gave Lavinia a long, appraising look.

"So, you're really going on this trip?" she asked.

"I have to."

"You wouldn't consider a nice cruise somewhere instead?"

"Too many people on a cruise."

"True. But think how soothing all that open water would be."

"The open road will suit me just fine."

The couple on the dock had stopped shouting. They walked back to the bank, then went separate ways. Why was love so bloody complicated? None of Lavinia's kids had a significant other, though Angie had had a couple over the years. The last was a graduate student who cheated on her. Before that, when she was in college, she'd fallen in love with one of her professors. The twins tended to avoid men, probably because the idea of becoming a trio was difficult. Eventually, though, one would want a romantic relationship that lasted longer than a few weeks. Foster kept to himself, though some of his better friends were female. That left Timothy, who'd had a disastrous affair in college and showed no signs of wanting to engage on that level with someone else. Unless this roommate, this Sam/Samantha, were to become a contender.

"What do you think of that girl Timothy's living with?" Lavinia asked.

"I like her."

"You've known her for a while. She works at Lindell, right?"

"As an aide. She's got a good attitude for dealing with the elderly. Very no-nonsense, but not brusque."

"Any romantic possibilities there for your brother?"

"Oh, I don't know. I don't get that sense, but they're always very polite when I'm there."

"As if they're hiding something?"

"Aren't you the suspicious one!"

Angie had to know why she was that way. Keeping her father in line had taught Lavinia to be on high alert all the time. Like having a sixth child, one with a drinking problem.

The hostess said it would just be a few more minutes. Did either care for another round of drinks? Angie shook her head. Lavinia considered, then also declined.

chapter nine

Daisies bordered the brick walk leading to Timothy's front door. Someone had been down on bended knee, turning earth. The door, which had been brown before, was now pale green. So were the shutters. A shiny brass knocker stood in place of the old black one. Lavinia rapped with her knuckles, instead. When there was no response, she turned the knob and stepped inside. She was met by a pungently floral smell, which she saw at once came from a huge bouquet of pure white lilies in a tall vase on the living room coffee table. That Mel had recently bought her lilies made her realize that it was summer again, not that she'd forgotten, exactly. It was just one more thing she might have been more aware of if her circumstances were different.

She sat on the couch by the flowers. There were voices in the kitchen, around the corner. She leaned back and closed her eyes. She wasn't particularly tired, having slept better than usual, probably because she'd only allowed herself one glass of wine. Alma had had three. Their drinking together seemed to have become a nightly affair. She'd told her about Mel's wanting to propose.

"God help us!" Alma said.

To which Lavinia added, "Amen!"

He'd called that morning to say hello and to ask if she were looking forward to her trip. Lavinia chose to be pleasant. She said she was, very much, that she'd be sure to send lots of postcards because in this era of instant communication it seemed like such a quaint thing to do. Then she apologized for being so ragged with Potter at dinner.

"You're still in love with him, aren't you?" he'd asked.

His question was startling, despite what Angie had shared yesterday. Mel was seldom blunt, except when he was making fun.

"He's the father of my children."

He let it go. She'd promised to call before she left.

"Hi!"

A tall, overweight young woman smiled down at her. She had a small piece of something green, probably spinach, in her teeth.

"You're Samantha," Lavinia said.

"Sam. And your Timothy's mom."

"Yes."

A large hand was thrust into Lavinia's much smaller one. The grip, however, wasn't particularly strong. Sam was trying to be gentle, Lavinia decided. Timothy had probably told her to go easy.

"We didn't know you were here," Sam said.

"I stopped to admire the flowers."

"Aren't they great? They were left over from a memorial, at Lindell."

Lavinia's expression must have made Sam realize how close to home this was, because she said she was very, *very* sorry to hear about Lavinia's husband.

"Thank you."

Sam continued to loom over her.

"Timothy's out back," she said.

"Okay."

"I'll just go and let him know you're here."

"No need. I'll come along."

Sam headed off, and Lavinia didn't budge. Orange pollen had drifted from some of the flower petals onto the table. She wiped it away. Her fingers were now stained a deep yellow. It was a sickly color, a dying color, and suggested nothing of the beautiful thing it had come from.

She forced herself to stand up and go into the kitchen, which was mercifully empty. Timothy and Sam were in the backyard. Angie was there, too. Where was Foster? He always came late to parties. The social anxiety he'd suffered from as a boy remained. He worked in a veterinary office. No doubt he was much happier around patients who couldn't speak.

Timothy saw her through the window and motioned her to come outside. Still, she hesitated. She felt out of place, yet this was the house her late husband had bought; those were two of her own children in the yard, talking and smiling. It wasn't the first time she'd experienced this ache of alienation. When her kids were young, after she'd gotten them all to sleep and Potter was drinking alone in his little room off the kitchen where he'd installed a train set he never used, she'd sit by herself at the kitchen table, the fixture overhead always giving off the same harsh light no matter which house they were renting at the time, and bathed in that cold, yellow glow, her heart filled with the most wretched loneliness, a loneliness she'd had all her life and had done everything in her power to kill.

She stepped through a block of bright sunshine into deep, cool shade where there were chairs set up. Timothy stood, kissed her cheek, and gestured to the empty seat between him and Sam. Angie stood, too, and patted her arm. Lavinia still found all these gentle gestures cloying, though she knew they were heartfelt.

Timothy offered her a drink. He'd gotten a good bottle of gin because he knew she preferred it in the summer. Lavinia said a gin and tonic would be lovely. Timothy went inside to make her one. Sam asked if she were hungry. Lavinia said she wasn't. She remembered that she'd left Timothy's gift in the car. It was a CD by a local jazz artist. She had no idea if Timothy liked jazz. She'd gone to the store looking for a DVD to go with Potter's player and been distracted by the music section. The cover of the CD that caught her eye featured an intense-looking young man bent over a keyboard. His passion reminded her of Timothy.

"I hear you're going on a trip soon," Sam said.

"Yes. Tomorrow."

"Fun!"

"I hope so."

"Not looking forward to it?"

"Oh, I am. I'm just not ready yet. Well, more ready than I was. Finished packing this morning."

"Where are you going?"

"Don't really know. Just west somewhere."

Sam said she'd gone to Los Angeles a few years before, just for the hell of it. She got sick of Dunston, her mother, and the memory of her dead grandparents who'd been the biggest couple of judgmental jerks around. She'd worked in a motel there. She'd made no friends, except for her upstairs neighbor, a Japanese woman who turned out to be a prostitute.

"You were friends with a prostitute?" Angie asked.

"Yup."

"What was she like?"

"Petite. Tiny, really. Her English was bad. She dressed well and had a lot of nice things in her apartment. She wanted to go home and visit her family, but her brother flew all the way to L.A. to tell her she wasn't welcome."

"They knew what she did for a living?" Lavinia asked. The story interested her.

"Obviously."

"Did she tell them?"

"She must have. They wouldn't have known, otherwise. Not from that distance."

"That's the craziest thing I've ever heard!"

"She probably just wanted to be honest."

Angie disagreed. She thought it more likely that the girl had been testing their affection for her. Either that, or she deliberately wanted to make them unhappy.

Sam said if so, it backfired on both counts.

"How did you feel about it?" Lavinia asked.

"Her turning tricks? I thought she was stupid. With her looks, she could have done pretty much anything, and stay in good with her folks."

Lavinia detected more than irritation in Sam's voice. There was a clear ring of jealousy.

Timothy returned with Lavinia's drink. She took it from him. Before she could taste it, a pair of hands covered her eyes from behind.

"Oh, Foster," she said. He'd done the same thing as a little boy, usually when she was deep in concentration over her checkbook.

He appeared in front of her, grinning just the way he used to back then, too. Then he became serious and asked how she was doing.

"Never better!" she said, and drank.

For once, they weren't all watching her; their attention was turned to the grill. What should go on first, burgers, or chicken that had been marinating in teriyaki sauce? And what about the corn on the cob? Did the ears need shucking?

Sam had already taken care of the corn.

"You're just like that, aren't you?" Lavinia asked her.

"A shucker?"

Soft laughter from the group.

"No, I mean practical, willing to get at it, whatever it is. I assume you're responsible for the flowers along the walk and the new paint outside."

"Yup."

"You're very lucky, Timothy, to have such an energetic … roommate."

Timothy leaned over and rubbed Samantha's back. Lavinia couldn't tell if the gesture were romantic or just friendly.

While Timothy and Foster managed the grilling, Sam and Angie talked about some of the residents at Lindell. One was losing her marbles and needed to move up to the next level of care, but the family was resisting. Another had fallen again, and different medication was being prescribed to make her sleep less restless. Sam said she'd miss some of them, Mr. Mosher in particular.

"Quitting?" Lavinia asked.

"Yeah. I'm going to school."

"Really? For what?"

"Poetry."

"Well, that's really something."

"I've been thinking about it for a while. Then I came into a little money."

"I see."

"It's true," Timothy said from the grill.

Had she sounded skeptical? She hadn't meant to.

"I hope you didn't lose someone, too," she said.

"Nope. It's from my father, though I didn't know him when I was little. But, he was around all the time, saving some bucks for me."

"That's wonderful."

A few years ago, Lavinia had told Chip she was thinking of getting a degree. He encouraged her to. Why hadn't she followed through? Because being safe and secure sapped her energy? Made her lazy? When she regained her balance, she could apply, not to the University—that was Ivy League—but to one of the smaller, state schools around. Angie had gone to SUNY over in Cortland. Lavinia didn't mind the thought of all those young people wondering what she was doing there. It was that she had no idea what she wanted to learn. She'd have to get a solid handle on that before she could even think of taking the next step.

She used to love books—fusty old novels about people whose lives were completely different from hers. Women in manor houses, steering their daughters toward good marriages and their sons to lucrative pursuits. As she sat in that cool, almost soothing shade, going from one child's face to the next, even including Sam in that group for the moment because she'd felt a strong connection to her, she thought maybe she wasn't so different from a fictional character after all. She wanted the best for everyone. All her life, best had meant money. Best could only ever mean happiness, though. And there were many paths to that door.

Another old love was houses—seeing their potential, restoring them, stripping away all the wrong decisions and bad taste. She and Potter had never owned a home together, yet she'd rolled up her sleeves to the benefit of every landlord, getting a reduction in rent in return for her sweat equity. When Potter bought his childhood home—with his sister Patty's money—he set about restoring it. That was after they'd divorced. Even so, he called her in to consult on finishes. Then the fool he was working with set the place on fire. Not on purpose, everyone assumed, but because he'd gotten drunk and left the camp stove he'd been using get too close to a plastic tarp.

Chip's house was a relic, built in 1920 in a grand Greek style that was so popular then. The only remodeling she'd done was in the basement. Otherwise, she'd painted, chosen new wallpaper, and replaced the furniture, but she could have done much more. Chip wouldn't have minded. She'd had no interest, though. Had she felt that the house was never really hers?

The question, which had been floating in the corner of her eye, was whether she'd go on living there or not. She might buy some vacant land and build on it. A huge, modern home. A family compound where they could all live together. Angie might go for it, and Foster, but Timothy wouldn't want to because he had the house Chip bought him and which Lavinia now owned. The twins probably would never want to leave the city. So much for that idea.

Another one bites the dust!

"Dad said you had dinner together," Timothy said.

"By accident. That is, they walked by our table, and Mel, the dope, invited them to join us. The wife was eager to. I'm sure your dad would have high-tailed it out of there if it had been up to him."

"You had dinner with your ex?" Sam asked. She looked amused.

"Well, yeah, as I say, by accident."

"Did the fur fly?"

"Not at all. It was very pleasant."

The remark went unchallenged. Lavinia had always been a smooth liar.

Food was offered. Lavinia declined. She just had no appetite. She'd have to make sure she ate enough on the road, Angie warned. Lavinia promised to take care of herself. And to check in regularly.

Though she had only the one cocktail, it was as if she'd had many more, the way she sank into herself while the others ate, cleared away, enjoyed the cake Angie had made, and opened gifts. If Timothy had been unhappy with hers, he hid it well. He even said he knew the artist she'd chosen. His gratitude bordered on profuse.

chapter ten

At first, she didn't remember the way. A month ago, she could have driven it in her sleep. Winding out of the Heights, across the state highway, past about three miles of farmland, then right on Cherry Lane. But which was Karen's street after that? Spruce or Sycamore? A house with a mailbox in the shape of a small windmill made her realize the turn was coming up fast. She slowed just enough to avoid losing control of the car. Her tires screeched on the surface of the main road, then sent gravel from Karen's driveway flying. Had someone been in the yard, gardening, running the mower, stretched out on a chaise lounge bagging rays, he or she would have been peppered.

Lavinia got out of the car. Karen was looking at her through her front window. The surprise on her face was clear. They were supposed to meet at the restaurant Karen had chosen an hour from then. Lavinia decided she couldn't stand being at the mercy of a slow server or a backed-up kitchen, because she was ready to hit the road. Karen was her last stop.

"Aren't we going to The Inn?" Karen asked as she opened the door.

"I'm sorry to change plans on you like this. I'm a little worried about my timing, so I brought lunch. It's in the car."

Karen was all dressed up in black jeans with metal studs down the outside seams. Her tank top was black silk, or maybe rayon, with spaghetti straps. She looked like a hooker. A cheerful, well-meaning hooker.

In honor of the hours she'd spend behind the wheel, Lavinia wore a comfortable jumpsuit. It wasn't new. It had been in the back of her closet with three others. Her passion for jumpsuits waned during the years with Chip. That morning, she wondered if it would still fit. To her surprise, it was looser than before. The fabric was soft, pale blue, and sadly plain. She'd dressed it up with her peacock brooch, which she'd never liked but felt Chip, wherever he was, would be glad to see her wearing.

That it was completely wrong for her outfit showed in Karen's eyes.

"Aren't you looking fancy!" she said. The house smelled of fried fish, with an overlay of something sweet. She ushered Lavinia past the dining room table that was covered with old newspapers and magazines, just as it had been when Lavinia was last there, several years before. She once thought Karen's poor housekeeping meant she was a free spirit. Then she decided she was just a slob.

A mechanical whine rose from the open door leading down to the basement. Lavinia turned angrily in its direction. She hated loud noises. She went to the far reaches of the house when Alma vacuumed.

"Phil's refinishing an old chest. We're giving it to Lily. She's having a baby this fall," Karen said.

"What's Phil doing home?"

"School's out."

"Is it?"

"As of two weeks ago."

"Yes. Of course. Oh, and congratulations on becoming a grandmother."

"Thanks! It's wonderful news. Lily hasn't been feeling very well through the whole thing, but she's sturdy. She'll be fine."

They stood, listening to the whine spiraling toward them. Lavinia hoped Phil would stay down below, his dreadful noise notwithstanding. She wasn't up to being polite to both of them at once. Then there was the matter of the lunch she'd brought. There were two chicken salad sandwiches. She supposed they could be split three ways. The idea upset her. She liked order when it came to food. And everything else.

The fish smell seemed to grow stronger.

"Look, we can still go to The Inn, if you like. There's plenty of time," Lavinia said.

"Okay. But what about your lunch?"

"Leave it for Phil?"

"Good idea."

Lavinia went and returned with the brown paper bag from the grocery store. She realized it was a paltry offering and would have made a meager eat-in meal. How proud she'd once been of her good taste in everything! She used to have quite a flair. Dinnertime was a work of art after she married Chip. It always pleased him. Before that, meals were an exhausting affair of quickly thrown-together plates, raised voices, arguments around the table, and a sink full of dirty dishes she often ended up washing alone. The lame sandwiches she brought suggested that she had gone back in time, past her marriage with Potter, to the days when she lived alone in a small apartment with stained wallpaper and scuffed floors. She worked in a record shop and made herself a sandwich every night. If she kept up her backward flight, the next stop would be sitting unhappily at a small table with metal legs and considering before her the soft-boiled egg, headless in a cracked blue cup, and cereal served in a yellow bowl, the staples of her childhood.

"I'll just get my purse," Karen said. She went down the narrow hall to the bedroom.

The howl from the basement stopped. There were footsteps on the stairs. Phil emerged. He was a big man with ginger hair and a generous double chin. He wore a striped apron, the kind that looped over the neck and tied at the waist. Leaning out of one of the front pockets were the fat, orange fingers of a rubber glove. He took Lavinia in from head to toe, taking an extra moment at the brooch pinned to the left side of the jumpsuit's V-neck.

He embraced her roughly and stepped back quickly. He smelled of cigarettes and something spicy, an antiperspirant, maybe.

"How have you been?" he asked in a voice rich with sympathy.

"Fine. You?"

"Can't complain. Always good to get done for the year. And I'm not teaching summer school this time, though God knows we could use the money."

He looked at her probingly. He might have been remembering Karen getting laid off, although it had been several years.

"Karen says you're going on a trip," he said.

"Yes. Today. After lunch."

"Where to?"

"West."

He nodded. Again, the probing look.

Karen's high heels tapped down the hall. Her fringed suede purse flapped as she walked.

"Ready?" she said to Lavinia.

"Sure."

"There are sandwiches in the bag," Karen said to Phil. She didn't look at him.

"You bought sandwiches?" Phil asked.

Karen was already out the door. Lavinia followed her. Karen got into her pickup truck. The passenger door was dented and difficult to open. Lavinia would have preferred to take her car. She could keep control of the situation that way.

The truck came to life reluctantly. The engine was rough. Karen backed down the driveway, then into the main road without once consulting the rearview mirror. Here was a woman bent on flight.

"What's wrong?" Lavinia asked.

Karen pulled up close behind the car in front of her. She swore.

"Karen?"

"Sorry."

"What's going on?"

"I'm through."

"Meaning what?"

"I'm divorcing him."

"Jesus. Really?"

"I told him last night."

"He sure wasn't acting like a man who's being given the boot."

"Didn't register. Nothing ever does."

"You guys have been married so long, though," Lavinia said. As if that made a difference when you finally realized you'd had enough.

"Twenty-eight years."

"It's not easy to start over."

Karen glanced at her quickly. Her smirk was unmistakable. She was probably figuring that Lavinia's words were hollow, given how easy she thought it would have been to marry Chip's bank account.

"Not just financially. There's the emotional side to being single again," Lavinia said. Now *she* thought she sounded like a horse's ass.

"I'm seeing someone."

"Already?"

"Still, you mean. I have been for a while."

"Does Phil know?"

"No."

"Are you going to tell him?"

Karen shrugged. They were at a red light. Lavinia realized they were going in the opposite direction from the restaurant. She mentioned it.

"I know; I just needed to put a few more miles on this old beast so I could calm down a little."

The lunch hadn't been to wish Lavinia well or see how she was doing in her new widowed state. Karen wanted to talk.

They were on the outskirts of the college now, crossing one of the gorges. Students in shorts and flip-flops meandered along the bridge. A few were at the rail, looking at the rushing water below. Sometimes one of them jumped, usually at the end of the semester when they realized they were about to flunk out. A boy in Timothy's fraternity had plunged over one winter. He'd been drunk, and there had been speculation that he'd fallen from the path that ran down one side of the ravine. A note found in his room clarified that his intention had indeed been to destroy himself.

"Forget The Inn. We'll find something around here," Lavinia said.

Karen agreed.

Parking was a challenge. Lavinia suggested a space in the lot by the grocery store, though the sign clearly said these were for customers only. Lavinia promised that they wouldn't get towed. Karen was firm; they'd keep looking. Fifteen minutes later, a spot opened up on the street. Karen wasn't very good at parallel parking. She made three tries before wedging the truck between two much newer cars. She tapped the bumper of the one in back. Then she spent a good two minutes assessing if there had been any damage. She asked Lavinia to look and see. Lavinia bent down, peered, and saw nothing. She wondered how long it would take to get a cab to come pick her up and run her back to Karen's place, where she could jump in her car and flee.

When Karen decided that the bumper was unscathed, she turned to Lavinia and said, "So, where to?"

The area had changed since Lavinia had last visited. In place of burger and pizza joints were upscale restaurants advertising locally sourced ingredients and award-winning wine menus. One looked reasonable. The interior was dimly lit, with soft music in the background. A young woman in a long, black skirt and high heels showed them to a table by the front window. Lavinia asked if there were any booths available. The woman led them deeper into the restaurant. The booth she indicated was close to a swinging door that obviously led to the kitchen. That wasn't ideal, either, but Lavinia let it go. She sank gratefully onto the faux leather banquet seat. The wall next to her was decorated with three watercolors in a line, each depicting some natural facet of the area in and around Dunston. One was of the lake; the next, the bell tower on campus; and the third showed the falls seven miles outside of town. Each had a small, discreet sales tag taped just below. The artist was asking two hundred and fifty dollars apiece.

Karen read the menu. Everything on it was written in script. Lavinia looked, too. Nothing seemed appealing, but she had to eat something. She thought a slice of roasted tomato quiche would be nice. And a glass of Chardonnay. She shared this with Karen, who said she was in the mood for a Scotch on the rocks.

When the server came, they ordered their drinks and food. Karen was going for the lamb burger with bleu cheese. Lavinia thought that sounded revolting. She told the server she wanted to buy the artwork, all three pieces. She pulled out her credit card and handed it over. The server said she'd have to check with the manager.

"Are they for sale or not?" Lavinia asked. Yes, the server said. They were.

"Well, there you go." Lavinia shooed her away. She took the pictures off the wall, examined them, and set them on the bench beside her.

Karen seemed to have been lost in thought during the entire transaction. Then she focused on Lavinia.

"What did you just do?" she asked.

"Bought those watercolors."

"Oh. Why?"

"Why not? I'll look at them from time to time on the road and see if they remind me of home."

Karen nodded.

Lavinia asked who the guy was, the one she was seeing.

Someone she'd met through her bowling league. He was divorced, with two grown sons. They got along well. Shared the same values. Lavinia couldn't say what those values were. Their entire friendship, before and now, seemed to consist of a series of complaints one of them had about something. That, and the fact that they both enjoyed alcohol. She supposed there were flimsier reasons why people connected.

"So, you're in love, is that it?" Lavinia asked. Her wine had arrived, and she was admiring its gold tone.

"I guess so. I mean, I think so."

"And him?"

"He says he is."

"But what you really want is out. And this guy is a way."

"I'd go anyway."

"That bad?"

Living with Phil was like being trapped in a painting, Karen said, just as fake as those watercolors of Lavinia's. Everyone thought they were totally happy. Only Phil was happy. And that was because he was oblivious to what went on inside her. Even if she screamed at him, he just looked confused, then smiled like an idiot and went back to the basement to work on some stupid project. Not that the chest for Lily was stupid; she didn't mean that. It was the way he used his hobby as an excuse to avoid thinking about anything difficult.

You could never be sure what someone else was actually thinking, Lavinia said. Take Potter. When he was drunk, his mind was always running over something that pissed him off, and he made sure Lavinia heard all about it. But when he was sober, he often fell silent, and for a long time Lavinia assumed that all was well inside his head, that he wasn't mulling or agonizing over anything, and then *POP*—out of the blue— he'd say something weird.

When Angie was having trouble with that professor she was in love with—she'd mentioned that before, right?— Lavinia assumed it was just a matter of time before she bounced back, but while she did recover, it wasn't complete, as if something had gone out of her forever. When she told Potter in passing, probably when she was picking up one of

124

the kids—this was after they'd split up—that she was surprised Angie had been so deeply affected, he said, "Not everyone is as tough as you." And his saying so meant he'd long thought it, probably the whole time they were married. She never knew he saw her like that. She always thought he saw her as desperate, needy, and scared, but that was only because that was how she felt, herself. What she'd felt and what he'd observed were two different things.

Karen had clearly drifted again while Lavinia talked.

"My point is, don't be so sure he'll take all this lying down," Lavinia said.

"Doesn't matter how he takes it. I gotta do what I gotta do."

"How about Lily? Does she know?"

"Not yet."

Lavinia had barely touched her quiche. Karen had made it through half of her burger and was staring at what she'd left on her plate. She suggested another round of drinks. Lavinia said she needed to keep a clear head if she was going to make it to Buffalo.

"Phil and I went to Buffalo once. Lily was still small. I was going nuts. I had to get out of the house, so he put us in the car and we took off."

"Sounds like fun."

"It sucked. Lily threw up in the car, I hadn't packed enough diapers for her, Phil's credit card was over the limit, and we had to spend the cash in my wallet—that I'd been saving for a bookkeeping class at the college."

"But you guys did all that traveling later. Weren't those good times?"

"No."

They sat. Karen's mood darkened. The look in her eyes when she finally met Lavinia's was almost wrenching.

"Look, I have no right to ask you this, but would you put off leaving for a little while longer? In case ... I don't know, in case something rotten happens?" she asked.

"Like what?"

Karen shook her head.

"Nothing's going to happen. You know what you want. Just go and get it."

Karen signaled the waitress and asked for another drink. It arrived immediately. Karen drank it quickly.

"Everything's so easy for you, isn't it?" she asked.

"I just lost my husband!"

"And just how much does that hurt?"

The blood rushed to Lavinia's face.

"I loved him, you know," she said.

"Did you?"

Lavinia paid the bill with the card the server had finally returned from the purchase of the watercolors; said she needed a brown paper bag to put them in, which the server provided reluctantly; and asked Karen if she were sober enough to drive.

"Of course."

Even so, Karen seemed a little wobbly behind the wheel. When she sniffed, Lavinia realized she was fighting back tears. She was so glad to see Karen's driveway come into sight, she turned down her invitation to step inside for a moment and freshen up. That was what gas stations were for. She promised to call and check in regularly.

"I'm sorry about what I said," Karen said once they were both out of the truck.

"It's okay."

"I'm just … scared as hell."

"I know."

Karen gave her a damp, meaty hug and walked away.

chapter eleven

The light woke her. Yellowish white, in angled bars allowed by the cheap blinds. She brought her wrist within view. Her watch said it was just after six. She'd checked in late because there'd been roadwork for miles on the interstate. She ate at the diner across the street. Chicken fried steak, a dish she hadn't seen since she was a kid. She devoured it. All those days of light eating and too much drinking had hollowed her out. Then she slept hard, which she'd assumed she wouldn't be able to. She always had trouble with strange beds.

She got to her feet. The new nightgown she'd bought clung cozily to her legs. Nightgowns were another rediscovery. She'd worn them for years, then switched to pajamas when she married Chip. She pulled up the blinds. The strings were out of sync, so one side lifted much higher than the other. The view was of downtown. Glorious Buffalo! Not much seemed to be going on at that hour, though she could hear traffic rumbling on the highway, visible in the corner of her slanted view.

Despite the delays, the drive had been an intoxicating rush of freedom. She'd seen some remarkable things: a family of six or seven people waiting patiently on the shoulder while the man/father changed the tire of their ancient Volkswagen bus; a discarded lawn chair, also on the shoulder; and a child's pink shoe, dead center in the right-hand lane. Also, a few smashed-up animal carcasses, one clearly a raccoon, which made her recall the raccoons of her youth, banging around at night in their metal trash cans, and her father lurching to his feet and out the door after them, rifle in hand.

The shower curtain had a daisy pattern. The tub was yellow. So were the basin and the toilet. Lavinia took it as an affirmation of the shift occurring within her. Yellow was the color she hated most, yet here it was, all around, and it didn't bother her at all. She even admired it, a little. The hot water took time to come up. Lavinia thought she'd mention it to the manager, a frail little man with a nasty cough, though he probably wasn't on duty in the daytime.

He'd looked at her skeptically as she came through the door. When she filled out the reservation card and had to indicate her car's make and model, he stared at it for a moment as if he suspected some sort of subterfuge. The motel was clean but very plain, not at all the kind of place Lavinia would have stayed before Chip died. The place was more Karen's speed. Lavinia thought she might send her a postcard of the building, and asked the manager if he had any. He produced one from underneath the counter.

She took a long shower. The bath towels were scratchy, but not unpleasantly. With one around her and another around her dripping hair, she pulled her clothes out of Foster's borrowed backpack. She chose a white silk tank top and a blue linen skirt. She slipped on her newest pair of sandals, the ones she'd worn to the brunch with Angie, and ambled across the parking lot to the diner. The smell of fresh coffee greeted her. Also, bacon frying. She was famished.

She sat in a booth and gazed euphorically through the grimy window. She hadn't dried her hair, and it hung damply down her back. With the air conditioning on high, she shivered. She needed a cup of hot coffee. No one was around.

"Hello?" she called out.

She rose and walked behind the counter. She pushed open one of the swinging doors that led to the kitchen. It was empty. Several strips of bacon were sizzling on the grill. She approached and assessed them. They were close to burning. She turned off the grill. A man came out of a storeroom carrying a cardboard box. He stopped and stared at her.

"Your bacon's about to go up in smoke," she said.

"Who the hell are you?"

"Your first customer of the day, and I'm all alone out there."

The man put down the box and asked Lavinia to take a seat, he'd be right with her.

He appeared a moment later with an empty coffee mug that he put on the table before her. In his other hand was the coffee pot. He poured some into her cup without asking if she wanted any. He had a laminated menu under his arm. He put that down, too. Lavinia looked up into his face. It was jowly and red-cheeked. A small nick was on his chin, probably from a hasty shave that very morning. He seemed about her age, in his early fifties, but then, she'd never been any good at guessing how old someone was.

"That must have been your breakfast I turned off in there," she said.

"Yup."

"I hope you don't think I'm just an old snoop, poking around for the hell of it."

He asked if she wanted cream and sugar. She said black was fine.

"I'm not too keen on bacon, myself," she said.

"Lots else to choose from."

He finally seemed to realize that she was trying to be friendly. He nodded and said he'd be back in a minute to take her order.

A woman came through the entrance wearing a red and white checkerboard dress under a white apron. Her hair was up. She put her purse behind the counter, took note of Lavinia, and stuck her head into the kitchen. She said something to the man.

He replied with, "Goddamn it!"

The woman went all the way in. Their voices rose and fell for a few minutes. Lavinia sipped her coffee. She studied the menu. Pancakes? Way too heavy. Eggs over easy? They had to be done perfectly. Scrambled was always a safe bet.

The woman emerged, flushed, tense as a bullet. She marched over to Lavinia and removed her order pad from the pocket of the apron.

"What can I get for you this morning?" she asked. Her voice was light and pleasant, despite her outward appearance.

Good fake job there, girl!

"Two scrambled eggs and a slice of sourdough toast."

"That all?"

"Yes."

"Don't eat much, do you?"

"That's actually quite a big breakfast for me."

The telephone on the wall by kitchen rang. The waitress stared at it in silent fury. She returned to her station behind the counter without answering it. The man emerged, spatula in hand, and put the receiver to his ear. He didn't say hello. After a moment, he said, "Not this time. I told you that before." He slammed the receiver into the cradle, took the piece of paper with Lavinia's order that the waitress had set on the counter, and shoved his way back through the swinging doors.

While she waited, Lavinia took out her cell phone. Marta had called her the evening before, late, after she had silenced it for the night. There was also a call from Angie and one from Mel. Timothy had texted to say he hoped she was having a blast. Alma had left a long message about the garbage bin, which she had finally taken upon herself to steer down the driveway. Of course, collection day wasn't until the end of the week. She wondered where she should stow full trash bags in the meantime. Probably in the garage. Then she could put them out, too. Did that sound like a good idea? Well, she'd figure it out, but if Lavinia had any suggestions, she should give her call. Oh, and remember to have fun out there, wherever the hell she was!

Lavinia put her phone away when the waitress returned to refill her coffee cup. Her face was red and blotched.

"What's it all about?" Lavinia asked. The woman looked her in the eye in such a direct manner that Lavinia was temporarily unnerved.

"My son got himself arrested. Again."

"I'm sorry."

"He has a drinking problem. They took away his license. He drove anyway."

"And he got pulled over, and that was that."

"Pretty much."

"How old?"

"Twenty-seven."

Lavinia thought of Foster, Marta, and Maggie, her three twenty-somethings.

"He's looking at jail time now," the waitress said.

Lavinia nodded. She'd gone into a realm she wasn't entirely comfortable with, though she knew she'd walked in all by herself.

The waitress took herself off. Lavinia stared out the window and considered the misery of young people. Timothy and his rocky moods. The twins, in their selfish, fragile world. Angie's sullen years, her rebellious spirit. And Foster, with his constant anxiety. The problem with being young was that you were unaware that nothing lasted, good or bad. Knowing the temporary nature of distress was helpful when trying to keep one's head above water.

Now, as to why this young man drank, who could say? Some kind of pain, obviously. Why he overdid it came down to either laziness, or weakness. Maybe they were the same thing. Or maybe sometimes laziness was a kind of stubbornness, digging in your heels and not doing what you had to. Potter didn't like working; that had been his laziness. He didn't feel he should have to if he didn't want to. No, that wasn't it, either. He hated having to drive a delivery truck, stock shelves, or sweep floors for people who weren't as smart as he was, but who were better educated. There were ladders he could have climbed even so, if he'd been more patient.

It seemed, looking back, that the whole time they were married, Potter had been in a state of panic. Another man might have reacted by striving to achieve and accomplish, but Potter shrank away and clutched whatever he could hold onto. And that, more often than not, was a bottle. He was like a refugee standing on a piece of land that got smaller and smaller as the years went by. That land had been Lavinia's opinion of him. The more disdainful she became, the more he drank. If he only could have taken himself in hand and sobered up long enough to make a real change in his life—in their lives together.

If wishes were fishes.

He'd needed her to help him. To believe in him, to say he could. She had nothing to give him. Everything went to the children, to working, to running the house. Her burdens,

135

carried on her shoulders alone, made her hard, unsympathetic, and ultimately cruel. Love hadn't been enough to get them through the challenging times. Love hadn't been able to keep them together.

He'd moved on. He was working for Mary Beth in her construction company. He made the first contact with homeowners and got a sense of what they wanted to do and how much they could spend. He was attentive, calm, and polite. He inspired confidence. When there were conflicts, he solved them. He'd learned a lot listening to Lavinia's complaints over the years, or so it seemed. And now his life was working.

Lavinia's wasn't, even before Chip got zapped.

She never really thought about divorcing him. She assumed, when despair crept in, that she'd come around, kick herself in the pants, and find something that gave her life meaning. She could open herself and remember that they'd once had a lot of fun together. He appreciated her business acumen. He could make her laugh. She'd liked working for him more than she'd enjoyed being his wife. On the job, he was blunt, swore a lot, and made fun of customers. When they married, he became guarded and deferential. She'd married two men who were afraid of her.

The waitress brought her plate. Lavinia ate quickly, fighting back tears. More people entered the diner. A family with a wailing child sat two tables away. Lavinia studied the infant's red, damp face and wondered what nonverbal thoughts were racing around in his developing brain. His mother moved him off her lap and dropped him roughly on the seat next to her. When he tried to get back in her lap, she pushed him back. The man with her remonstrated.

"You take him then," the woman said. The man didn't move. He was studying the menu. The woman wasn't.

The waitress brought Lavinia's bill. She appraised Lavinia's changed mood. Something like understanding, or at the very least acknowledgment, brightened her eyes. Lavinia nodded. When the waitress had gone, Lavinia left a fifty-dollar bill on the table, secured with the salt shaker. The tab had come to $9.85.

At the motel, she dried her hair, pinned it, stuffed her toiletries in the small backpack, and left. She was heading to Niagara Falls. The grand rush of water would block out her thoughts. The map she'd taken from the motel office the night before was spread out on the seat next to her. She didn't consult it after seeing several road signs telling her the way. It was still quite early, and there was little traffic. Her cell phone buzzed. She didn't look to see who it was. She thought about tossing into the Falls when she got there. People probably did that all the time—throw away remnants of their damaged lives. She bet a lot of wedding bands had been donated, packets of letters, lockets with pictures of the morally bankrupt. If she trashed her phone, though, someone would flip out and call the police.

A large billboard advertising a flea market caught her eye. *7 Days a Week. Turn Left on Lincoln, follow the signs.* Lavinia did exactly that, and soon came to a street bordering a large, grassy field where several rows of tents were installed. A few cars were parked randomly because no formal spaces were marked. Lavinia pulled up next to a pickup truck that looked very much like Karen's, only older. She punched her number into her cell phone. The call went right into voicemail.

"Hi, Karen, it's me, out here in the wilds of Buffalo. Hope you're well. Feel free to give me call. If I don't pick up, I'm driving, but I promise I'll call back. Great seeing you ..." For a moment, Lavinia couldn't remember when that had been. Was it only yesterday that they had lunch? Getting on the road had stretched time, pulling recent events into a psychic space that made her feel far away. She hung up.

Though the air was cool, the heat of the sun said it would be a warm day. The grass still held its morning damp, and Lavinia's toes, in her elegant sandals, soon grew chilly. At first glance, much of what was for sale was used furniture: dressers, coffee tables, side chairs, lamps, cribs, changing tables, and a few bedroom sets. Some pieces were handsome, even stately, but much of it was scratched, leaning, missing knobs or feet, stained, nicked, and dirty. The people selling them often looked just as beaten up, with a cheerful veneer, friendly words, a warm invitation to take a closer look. One man had an electric coffee pot connected to a long orange cord that met a small generator at the back of his tent. The coffee was for customers, yet the noise of the machine made it unpleasant to linger. His table was covered with trays of costume jewelry, some of it decent. Chip would have been delighted with the bumblebee pins. The man admired Lavinia's peacock and asked if it were real. When she cupped her hand behind her ear, he turned off the generator and asked again.

"Yes."

The man whistled. He assumed she'd have no interest in selling it.

"How much?" she asked.

He wondered if he could see it. She removed it and handed it over. He pulled a loupe out of the pocket of his plaid shirt, and from the way he peered closely at the stones, he knew about gems.

"Couldn't give you more than six hundred, but it's worth closer to twenty-five hundred," he said. His meaty hands and thick fingers held the brooch lovingly.

"No one around here would buy a thing like that."

"At a flea market? No way. I've got another store in town, a jewelry exchange."

"You mean a pawn shop."

"If you like."

"I don't think I'm ready to pawn my brooch."

"You don't look like you need to, that's for sure. But it never hurts to ask."

He returned the brooch, then turned the generator back on. As Lavinia was moving away, he offered her a cup of coffee by making a pouring motion. She shook her head.

In the next row, racks of clothes were for sale. Oversized sweaters a few decades old, ties, snow boots, high heels in many colors (usually black or red), belts, a couple of fake fur vests, and a raccoon hat dangling from a string overhead. Next door were dishes, trays of tarnished silverware, many sets of chopsticks, teapots, and candlesticks. Lavinia looked at everything closely, imagining where these items might have once resided, the hands that held them day in and day out. A china vase had visible cracks. Broken, and glued carefully back together. Lavinia asked the woman at the table how much it cost. The woman said the price was taped to the bottom. Seventy-five cents. Lavinia turned the vase upside down. A single dried leaf drifted out. The blue glaze was uneven and cracked. Lavinia was sure someone had purchased it in one of those paint-it-yourself places. It didn't matter. She loved the color. She gave the woman a dollar and asked if she had a bag. The woman didn't. Lavinia tucked the vase under her arm and continued.

At the end of the row, a table had box after box of black and white photographs. Some had writing on the back with a year, a name, a place—*Beverly Falls* or *North Platte River*—but most were blank. Many had scalloped edges that Lavinia remembered from the albums of her youth. Her mother had been meticulous about her pictures, most of which were from her own early years, before she married Lavinia's father, at which time the pictures stopped abruptly. What happened to them? Black construction paper pages, and notations written in silky white ink.

Lavinia had taken pictures of her children as they grew up, until each became a teenager. Then there was too much resistance to sitting still while Lavinia fiddled with her camera. Some went in albums, most were in shoeboxes, like the ones here on the table. They came with her to Chip's house and lived in a closet in the converted basement. She assumed that one day, if any of her kids became parents themselves, they would want them. It went like that, didn't it, the life cycle of children and parents? A new baby is cause for great joy and wanting to capture the moment. Then the child grows up and the moments are less joyous. Memories get locked away, then it begins all over again, years later, and for a while everyone is awash in wonder and delight.

You're turning into quite a philosopher, Lavinia.

The shots in one box were all of one family, standing awkwardly in front of the same house, moving forward through time. The house had columns and a set of steps that served as the stage for the group of seven. They kept the same position—parents seated, two boys on the right, two girls on the left, and a son standing behind them all. Lavinia went through them, watching them age. The mother looked increasingly frail, though her eyes retained the same spark. The clothes evolved, too, from the severe 1880's garb to what had to be the climbing hemlines of World War I. The oldest boy was in uniform in the last picture. That there were no others suggested that he might have been killed.

Lavinia asked the woman seated behind the table how much it would be for the whole set.

"Dollar," she said. She was knitting something with yellow yarn. A white dog lay at her feet, snoring.

"Yours?"

"What, the people in the pictures? Nope. Found them in my attic when I bought the house."

"Is this your house then, with the columns?"

"Nope."

Someone's life in a box, left behind for her to find.

Lavinia gave her the dollar, then took the eleven snapshots and dropped them one by one inside the vase. The mouth was large enough for them to go in easily. The knitting woman paused to watch Lavinia insert them.

"Handy," she said.

Lavinia turned away. The air was cooler, and the sun had dimmed. Clouds moved in, and the wind lifted. Thunder sounded. Lavinia stopped. There had been only a little rain in Dunston since the day of Chip's game, none with thunder or lightning. Hearing it now, gauging its distance and direction, Lavinia understood that for the rest of her life that one sound would command her attention and fill her with despair.

"You okay?" the knitter asked.

"There's a storm coming."

"Doubt it. Moving off to the south, see?"

Lavinia looked at the corner of the sky the woman had indicated. The clouds were drifting away. For a moment, it was as if they were pulling her along behind them. Would it be so bad to be lifted and carried aloft?

She continued her survey of items for sale: candles, egg holders, butter knives, hacksaws, rakes and spades, spools of ribbon, a bolt of lace cloth. Two green velvet pillows reminded her suddenly of Alma. Alma liked to pad around in a pair of green velvet slippers that were at odds with her stretch pants and plaid shirts.

Dear Alma.

A woman at the last stall was on her phone.

"No way. Not now. Can't you deal with it?" she said. She blushed. She hung up. When she looked at Lavinia, her face grew even pinker.

"Didn't mean to eavesdrop. Bad habit of mine," Lavinia said. Her eyes dropped down to the wares on the table. Bookmarks. Hand painted, embroidered, woven, usually in purple and red, which Lavinia always thought was a sad combination. Some were laminated, others depicted the Falls. Next to the bookmarks was a tray of silver thimbles. A few looked quite old. Lavinia asked the woman how she'd come by them. Her grandmother had had a passion for needlework, and collected them over the years.

"Don't you want to keep them, for sentiment's sake?" she asked.

The woman's face was no longer red, but her eyes were hard, like bitter marbles.

"Need to raise money," she said.

"Tight?"

Again, the bitter glare.

"None of my business. I'm sorry."

Lavinia went on admiring the thimbles. One had a floral pattern, another twining vines.

"I'll take the whole tray. How much?" she asked.

"Name your price."

Lavinia put three one hundred-dollar bills on the table, then dropped the eight thimbles, one by one, into the vase.

"Wait," the woman said as Lavinia turned away. She was quite a few steps away when the woman appeared at her elbow, saying Lavinia must have made a mistake.

"Many, but not this. Take it, and good luck," she said.

The woman went on looking reluctant, then gave Lavinia a quick, rough hug.

Her cell phone buzzed again. It was Marta's number. This early?

"What are you doing up at this hour?" Lavinia asked.

"Maggie got arrested."

"What the hell?"

"Last night at a gallery opening. She got mad at the owner for not showing her work. She said she should be hanging on the wall, not the hacks up there now. He asked her to lower her voice, and when she didn't, he told her to leave. She threw her drink at a painting. The cops got there in no time."

"Where did they take her?"

Marta named the precinct in the West Village.

"Are they going to release her?"

"On bail, yes."

"How much?"

"Five hundred dollars."

"You've got that."

"Well, actually …"

"What do you mean? I just sent you a big check."

Marta hadn't wanted to say anything, but she was investing in a small theater troupe. The guy running it was someone she'd met the year before in a workshop. He'd been turned down for as many parts as Marta had, and decided to take matters into his own hands. He had a script from a brilliant new playwright from England, Lucas Somebody, and had wrangled a small performance space upstate somewhere, Marta couldn't remember.

"How much money did you give this clown?" Lavinia asked.

"He's not a clown. He's very smart."

"Smart and broke."

"That's not his fault."

"No, especially when he knows how to pick his friends."

Marta grew exasperated. What with Maggie getting hauled off, and her bank account unable to get her out today, she was in a pretty bad mood, thank you very much.

"Use your credit card," Lavinia said. She didn't know if bail bondsmen accepted them or not.

"Well, see, that's another issue."

"You maxed it again. For the genius producer."

"No!"

Lavinia took her wallet out once more and gave Marta her credit card number.

"And I better not see any other charges on there. When you get Maggie out, call me right away. I want to hear from her exactly what happened."

"Okay."

There followed a long pause. In the background, a cat meowed insistently. Lavinia didn't know the twins had gotten a cat.

"Go get your sister, then call me back," Lavinia said.

"Okay."

Lavinia knew they wouldn't call once the problem had been solved. That wasn't her role, receiving good news. Only bad.

She put her things in the car, and headed out.

chapter twelve

Four days later, Lavinia woke to the peals of a church bell. She was in Rapid City. Between the motel she left each morning and the one she checked into at night were over five hundred miles. Watching the land change from rolling to flat and back again fascinated her. She noted every new feature with awe.

It was nine. That was the latest she'd slept since getting on the road. Her rest the night before had been unusually peaceful. As she lay listening to the bell, she realized it was the Fourth of July. That was not a remarkable thing in and of itself. The only remarkable thing was that it was also exactly one month since Chip died.

He came to her then, in all his bumbling awkwardness. His hand, spotted with brown, rested on her knee as they sat on the patio, watching the twilight drop deliciously down through the trees. His voice was low and rich as he detailed something funny he'd seen that day, which often included the antics of her own children. He'd loved them all in his way. She'd asked him once if he minded the estrangement with his two sons in Texas. He said at first he had, a great deal, then came to accept that blood ties weren't always enough to keep someone in your orbit. He struck her in that moment as being very brave, or very wise. He inspired confidence and made her think he was a man with a keen understanding of the human condition.

Yet most of the time she hadn't thought so. She thought his reluctance to offer opinions meant he was stupid, or at the very least out of touch. And what had she asked him to judge? Just about everything, really. A piece of furniture, a story in the newspaper, a driver in front of them who didn't signal a turn. He noted everything blandly, without anger. Aside from that one time when he yelled at his son on the phone, he never got mad. Except at her.

"Yeah? Well too bad about that," she said to the empty room.

She dressed in a pair of khaki shorts and a white tank top. The jumpsuits were now at the bottom of her pack, below the T-shirts and blue jeans she'd also brought. She'd gotten herself a pair of hiking sandals, the kind you can also wear in water.

The shorts were loose. That was because she only had an appetite at dinner. After her first hearty breakfast on the road, she now had only black coffee. Lunch was a piece of fruit. Sometimes she was overwhelmed with the desire for a candy bar. She'd allowed herself one in Gary, Indiana, when she stopped for gas. Sitting behind the wheel, staring through her bug-smeared windshield and chewing on chocolate and caramel had been heady. She sat so long at the pump the man in line behind her asked if she were having engine trouble.

One more long day of driving would bring her to Helena, Montana, where her former sister-in-law and husband lived. She hadn't told them she was coming. If they didn't want to receive her, she'd find yet another motel and be on her way the following day.

She was no longer transporting the photographs and thimbles in the vase. Those were now in a pair of plastic containers she'd purchased at a local grocery store in Iowa the day before. The vase was put to its original use and positioned carefully in the foot well of the passenger seat. Yesterday's arrangement had been daisies. Today, she'd look for roses. Her first stop after leaving the motel was the grocery store two blocks west.

She consulted her phone as she walked across the parking lot. She hadn't looked at it for a while. Maggie had texted two days before (*I'm free!*), but there'd been nothing further from either of the twins. Alma had left a long, cheerful voicemail saying the trash had been collected, the old clothes, too, and that the bird bath was currently home to a pair of robins several times a day. Angie had been over to see how she was getting along in Lavinia's absence. Angie really was the most thoughtful young lady. And that oddball Timothy was living with had dropped in to see if they had any spare paintbrushes in the basement she might borrow. Seemed like she wanted to turn their kitchen dark blue so that the white cabinets they just refinished would pop.

Then she went into a monologue about the neighbor's cat going way up one of their trees and taking its own sweet time to come back down. Just sat up there yowling like an idiot. Alma had had a mind to pitch rocks at it until it took itself off, but figured the neighbor would get up in her face for that, and as Lavinia well knew, that old Mrs. Burridge was one piece of work. Hell, she'd have the mayor on the phone before too long if Alma, or anyone, raised a finger against her precious Fluffy.

Karen had left a message saying she'd only just picked up the one Lavinia left the day before. She said she was fine, that things were … progressing.

There was also a message from Mel wishing her the best and begging for a phone call in return. Lavinia had meant to get in touch with him ever since she'd left town and just couldn't bring herself to.

Foster texted her about work, saying he was being considered for a full-time position at the vet's office, but it would be in the reception area, not back with the animals, which wasn't something he really wanted to do. Lavinia could infer the strain from the printed words on her screen. Foster was a born worrier.

The grocery store was bright and empty. Lavinia was overcome with melancholy the moment the automatic doors slid apart to admit her. She couldn't find the baskets, so she pulled out a shopping cart, which struck her as absurd for carrying a simple bouquet of flowers. The floral department was overrun with Mylar balloons featuring cartoon characters and peppy slogans. *You're one of a kind!* and *Give it all you got!* On a low table were some small teddy bears with red ribbons tied around their furry necks. One in a blue sweater caught her eye, and she picked him up.

Oh, why the hell not?

The roses were surprisingly fragrant.

"Buy them by scent, not looks," she'd always tell Chip when their anniversary rolled around. Still, the poor clod always produced stale bouquets that wilted within a day.

The image of him, flowers in hand, returned. She wiped her eyes. She picked pink roses, then headed to the aisle where bottled water was sold. She hadn't filled the vase at the motel.

The woman at the check-out line handled everything with great care.

"I'm sorry," she said.

"For what?"

"Whoever's sick."

She pointed to the bear's sweater.

Get well soon!

"Family or friend?" the woman asked.

"Both."

The woman nodded. Lavinia swiped her credit card. It was declined.

Maggie and Marta!

She used another one. It went through.

Did she care for a bag?

"No. Thank you."

The overcast sky had given way to rushing clouds and glimpses of blue. The change both made her restless and filled her with hope.

She put the bear on the passenger seat. She poured water into the vase and arranged the roses. The vase was kept in place with a pair of bricks she'd found in the parking lot of the motel in Gary. Sadly, they'd damaged the glaze even more.

After settling herself behind the wheel, she realized she hadn't had any coffee. She went back into the store. At the far end was a kiosk serving lattés and espresso. She asked for the drip of the day. That made her think of Mel, and she laughed suddenly. The server took it in stride. He looked like he'd been up for hours, judging from his dark circles. He asked if she wanted anything else. She pointed to a banana sitting in a basket on the counter. That would take care of lunch, too.

Back in the car, she sipped her coffee, then slid it into the holder in the console. She called Maggie's phone, knowing it was too early for her to be up and that she'd be sent right into voicemail.

"Hi, dear, it's Mom calling you from Rapid City. I'm glad you're out of the pokey, but we need to talk about the card number I gave Marta. You guys just got a shitload of money from me, and you're going through it faster than a hot knife through butter. So, put the damn brakes on, okay? Take care. And don't pitch anymore fits. At least not in public."

She tossed the phone on the seat next to the bear.

"Ask me before you use that," she said.

She drove. She told Chip that yes, she was talking to the bear, and no, the bear was not talking back.

You knew that about me, right?

He would laugh when she insulted the food she was cooking.

"Get busy, and don't burn," she'd command her sautéed onions.

"Oh, what the hell's wrong with you now?" she'd demand of the living room curtains that always caught when she closed them.

155

His arms would go around her from behind.

"You tell 'em," he'd say and kiss her neck.

She drove. The flowers gave off their lovely scent. The bear kept quiet.

Her cell phone buzzed. A few minutes later it buzzed again. After twenty more minutes, another call came in.

Lavinia answered.

"What?" she shouted.

"Who's this?" It was a man's voice.

"Who the hell is *this*?"

"Where's Georgette?"

Lavinia couldn't tell if he were angry or scared. Maybe both.

"You've got the wrong number," she said, and hung up. She navigated back to the right-hand lane, signaled, then pulled slowly onto the shoulder. She examined her call record. The man had called twice. Another was from Angie.

Lavinia punched in her number.

"Where are you?" Angie asked.

"In my car, on the shoulder, on the highway outside of Rapid City. What's up?"

"You pulled over to call me back?"

"Obviously."

Then Angie felt bad for disturbing her. It could wait. Lavinia said to just please get it off her chest. Angie said she was planning to go down to the City and check on the twins. She'd heard about Maggie's arrest. Marta had called asking for money.

"Wait, when the hell was this?"

"Day before yesterday."

"You didn't give her any, did you?"

"I didn't have it to give. So, no."

Lavinia shared her side of the saga. Was it possible that they'd gotten into drugs?

"I doubt it. I think this is just some random thing. Maggie got mad at the gallery because she's unhappy about her painting in general, and Marta is really trying to do something with this theater guy. They're not good at sticking to a budget. They never have been."

But she still wanted to put eyes on the situation, as it were.

"Let me know how it goes," Lavinia said.

They signed off.

The day wore on, warmer by the hour. Just before noon, the digital thermometer on her dashboard said it was ninety-four degrees. She pulled into a rest area that was pleasantly shaded. She took her banana, bear, and bouquet to a picnic table along with the second bottle of water she'd gotten at the store. She sat, nibbled the banana, tapped the bear on its head, and enjoyed how the shade had managed to make the pink blossoms an even richer hue. Then she pulled out her phone and snapped a selfie.

Taking time to smell the roses!

She took a picture of the bear next to the flowers. She went back to the car and dug out the plastic container of thimbles, which she arranged in a circle on the surface of the table. With the bear in the middle, she took another picture, then one of the vase similarly encircled. She imagined showing these to her children and watching them puzzle over the meaning of it all.

Last night's dream, ended by the pealing church bells, replayed.

She watched a line of mountain climbers scale a rocky slope. The landscape was barren, no trees, no streams or lakes, all under a muted light, as if an eclipse of the sun were taking place. The ascent was slow, though the grade wasn't particularly steep. It wasn't clear if she should join them or simply go on observing their progress.

Then she was on the edge of steep ravine, and a woman was walking along the bottom. She looked up, eyes shaded, and yelled for Lavinia to throw down a rope. Lavinia did. With the rope secured above and tied firmly about the woman's waist, she began to pull herself upward by wedging her hands and feet into nicks in the wall.

Lavinia had woken before the woman made it out of the ravine. She seemed like the kind of person who wouldn't give up. Lavinia understood that she was both the woman in the ravine and the one who'd thrown the rope. Given where she was now, that made perfect sense. Who were the people climbing the mountain, though? And why hadn't she felt like joining them?

"You blaze your own trail, Lavinia."

How Chip had admired her drive! Her determination to succeed. She sold more manufactured homes than anyone else in his company, month after month. She knew what made people tick. She could see when they were susceptible to being oversold. She would talk wistfully about how lovely it would be to have that extra bedroom, even if it meant more money. It was always the wife who wanted the space for herself, a place to craft or paint, sometimes just to sleep apart from a snoring husband. The men always wanted the optional side awning so they could sit outside and drink or smoke or read the paper in peace.

She realized she was being closely watched by a guy with a lot of tattoos. The dog he was walking was some small, energetic breed, a terrier mix, probably. It darted back and forth in front of him so that he had to switch the leash from side to side. After a moment, he approached the table where Lavinia sat.

"Stood up?" he asked.

"Sorry?"

"Guy stood you up?"

He must have thought, from the objects on the table, that Lavinia was holding a celebration.

"No. Just me."

"You mind?" he asked, gesturing to the seat opposite.

"Help yourself."

He sat. Up close, Lavinia could see life had worn him hard. His eyes were wary, his friendly manner false. Under different circumstances, Lavinia might have been afraid. But there, in a well-populated place, she wasn't.

He studied the circle of thimbles and the bear. Lavinia studied his tattoos. The name Angeline was written in cursive on one forearm.

"Daughter?" she asked, pointing.

"Ex-wife."

"Ah. My daughter's named Angelica. Goes by Angie."

He nodded.

"Bill," he said, extending his hand.

"Lavinia."

160

"That's some name."

"Bovine."

"Come again?"

"Sounds like what you'd name a cow."

"You're no cow."

"Moo."

His eyes bore right into hers. She could see him trying to decide if she were nuts.

"Where you heading?" he asked.

"Montana. See my sister-in-law. Ex-sister-in-law, actually."

"You divorced?"

"Widowed."

"Shame. Recent?"

"A month today."

"Wow."

His buzz cut was bluntly familiar. So was his cold, observing manner.

"Are you a cop?" she asked.

He removed his hands from the top of the table.

"It shows that bad?"

"A little."

He had been, until about two months before. He'd taken what some called early retirement. That's all he cared to say, but she could take it from him, it hadn't been his choice.

The tattoo on his other arm showed a serpent with a red, forked tongue.

"And you thought I looked like I might be in trouble, sitting over here all by myself," Lavinia said.

"More or less."

"Well, I'm not."

"Good to hear."

The dog stood on its hind legs and pawed at the man's arm.

"You'll be on your way soon, I expect," he said.

"I expect so, too."

He stood and wished her well.

She thought it was no wonder people were afraid of the police, if it was that hard to tell them from crooks. She told the bear it was time to pack up and hit the road.

She drove until sunset, which brought her to Bozeman. Her pleasure in the passing land had been high all afternoon as the prairie rose and fell, with white jagged peaks always in the distance. The motel she chose, like all the others, was close to the highway, modest, clean, and near a diner. This one was called Nell's. Lavinia found it a happy coincidence that her grandmother had had the same name. Half a block down was a laundromat she'd make use of right after dinner. A great sense of peace settled within her, aided by not having any new calls on her phone.

The fried chicken had been dipped in a honey batter with lots of black pepper. In between large bites, Lavinia contentedly shoveled in the mashed potatoes and steamed carrots. Fried chicken had been one of her specialties back in her cooking days. This recipe was better than hers. She'd ordered a single glass of red wine, and decided she could treat herself to a second. She'd get to Helena in no time at all tomorrow, if that were still her destination.

She opened the large road atlas she'd bought at a gas station back in Buffalo. She could have gone into Canada, if they hadn't changed the law. Now you needed a passport. What if she went south for another three or four days and ended up in Texas? Then she thought of Chip's cold-hearted sons living there, selling their plumbing supplies, waiting for Chip's lawyer to get them their share of the estate. If she recalled correctly, they lived outside of Dallas, which would be easy enough to avoid. But then, there was no chance in hell she'd ever run into them, unless she needed a faucet. Thinking that made her recall Mel's remark at dinner with Potter and

Mary Beth. She was struck suddenly with the irritating truth that she missed him.

A child was at the table, staring at Lavinia's stuffed bear. The bear was propped up against the sugar dispenser. The child, a little boy with large brown eyes, couldn't have been more than three. He looked Hispanic. A moment later a man came and moved him along, but not before giving the bear a good look, too.

"You're always attracting attention," Lavinia said, and put the bear on the bench seat next to her.

After the waitress gave Lavinia her second glass of wine and cleared away her polished plate, Lavinia called Mel.

"Are you all right?" he asked.

"I'm great!"

"I've been worried about you."

"No need. Things are going swimmingly."

She told him about the flea market, the daily flowers, the bear, and about Bill the cop.

"You got pulled over?" he asked.

"No! He came up to me in a rest stop and started talking, that's all."

"Looking for a date?"

It occurred to Lavinia for the first time that this might have actually been the case.

You're no cow.

"He was still wet behind the ears, Mel," she said.

They talked for a few more minutes. Sandy was fine, he said, though the housekeeper had quit. He thought she might have overheard him calling her a hippo under his breath. Lavinia said it served him right.

"It was just that slow, lumbering gait of hers," Mel said defensively.

"You want someone young and speedy, pay more."

Mel said he'd gone back to the golf course. The place just wasn't the same without Chip. He paused, then talked about his Jeep, how the tire was now repaired and he'd put an ad in the paper. It was time to get rid of it.

Lavinia asked him why he told Angie he wanted to marry her. She hadn't intended ever to bring it up, but sitting there, looking at the Montana scenery out the window, her stomach full and the wine starting to work its magic, something opened inside her.

"Because I do," he said.

"Why?"

"What do you mean, why? Why does anyone want to marry someone?"

"Sex, drugs, and rock and roll."

"Lavinia."

She laughed so hard, tears formed. The waitress looked her way.

"I'm sorry," Lavinia said.

"I was going to talk to you about it when you got home."

"And if I never come home?"

"Then we'll talk about it now, I guess."

Lavinia admired his practical turn of mind.

She had to know how he felt about her, how he'd felt about her for a long time. He didn't expect her to feel the same thing in return. They were mature, level-headed people. He thought they'd make a good team because they shared the same outlook on life.

"I hate golf," Lavinia said. She was thinking about ordering a slice of key lime pie.

"You don't have to play golf."

They could travel, Mel said.

"I'm already traveling," Lavinia said.

"I mean together."

Lavinia considered having Mel ride shotgun. It wouldn't be so bad having someone to talk to, although the bear was doing a good job in that department.

"I didn't know you were so lonely," Lavinia said.

Mel took his time responding.

He wasn't lonely, he said. He was used to living alone. They weren't the same thing. He didn't want Lavinia because he was bored with himself or how he spent his time (and here Lavinia wondered exactly what kept him busy, besides golf). He wanted her because, well, it should be obvious, because he loved her.

"Why?"

"Oh, Lavinia!"

"How can you? I'm such a pain in the ass!"

The child's father looked at her disapprovingly from two tables away.

Mel resumed. Did it ever occur to her that her spirit was highly attractive? She was a straight shooter. He always knew where he stood with her. She didn't pull her punches. Lavinia wondered how many more clichés he'd use to get his point across.

Yet she was greatly touched. And that sense of being important to someone made her feel terribly lonely all of a sudden.

Aren't you supposed to feel lonely when you realize no one gives a shit?

"I need to go," Lavinia said.

"Call me tomorrow."

"Can't promise."

"Well, call me sometime."

"Okay."

She passed on the pie, but had a third glass of wine.

A few days of relative sobriety caused the evening's intake to hit her harder than usual. She was clumsy loading the huge washing machine at the laundromat, and dropped several garments on the floor. She was about to add her silk jumpsuits when she realized what a mistake that would be. They'd have to wait until Patty's house where she could clean them by hand, but her underwear and T-shirts were busy sudsing away.

She sat in a yellow plastic chair and reviewed her strange conversation with Mel. She asked the bear his opinion. He offered nothing. He just lay there, slumped over on his side, drawing glances from the other patrons, one of whom looked like she'd been crying. She sat at the other end of the row of chairs. Every now and then, Lavinia detected a sniffle. The woman glanced repeatedly at her phone.

Lavinia flipped through a magazine.

Too many smiling women, too much red lipstick. Lavinia disliked lipstick. It made her feel as though she'd been kissing a bowl of Jell-O. Makeup should always be minimal, though she didn't always follow that rule, herself. When she first married Potter, she was into heavy eye shadow. She wanted to look glamorous, exotic, probably because she was neither, only a woman stuck at home who'd had to give up her job as a sales clerk in a clothing store because her first pregnancy had made her sick as hell. The other three were no better. Potter was always happy to learn that a new baby was on the way; even when she told him they were having twins, his joy was evident.

Potter.

She'd love to hear his voice. She pulled out her phone. There was a message from Timothy. He just said he hoped she was having fun, and to thank Alma for the paintbrushes. She hadn't heard the phone buzz over the noise of the machines.

She could tell Potter she was worried about the twins—again. And he'd listen. They'd say the same thing they always did, that they were good girls with bad judgment. He'd ask about her trip, especially if Mary Beth were somewhere else. Lavinia looked at her watch. It would be about nine in the evening in Dunston, and Mary Beth was sure to be home, next to him on the couch.

She put the phone away. The wash cycle had another few minutes. What to do until then?

She could consult the atlas, but she'd put it back in her motel room after dinner. There was time to go and get it now. The woman who'd been seated at the end of the row was at the glass door of the laundromat, looking up and down the parking lot, pacing.

"Excuse me," Lavinia said, and reached to push the door open.

"What do I look like to you?"

"Someone standing at the door of a laundromat."

"Like someone who just got dumped?"

Lavinia decided the woman was on the level.

"Have you been?" she asked.

"Seems so."

Her husband was supposed to have been back over two hours before.

"Try calling?"

"About forty times. Phone's almost out of juice."

The woman was a head taller than Lavinia and smelled strongly of sweat. She wasn't young, maybe in her early forties. An age where she should have been used to the rotten nature of people, Lavinia thought. That was pretty damn cynical, though, wasn't it?

The woman resumed her pacing. Her distress was hard to watch. Lavinia put a hand on her wide, freckled arm and told her to sit down, take a deep breath, and then tell her all about it.

Her name was Delray, like the town in Florida, but she wasn't from there. She was from Arkansas. Both she and Kyle were. Kyle was her husband. They were going to Missoula where her brother lived. The brother had offered Kyle a job. Kyle worked construction, when he got around to it, that is. Her brother built houses. There was a building boom, he said. Lots of jobs. Regular money.

"And you? What do you do?" Lavinia asked.

"Just about everything, one time or another."

She'd waited tables, worked in a carwash, bagged groceries, drove one of those community service buses that old people took to go to their doctor's appointments. That had been an easy job, and she'd liked it pretty damn well, except she'd failed the random drug test they did. Sometimes she smoked pot, and to be honest, it messed her up way less that booze did. Pot was better for your head. Everyone knew that. But rules were rules, and they weren't going to bend her way, so she got the boot. Okay, fine, whatever.

Lavinia excused herself to transfer her clothes. Delray seemed to have forgotten about hers, so Lavinia asked which washer she'd been using, then looked to see how far along the cycle was. It had another twenty minutes.

When Lavinia sat down again, Delray said her son was the problem. He was a good kid, but he always got between them. He was twenty-two and had a nasty girlfriend. Kyle thought the girlfriend was okay, fine, in fact, because she had big tits. Delray hated to say it, but Kyle sometimes thought with his dick, and that was a fact. Delray knew for sure that the girlfriend took money from her son's wallet without his knowing. She'd seen her do it. The girlfriend said she'd had his permission, but Delray thought that was crap. Even so, she said nothing to her son, but she mentioned it to Kyle, who said she worried too much.

There were other issues with the girlfriend. She drank too much, she banged up the son's car, and she was generally a slob. When they decided to move to Montana, Delray figured it wasn't her problem anymore, except just the other day the son said he was running low on cash and could they spare some until payday—he also worked construction—and Kyle let him have a couple hundred bucks, which was a hell of a lot of money to people who didn't have all that much to begin with. Didn't Lavinia agree?

"Yes. Absolutely."

Well, Delray knew goddamn good and well that the girlfriend was the reason for the shortfall, and she told Kyle he was enabling her. He said she was making an accusation without any proof, because even though she saw her with the son's wallet on one occasion, that didn't mean it was an ongoing thing. Why couldn't she give the girlfriend the benefit of the doubt? Because Delray knew her son was dumb about women the way men get, the way Kyle used to be dumb about her, truth be told, way back in their early days when she thought it was smart to use her looks to get what she wanted. If Lavinia knew what she meant.

"I do."

So, they had a big fight, and Kyle dropped her off to do their laundry (because it had been at least a week since the last time), saying he was just going to go cool off and be back in about a half an hour, which was two hours ago.

"You don't think he turned around and went back to Arkansas?"

"No. He probably just went on to Missoula without me. He'd figure I'd get myself there eventually. Only the son of a bitch didn't leave me any money, and I got exactly seventeen dollars in my wallet."

"I'll give you some."

"You don't have to do that. Hell, you might figure I made the whole thing up just to play on your sympathies."

"Wouldn't matter."

Delray considered this. She blew her nose into a handkerchief. Lavinia hadn't seen anyone use one for years. Delray was old-fashioned in the way she dressed, too. Frilly skirt with a short-sleeved shirt; white sneakers with white ankle socks.

Lavinia said to come to the motel with her; she'd pay for a room, and in the morning, she could take her as far as Helena, with fare to get the rest of the way.

"I can't ask you to do that," Delray said.

"You didn't ask."

"I don't know when I can pay you back."

"You don't have to pay me back."

Delray looked at Lavinia, sizing her up.

"What's your story, anyway?" she asked.

"I'm loaded. In the financial sense. Also, a little in the booze sense, but the offer still stands."

They sat, lulled by the mechanical noises around them. Lavinia's phone buzzed. She ignored it. Delray looked at her own phone and was disappointed by whatever it told her.

"Well, I ain't in no position to refuse," Delray said.

"Looks like my stuff is dry. Finish up, come to the Days Inn at the end of this block, and call me from the office. Ask for Lavinia Starkhurst. I'll come down."

Delray nodded. Lavinia shoved her clothes into the backpack without folding them.

"You forgot your bear," Delray said as Lavinia was heading for the door.

"Would you like to keep him?"

Delray picked up the bear and stared blandly into his plastic eyes.

"Nah."

"Just as well. He'd get mad if I gave him away."

"Uh-huh."

"Well, see you in a bit."

In her room, Lavinia folded her clothes, pulled out what she wanted to wear the next day, sat on the bed, and brushed her hair. Then she counted her cash. She had just under eight hundred of the twelve hundred dollars she'd withdrawn the morning she left. That felt like such a long time ago!

She called the manager and told him to expect a woman asking for her. He was to rent her a room for one night and charge the card Lavinia had already used. He would please tell her that she had gone to bed and that she'd see her in the morning. Then he should call Lavinia back and give her Delray's room number, but not give her room number to Delray because she was turning in now and didn't want to be disturbed.

Despite the wine and being worn out from Delray's tale of woe, Lavinia didn't sleep for quite some time. Mel's voice on the phone returned, saying calmly that he loved her.

She dreamed of standing on an open plain with a single house in the distance. It appeared to be an ordinary wooden house, two stories, next to a large tree. It seemed peaceful and charming, but there was smoke rising from it and the roof was suddenly aflame. People ran with buckets of water. One poor old man was tugging feebly at a hose. The man was Mel.

There followed other dreams, sewn from memories of Potter and the children when they were young, of her father shoeing horses, and of Chip teaching her how to hold a club. The people in the photographs she'd bought were on the course, too, teeing off, smiling, urging her on. The youngest child wore a thimble on her forefinger.

She woke to firm knocking on her door. It was 7:20 a.m.

"Yoo-hoo!"

It was Delray.

Jesus. I told you not to give her my room number!

Lavinia put a sweatshirt on over her nightgown and opened the door. She was presented with a box of doughnuts and coffee in a paper cup with a white plastic lid. Delray was wearing denim overalls and a pink T-shirt. She smiled widely, showing two missing teeth Lavinia hadn't noticed the evening before.

Lavinia told her to come in. There was a table and two chairs in front of the window. Delray set everything up there and said Lavinia's room was a lot bigger than hers, not to complain or anything. Hell, she was damn grateful for a clean bed and what turned out to be a decent night's sleep.

"You hear anything from your husband?" Lavinia asked through the closed door of the bathroom where she was getting dressed.

"Nope."

Lavinia came out and joined her at the table. Delray had taken the liberty of adding both cream and sugar to the coffee she would have preferred black. She sipped it anyway. Delray was eating a doughnut and spilling powdered sugar all down her front. Lavinia went to the bathroom and ran water on a washcloth and handed it to her.

"You still want a lift to Helena?" Lavinia said.

"Yup."

Lavinia considered a chocolate doughnut. The glaze gave it a plastic sheen. She decided against it. Delray must have spent almost all her cash on breakfast, just to offer a gesture of goodwill.

"That reminds me," Lavinia said. She took three hundred dollars out of her wallet and put it on the table in front of Delray.

"I can't take that."

"Bull."

"I already said I can't pay you back."

177

"And I already said I don't care. Now put it in your purse, and let's get going."

Delray appraised the leather seats of Lavinia's car, the wood-grain steering wheel and dashboard, the Coco Channel sunglasses wedged in the console, and the bouquet in the foot well. Lavinia removed the vase, poured the water onto the asphalt, and put the flowers in a plastic box in the trunk which held the drying bouquets from previous days. The vase went on the back seat along with the sullen bear and Delray's bag—a vinyl-sided suitcase with a big red sticker in honor of the Arkansas Razorbacks.

After only a few minutes on the road, Delray turned glum. She sighed. Her face was turned away. Lavinia knew she was crying.

"No good keeping it in. Why don't you tell me what you're thinking?" Lavinia said.

Delray shrugged. The gesture was childlike.

Grief turns us all back into children.

"How about this? Pretend I'm him. Say what's in your head," Lavinia said.

Delray sighed again. Lavinia figured they'd reach Helena in about another ninety minutes. She could put up with Delray's blues until then, she supposed.

The day was clear, the light almost searing. Lavinia put on her sunglasses. A motorcycle raced past. The driver had a long, gray beard.

"I've always wondered what it's like to ride a motorcycle. I bet it's scary at first, then really fun. The wind in your face. Racing along under the open sky. You ever ridden one?" Lavinia asked.

"Nuh-uh."

"Maybe I'll get one in Helena. Hire someone to drive the car back east for me, then cruise the chopper back home. That would turn some heads, no?"

"It might."

Her phone buzzed. She'd placed it in the console for the drive. She picked up.

It was Angie, reporting on the twins.

"They're okay. Just rattled about what happened to Maggie. I told them they were spending way too much money and that you weren't going to stand for it. I said you'd cut them off if they didn't get their act together," Angie said.

"Bravo!"

"Where are you now?"

"Heading to Helena."

"Cool. Patty will be glad to see you."

"Probably not."

Delray was motioning to a herd of elk grazing on a bluff not far from the road. They were large, striking animals, oblivious to the rush of traffic.

"Wow," Lavinia said.

Angie didn't understand.

"There are elk out here, a whole bunch of them!"

"Look at the antlers on that one," Delray said.

"Who's that?" Angie asked.

Lavinia explained.

Angie said it wasn't the best idea to let a stranger in your car. Lavinia said not to worry, she'd check in later.

"I'll hold you to that," Angie said. They said goodbye.

"My daughter," Lavinia said as she replaced the phone in the console.

Delray just went on looking out the window. Lavinia was getting hungry. She hadn't bought any fruit. She asked Delray to reach behind her and get the box of doughnuts. One wouldn't kill her.

"You got chocolate, plain, or cinnamon," Delray informed her.

"Tear that plain one in half."

Delray gave Lavinia her share and ate the rest herself. Delray handed Lavinia a napkin she'd stashed in the pocket of her overalls. She put the box back where it had been, and sat, staring out the windshield.

A jaunty tune came from her lap. Delray produced her cell phone and stared at it. The music played for a good ten seconds before it stopped. Delray pushed the button in her armrest to lower the window, and threw the phone out. She raised the window and leaned her head against the glass.

"Hubby?" Lavinia asked.

Delray nodded.

"Ballsy move."

"Overdue, too."

"Calling it quits?"

Delray couldn't say for sure. One thing she did know was that she needed some time to think things through. When she had, she'd get one of those cheapo phones and call him, assuming he hadn't changed his number. And if he had, her son would know how to reach him.

"Makes sense," Lavinia said.

She wondered if she could offer Delray some advice.

"About?"

"Getting divorced. I speak from personal experience here."

Lavinia said it was a lot harder than it looked. At first, all you're thinking about is how you're going to get from under this huge, miserable weight, and you do, which is great, only there are all other kinds of things you didn't expect to have to deal with.

"Like?"

Well, like sleeping alone, for one thing. Especially if you'd been married a long time, it took some getting used to. And then there's how other people in your life felt about it—your kids, your relatives, any friends you had in common, which in her case weren't many (none, in fact), because she'd been too damn busy working and raising five kids to make friends. The only one she had made was her boss, the guy she ended up marrying. And, of course, Karen, who was basically on-again, off-again.

And then there were the feelings you had for your ex. Even if things between you totally sucked, you never really forgot that first rush of love. You'd be in the middle of doing something, and suddenly you remembered the good times, the happy times, the loving times, and you got lonely. You second guessed deciding to leave. The worst was when you ran into each other and saw how things were going for him, how he'd cleaned up his act without you and showed signs of being the man you'd wanted him to be all along.

"You okay?" Delray asked because Lavinia's voice had broken. Tears flowed. Her arms weakened. It was hard to hold the wheel.

"I made him so unhappy," she managed to get out.

"Maybe you oughta pull over."

Lavinia signaled, moved to the right-hand lane, slowed, and eased the car onto the shoulder. She put her head on the wheel and wept until her chest hurt. After a moment, she lifted her head. During her wretched weeping, Delray had reached over and turned off the engine.

The episode slowly passed. Her face was hot, her eyes stung, and her shoulders ached.

"Things always this close to the surface with you?" Delray asked.

"Didn't used to be."

"What changed?"

"My husband died."

"Thought you was divorced."

"Got married again."

"You get around."

Delray didn't say this meanly.

The speed of each passing car caused Lavinia's to rock slightly. It was no good just sitting there.

"You want I should drive?" Delray asked.

Lavinia shook her head. She'd already given up too much control, breaking down like that. No more tears, no more sobby confessions, just the road ahead and getting where she needed to go.

chapter thirteen

Years before, Patty and Murph had lived in a double wide, just like the kind Lavinia used to sell. Since then, Murph had done well with his remodeling business, Patty had done well with the restaurant she owned, and between the two of them they socked enough away to buy a big place on the edge of town. It was a work in progress. The living room walls were clad in fake wood paneling that reminded Lavinia of her father's tiny office at the university stables way back when. The windows needed to be replaced. Half of them had broken sashes and wouldn't open, so several high-powered fans had been strategically placed. The downstairs bath, which Lavinia used, had baby blue fixtures and a fluorescent overhead light that made her skin a sickly gray. The floor of the back porch was riddled with holes at the far end through which mice tended to come and go. Lavinia heard them in the crawl space below her first-floor room.

The work so far had all gone into the kitchen and upstairs master suite. Lavinia would have done the same. The kitchen had a large quartz island, and the adjoining sun room was furnished with oversized couches and grass rugs.

Her arrival had been expected. Potter had called Patty to alert her. Lavinia would have loved to know how that conversation had gone. She and Patty were former enemies. Their rancor dated back to when Lavinia and Potter first got together. Patty thought Lavinia was stuck up; Lavinia thought Patty was overly protective of her older brother. When Lavinia walked out on Potter, Patty came east to look after the children for a couple of weeks. Patty got a chance to see first-hand how useless Potter was around the house, and her sympathy for Lavinia grudgingly increased. When she and Murph decided to marry, they wanted to do it back in Dunston, and Lavinia had offered them Chip's large backyard for their June ceremony.

For two days, Lavinia sat around Patty's house, steeped in misery. On the third day, she got up when she heard Patty moving around in the kitchen and appeared fully dressed in one of the jumpsuits she'd washed in the bathroom sink and dried on the porch, well away from the infuriating mice.

Patty poured coffee into a hand thrown mug decorated with yellow flower petals and handed it to her.

"Sleeping better?" Patty asked.

"Some."

"Never easy, in a strange bed."

"No."

186

Murph was already out for the day. His crew was remodeling a wing of a local nursing home. At dinner, the evening before he described some of the residents gathering in their wheelchairs to watch them come and go like a bunch of lions who'd lost the urge to pounce. Lavinia was reminded of the Lindell Retirement Home and the fiasco of the grief group. No matter how nice Lindell was, or the place Murph was fixing up, old people were just warehoused while they waited for the inevitable. She sipped her coffee, determined to ignore that thoroughly depressing thought.

Patty put a bowl of fresh strawberries on the table and invited Lavinia to help herself. Lavinia chose the reddest. It dripped down her chin and filled her mouth with a rich, tart sweetness. She took a napkin from the wooden holder Patty had on the table and dabbed.

She tasted again her mother's delicious strawberry tarts. Baking had been a lovely refuge for them both. Lavinia would sit on a blue wooden stool and watch her mother chop a stick of shortening into the flour with a pastry cutter. The strawberries simmered on the stove, then were cooled before being poured into the dough-lined pie tin. Her mother trimmed thick strips of the remaining dough and wove them across the top, over, under, over, under without tearing or breaking them. She brushed a beaten egg over the dough and sprinkled everything with sugar.

Lavinia had had no interest in learning how to bake. Now she wished she had.

"Some say it's easier when a loved one takes their time dying. Gives you a chance to prepare yourself. Someone goes the way Chip went—all of a sudden—you're thrown down the rabbit hole without a parachute," Patty said.

"I guess so."

"Thing is, that's not necessarily true. My mom was sick a long time before she died. You remember, right?"

Lavinia did. Potter's mother had been a small, silent woman whose blue eyes were on fire. When she fell ill, that fire remained, even as the rest of her dimmed.

Patty had gone back to Dunston when the end was near. Potter begged her to, otherwise she probably wouldn't have. It was no secret that she and her mother weren't exactly chummy. Damn woman managed to disapprove of everything she did— her choice of men, the way she dressed, the length of her hair, the fact that she had a raucous spirit of adventure. Patty was supposed to settle for a dull, lonely life, just like her mother had, with the same kind of overbearing, heartless man her father had been. Did Lavinia remember how he could shut down a conversation just by walking into the room? Didn't have one drop of love in him, which Patty knew from her earliest days, of course. She could see the yearning in her mother's every move. Patty couldn't bring his face to mind, not without looking at a picture, but she knew his back by heart. Didn't that say it all?

Anyhow, things took a turn for the worst, and Patty's mother had something to tell her and Potter before it was too late. They went to her room, which was shuttered and stifling, and stood solemnly by the bed. She was propped up on about four pillows. The hospice nurse was a madwoman about those pillows, always hauling and punching them. Her mother's eyes were huge, as if somehow that was all that was left of her. But her voice, when she spoke, had a new power neither she nor Potter had heard before.

"I want you both to know here and now that I was untrue."

Ed Slocum, their neighbor, was the one she'd sinned with. It was hard to believe. He wasn't particularly tall or handsome, but he smiled a lot and laughed at little things. A sense of humor was important in a man, didn't Lavinia agree? It suggested a warm heart, and God knew, Patty's mother needed that. It went on for years until Slocum's wife finally got suspicious. She had a job in town that had her out of the house early. Patty's mother waited until Patty's father was off with his herd or fixing fences or holed up in the barn with another one of his damn wood projects. They came back now to Patty as if it were yesterday, all those broken-down pieces of furniture he picked up from neighboring farms, things he swore he'd repair and make good money on, though Patty never remembered a single item being sold. Anyway, they had to call it quits because Slocum wasn't willing to leave his wife, despite his feelings for Patty's mother.

The break must have come in Patty's last year of high school, when her mother became even more withdrawn and sometimes went to the window and stared out—always in the direction of Slocum's farm. At the time, Patty thought nothing of it, though she disliked her mother's harsher stance, since it was usually directed at her rather than at Potter. When she did the math, she reckoned that her mother had lived another fifteen years after she stopped seeing Slocum. That was a long time to grieve over losing someone you cared for.

"So, she loved him?" Lavinia asked.

"I thought that should have been obvious."

"Well, she wanted the sex, certainly. But love is something else, right?"

"Maybe. All I know is I had a hell of a lot to process afterward. What she told us changed things. Changed everything."

Lavinia said her case was similar. Even though Chip's death was sudden, she, too, was processing, remembering, going back to things that at the time were unimportant but that now came back in a new light.

"Like what?" Patty asked.

Golf. Wasn't that ironic given … well, Patty knew what she meant. Chip wanted her out there with him on the green. She thought it was a stupid game, a boring game, a game for old men and women. But Chip didn't play golf because he was old or boring, but because it relaxed him and made him feel that things were all right. When something worried him, he grabbed his clubs and went. He had wanted to share that with Lavinia. Being peaceful and happy together was an intimacy for him. Lavinia hadn't seen that. She saw it now, though. Only now was too late.

"Not if you've learned something. You can't change the past, only your understanding of it," Patty said.

Lavinia ate another strawberry. Her mind stayed on the green with Chip a few moments longer, then turned where it so often went.

"Did Potter have a hard time with your mother's confession?" she asked.

"Hard to say. That was right after you'd left him. He was in a bad way all around."

Oh, how she remembered! He kept calling, needing to talk, saying things would change—that he was already drinking much less. His mother was sick, and going fast. Couldn't Lavinia spare just a little of herself then to tide him over? She said she was sorry about his mother but that he shouldn't call her anymore after that unless it had to do with the kids.

"Is he happy with Mary Beth?" Lavinia asked.

Patty regarded her coolly.

"You looking for some kind of redo on that one?" she asked.

"Don't be ridiculous."

Patty went on appraising her with her head tilted and her lips curled up on one side. It was the same expression she'd given Lavinia the first time they met. Patty had thought Lavinia was a fool for thinking her brother was someone she could improve. The notion wasn't disloyal on Patty's part, just realistic.

"I wouldn't say he's happy. He's not unhappy, either," Patty said.

"A typical marriage, you mean."

"No marriage is typical, is it?"

"Maybe not."

A lawnmower down the street came to life. Lavinia would have to remind Alma about having the yard service come back. She didn't want the grass growing out of control while she was gone. But then again, what did it matter? So what if it looked messy? When she listed the house for sale, it should be neatly trimmed. That was in the future, though, at a point she couldn't quite see.

"I heard about your dinner," Patty said.

"Must have made quite an impression on Potter for him to mention it. An unfavorable one, I'm sure."

"He's worried about you."

"No reason to be."

"He said you were hitting the bottle pretty hard that night."

"This, from him?"

"You know how much he's cut back."

Lavinia raised her hand to concede the point.

"And what about you?" Lavinia asked.

"What about me?"

"Are you worried about me, too?"

"Nah."

"Hm."

"I'm not being a hard ass. I know you'll be fine when you've had a little more time to figure out your next step."

Lavinia didn't want to tell Patty that she was the first person to say so since Chip died. It might sound too much like gratitude.

chapter fourteen

Every morning the light shocked. The dry air coupled with the altitude made the mountains crisp and clear. Could she see herself making a home there? Could she see herself feeling at home anywhere?

Not till I stop feeling like shit about Chip.

She'd heard it said that the first year of grief was the hardest. Like marriage. Or a new baby.

She offered to go to the store for Patty. She felt guilty for being snappish the evening before. Patty had cooked dinner, as always. Murph didn't help, as always. That struck a sour note. Lavinia had said it must be nice to be waited on all the time. Murph was taken aback. Patty glowered. Lavinia knew she shouldn't have made any comment about how they chose to live.

Before she started the car, she pulled out her cell phone and called Mel. He answered on the second ring.

"I'm not a nice person," she said.

"Of course you are."

"I'm a bitch. I've always been a bitch."

"You know that's not so."

"I *feel* like a bitch."

Mel paused. He seemed to be thinking.

"You've had a hard life," he said.

Many people had hard lives. Not all turned mean. She didn't share this idea with Mel. Neither of them spoke.

"How's Sandy?" Lavinia asked.

"In the pink."

"Any new words?"

"Yeah. 'Lavinia.'"

"Ha, ha."

Again, a hard moment of silence.

"I need to go. I'll talk to you later," Lavinia said.

"Lavinia—"

She hung up before he could say anything more.

When she got back to Patty's, Murph's silver pickup truck was in the driveway. He'd parked in the middle, leaving no space on either side for the Lexus, so Lavinia parked on the street and carried four bags in from there. She told herself it didn't matter. It was just a driveway, his driveway for that matter. She was a guest. She was lucky they seemed glad to have her.

So why was a little black seed of rage digging into her soul?

She put the groceries away, realizing that a lot of the nonperishable stuff was probably going in the wrong place. Patty would have to deal with that, herself.

Murph was out back, talking on his cell phone. He turned at the sound of her walking across the porch and waved. Their yard was deep and shaded by evergreen trees. Lavinia imagined a winding stone path with a bench here or there, a quiet place to sit and contemplate. Contemplate what, though? Letting one's mind go where it wanted wasn't always the best idea.

As Murph went on talking about getting an electrical permit for the nursing home project and needing to ping someone named Travis, Lavinia went across the grass toward the trees. At home, a lawn would be lush that time of year. There, in Montana, the grass was brown and dry. She'd noticed that on the drive, the tawny hills, shades of gold, yellow, and some spots of orange. The smell of pine was strong under the sun. Needles lay underfoot. In the novel *For Whom the Bell Tolls* Robert Jordan lay down to die "on the pine needle floor of the forest."

What a strange thing to remember! She'd read the book so many years before, pregnant with Angie, transported from their small rental cottage to the mountains of Spain. She had never understood why Jordan had joined someone else's fight. She couldn't remember if the novel had explained what his life

197

in America had been like. Maybe he was just bored. Maybe he felt he'd wasted too much time. Maybe he believed sacrificing himself would give his life meaning.

She bent to collect a handful of dirt and needles. She brought it to her nose. The smell was less strong. It must be the living cones that gave the scent.

"Yo!" Murph called out from the porch. Lavinia hadn't realized how far she'd wandered into the stand of trees. She must have been expecting to meet a fence that would tell her the end had come and it was time to turn back. She left the shaded shelter and returned across the dead grass.

"Hello," Lavinia said.

"What's up?"

"Just got back from the store."

He held the door open for her. She went inside. She crossed the living room and turned into the kitchen. On one end of the wide quartz countertop were pink hydrangeas in a heavy Mexican jug. They were wilted, petals browning.

"Those aren't native, are they?" Lavinia asked.

"What, the flowers? Not sure. Maybe. The florist would know. Got 'em at Green's."

"Apt name."

"Yeah."

"Special occasion?"

"Nope. I buy Patty flowers every Friday. Sort of a tradition, at this point."

Chip had done the same thing, although his day was Saturday. One arrangement for the round table in the foyer, another for the living room, the last for their bedroom. There was a sitting area in front of a brick fireplace. The side table was where they went, and because it wasn't very large, the vase had to be fairly small. It often held a single stalk of lily blossoms, or just two or three roses, or a few tulips in the spring and summer.

Chip didn't pick the flowers himself. Their florist handled that. Bella Cromwell. When she died, her son took over. His taste wasn't as good. Daisies and carnations made up most of his bouquets. Lavinia complained to Chip, who said he'd make a call and never did. She went to the florist herself and said she wanted higher caliber blossoms. Cromwell's son, Martin, was pale and pimply. He cringed visibly as she explained that daisies were plebian and carnations were cheap. Then Lavinia remembered that his late mother had been particularly fond of those two varieties. She had often suggested them when Lavinia went in to choose flowers for a party or to bring to Karen's or for the twins' birthday. At the time, she dismissed her gaffe. She told herself she couldn't be responsible for respecting the tastes of a dead woman. But she could have apologized to the son. She could have said something nice about the mother. One moment of grace wouldn't have killed her.

"What kind of woman gets rude about flowers?" she asked.

"The kind that's allergic to them?"

Murph had taken a beer from the refrigerator while Lavinia brooded. When he saw her looking at it in his hand, he asked if she wanted one, too.

"Sure."

He poured it into a glass held at an angle so the head wouldn't rise beyond the rim once he'd leveled it.

"Pretty fancy," Lavinia said.

"Used to tend bar."

"I didn't know that."

"Also used to landscape, haul trash, pump gas."

"You've had a checkered past."

"An unfocused one's more like it."

She tasted the beer. It was full and hearty. She didn't normally like beer. She used to find it so … lowball.

Lavinia sat on a stool. Murph took the one next to her. He rested his forearms on the counter. They were tanned and looked strong. Lavinia didn't know how old he was, only that he was younger than Patty, and Patty was … forty-eight? Forty-nine?

"Look, I want to say again how sorry I was to hear about Chip," Murph said.

"Thank you."

"We should have come to the funeral."

"It would have been a long way to go."

"That's what airplanes are for."

"You guys have busy lives. Making time is hard. And besides, I don't think anyone told you about it ahead of time."

"Angie called Patty."

Lavinia nodded. Angie was the force that held the whole family together. That had once been Lavinia's job. Now she couldn't even hold herself together.

Murph passed her the box of Kleenex from the other end of the counter. Lavinia hadn't been aware that she was crying. The physical sensation was becoming unremarkable. Did that mean she'd cry all the time now and not know? Would she become lost in her grief?

It occurred to her that she'd never felt so bad about anything before, even the child she aborted right after marrying Chip. She'd told him she miscarried. He was kind to her about it, and she accepted his kindness because she felt broken in the face of her decision. It wasn't a moral failure.

She believed it was her right to choose. What broke her was realizing she didn't have the emotional strength to have another baby. Up until that point, she thought herself strong enough for anything that came her way.

Murph patted her fondly on the shoulder.

He must feel awkward, sitting next to a weeping woman. Lavinia drew herself in tight and made herself stop shuddering.

"He was a good guy. A real good guy," Murph said.

Murph had met Chip when he and Patty came for Angie's high school graduation. They became instant drinking buddies. Laughter and the clink of glasses filled Chip's study. She assumed Chip enjoyed Murph's company because there was no one else to spend time with.

Then, when he and Patty came out to get married, they stayed with Chip and Lavinia, and the camaraderie resumed.

"A generous man," Murph said.

Lavinia nodded.

"We had a lot in common."

"Like what?"

"A taste for good whiskey."

"Yeah."

"Being driven by tough women."

"He said that?"

"I said it. He agreed."

Lavinia sank once again.

"I suppose Patty and I do more than our share of driving," she said.

"Which may be how come you guys didn't get along so great for a while."

"Years."

"She's a strong woman. You're a strong woman. A dicey combo, for sure."

"Things are different now."

"Clearly."

Murph didn't understand. He thought they got on better because they'd softened with time. Maybe Patty had, it was hard to know. But she hadn't softened. She'd disappeared.

Lavinia finished her beer. She wanted another one. He stood up and put his empty bottle in the sink. He didn't take another for himself, nor offer her one.

"Do you always finish this early?" Lavinia asked.

"Got as far as we could go. Waiting on the trades to come in over the next few days."

"You know Potter's wife is a contractor."

"Yeah. Small world."

She became aware of him studying her. She'd didn't like it.

"Maybe you should go take a load off. You look kinda beat," he said.

Lavinia said she'd do just that. In her room, she didn't sleep. She looked at her cell phone and was surprised to see that no one had called her so far today. The thought was oddly disappointing.

Isn't this what you wanted? Freedom?

chapter fifteen

Two days later, Lavinia found a job at Green's Flower Shop.

"Really?" Patty asked.

"Wandered in, thought I might pick myself up some posies, and got talking to the lady at the counter. Their business is booming, for the moment, at least. Summer weddings, and all."

"That would have been Sara Johnson," Patty said.

"You know her?"

"Small town."

Lavinia said now that she was gainfully employed, she probably ought to look for an apartment, something that rented by the week because you never knew when you would have to answer the siren call of home. And in fact, she'd made it clear to Sara that she didn't know how long she'd be in Helena but that she'd give as much notice as possible if her plans changed.

Patty said she was being silly. She could stay with her and Murph as long as she wanted. Lavinia wasn't sure she wanted to spend any more time there, but didn't say so. Instead, she told Patty she was truly grateful for her hospitality.

Then she called Mel about the job.

"I can see you in a flower store, surrounded by all that delicate beauty," he said.

"Oh, shut up."

He laughed. In the background, Sandy squawked something unintelligible.

Next, she told Angie, who was distracted by a work-related issue but promised to call back when she'd put all her fires out.

Timothy was surprised. He couldn't really see her waiting on customers. She reminded him that she'd sold prefab homes for years, and was damn good at it, too.

Foster took her news with little interest. He'd accepted the front office position at the vet's and was already regretting his decision. He was responsible for drawing up the bills, and people often argued about the cost of this or that. Some tried to bargain a lower fee. The one time he agreed, Dr. Salt, who ran the clinic, praised his compassion but said he should consult with him beforehand because not everyone who pled poverty was actually broke. Those in real need could make monthly payments, and sometimes an entire visit got written off when it was clear that money was just too tight.

Lavinia wondered how the hell Dr. Salt got ahead. You had to make a profit, right? Owning a pet was a choice, like having a child, and you had to be up to the financial commitment. Otherwise you ended up dumping on other people. She said none of this, though, realizing she'd sound like a bitter, old woman.

Maggie and Marta congratulated her and then asked if the new job meant she wouldn't be home for a while. Before she could answer, Maggie said she wanted to pay Lavinia back for what she'd spent on her credit card. Lavinia didn't know how she intended to do that since she didn't have a job, but then Maggie surprised her by saying she was training to be a barista. And get this—she'd gotten the coffee shop to agree to display some of her paintings! Marta was having second thoughts about the theater company. She wanted a greater role in deciding what got produced and who was given what part. The guy in charge wasn't returning her calls. She was thinking of asking for her money back. If he'd swindled her, she'd get a lawyer. Angie had clearly said just the right thing to each of them.

Alma was dismayed by Lavinia's news.

"You moving out there permanently?" she asked.

"No, of course not. I'm here just for a little while."

"So, the job's 'cause you're bored?"

"More or less."

Alma said things were fine at the house and that she'd invited her book club over just a couple of days before. Lavinia had had no idea Alma was in a book club. She hoped they'd behaved themselves and not gone through the place like nosy pests, touching her things, making remarks.

So what if they did?

Lavinia didn't know what to wear for her first day, and asked Patty where she could buy some new outfits. Patty suggested a store called Ray's. Lavinia asked if they specialized in Western wear.

"No. Just nice, tailored clothes," Patty said.

"Hmm."

She'd admired the cowboy boots and detailed button-down shirts she'd seen around town.

When in Rome ...

It was mid-morning, and already the sun was brutal. Lavinia made her way to a shaded street with old restored brick buildings. They were so like the nineteenth century gems in downtown Dunston—gray, red, three and four stories, packed in close, with stone stairs and metal railings.

Several years before, there had been a move to pull them down to make room for a new apartment complex. The buildings, seven in all, were owned by two people, Richard Bradley and Camilla Chase. Chase didn't want to sell. She wanted them restored to keep the town's heritage alive. Bradley had already been promised that his electric company would get the contract to wire the new complex, and was determined to push the deal through. It was up to the city council to decide.

Chase enlisted Chip to lead a citizens' group to pressure the council to let the buildings stand. One problem was that Bradley himself sat on the council, and his fellow members were reluctant to go against him. Chip's group had presented a few urban planners, historians, and architects who all said the buildings were living history and must be preserved. In the end, the council agreed.

Bradley was furious. He and Chip had sat on committees together and were both active in the Rotary Club. They stopped being cordial. Dunston was a small place, and it became awkward when Chip and Lavinia ran into him in public. Chip invited Bradley to the house for a private lunch. He refused, then refused a second time. Finally, he relented, perhaps because he thought Chip planned to apologize. Lavinia was asked not to disturb them. They closed both sets of doors to the dining room and sat for hours. They emerged, chatting pleasantly. Bradley and Camilla Chase were to form a non-profit organization and lease their property to it. Camilla had already given her approval. The organization then solicited money from some wealthy friends to renovate all seven structures. The city council provided some matching funds, and a grant from the state helped, too. Because public money was used, a competitive bidding process was required for all work to be performed. Bradley's company simply came in with the lowest electrical bid.

"But didn't he end up in the red?" Lavinia had asked.

"Of course. But it was worth it for the good will he generated."

After that, when the university erected some new dorms, Bradley got that work, too, because he pushed the point that he had a tradition of serving the community. The university's board of regents was suitably impressed.

"The whole thing was your idea, wasn't it?" Lavinia had asked.

"Yup."

"You knew about the dorms beforehand and figured you could persuade Bradley that he'd have an in if he took a loss with the city."

"Exactly."

"Very clever. You're quite the shrewd businessman, Mr. Starkhurst."

"Behind every great man stands a woman."

As Lavinia's gaze was drawn up the front of an 1890's brick building with arched windows and elegantly scrolled lintels, the memory pleased her. There had been good times. She'd just forgotten.

Billy Bob's Western Wear was on the next corner. A worn saddle was mounted above the door, and running down either side were rusty horseshoes. Just inside she was met by a wooden Indian whose lifeless blue eyes startled her. Behind the sales register, a pale teenaged boy with a mop of pitch black hair observed her coldly. Lavinia gave him her best smile and strolled deeper into the store.

The place was huge and hard to navigate. Boots were next to slacks for both sexes, followed by a rack of lady's shirts, then more boots, then several shelves displaying cowboy hats. Some had colorful bands, most often red, sometimes with a feather attached. Beyond the hats were belts. Mostly plain leather, some made from snakeskin or ostrich in alarming colors—teal, yellow, even pink. And the buckles! Silver, mother-of-pearl, turquoise, malachite, even lapis.

"Can I help you find something?" It was the sullen boy. Lavinia looked up into his face. His cheekbones, straight nose, and black eyes suggested that he was Native American.

"Everything, really. I need some boots, a few shirts, maybe some new blue jeans?"

He led her silently back to the boots. Lavinia took a closer look. Her eyes fell immediately on a pair in purple leather with red stitching. She pointed to them. He asked the size.

"Seven and a half."

"Have a seat. I'll be right back."

While she waited, a woman steered a wailing baby in a stroller around the various racks of clothing and then stopped before a display of bolo ties. Lavinia could see the kicking feet of the distressed child. One was bare. The other sported a striped sock.

The woman examined the string ties. She removed one and held it up for a closer look. She swiveled her head to the left, then all the way to the right, and dropped the tie in the baby's stroller. She bent down as if to wipe the child's face or put a fallen bottle of formula back into its eager mouth, but Lavinia was sure the gesture was just to make sure the tie was well hidden. The woman helped herself to two more before turning back the way she'd come. She stared at Lavinia, who had been seated behind her and therefore impossible to see. Her face was young, her eyes full of challenge but also fear. She made quickly for the exit, the heels of her cowboy boots falling hard across the wooden floor. The child, who'd not ceased its weepy protest, wailed its way out the door and off down the street.

That took a lot of guts!

The sullen boy returned with a stack of boxes. He set them on the floor.

"Didn't have the seven and a half. I brought the seven and the eight. Maybe one of them will work."

He left her alone to try the boots on. She'd gone out in sandals. She didn't relish the idea of pulling a boot on over a bare foot.

"Excuse me?" she called out.

She was about to call again when he returned.

"Do you have a pair of socks I could borrow? Just to try these on?

He stared at her bare feet. Her pink polish was still intact. She wiggled her toes. He met her eye and blushed. He left and returned promptly with three pairs of hiking socks in different weights.

"You're a dear," Lavinia said. His expression turned grim, and he left her once more.

The lightweight socks were a perfect match for the size eight boots. They were surprisingly comfortable. She pulled up the legs of her jumpsuit and strolled over to the floor-length mirror. She took herself in from a few different angles. She released the gathered-up fabric in her hands. The hem of each leg just grazed the top of the boot. She didn't mind that the jumpsuit was now too short. She'd never wear the boots with this outfit, in any case.

By the time she left the store, she'd chosen a pair of tight-fitting blue jeans with silver studs down the outside of each leg, three long-sleeved shirts with silk piping on the cuffs and breast pockets, a denim skirt, a flashy maroon cowboy hat, and a smart black leather purse with a huge silver clasp.

She toted her loot back to where she'd parked. In the window of a café, the shoplifting woman sat sipping from a paper cup, her baby in her lap. The baby had one of the stolen ties in its hands. He waved his meaty arms around, clearly delighted. Lavinia stood before the glass until the woman noticed her. She watched Lavinia. Lavinia watched her. The woman put her cup on the table and lowered the baby into the stroller. She buckled the straps of the stroller and stood. When she saw that Lavinia was still there observing her every move, a look of silent fury passed over her small, pretty face. She turned red all the way to the edge of her curly brown hair. Lavinia nodded to her, then went on her way.

When Timothy had gotten caught stealing an expensive leather jacket—one he could easily have afforded on his generous allowance—Lavinia naturally demanded an explanation. He said he didn't realize he hadn't paid for it. He'd tried it on and forgotten.

"That's bullshit," Lavinia said.

Next, he said it had been a dare from a frat brother.

"You're not that stupid."

Finally, he said he'd just wanted to see if he could get away with it.

"All that, for some lousy adrenaline rush?"

He just couldn't make her understand.

But later she did. Timothy felt ineffective in his life as a college student. His grades were poor. He wasn't interested in learning. Stealing a jacket was his way of telling the world that he was capable of something. That he could act. That he had agency.

In her own life, proving she could act had meant nothing. All that ever mattered were the tasks themselves and getting them done. To pit yourself against something for purely recreational purposes was fine, like wanting to become a better cook or dancer. But when the challenge was unsavory, that was unhealthy. Actually, it was self-destructive.

Frustration, failure, and anger turned inward could make a person hurt like nothing else. Lavinia hadn't realized it at the time, but she'd been depressed for years while married to Potter. That she was tired all the time didn't seem strange at all, given her load. Her pediatrician remarked on her weight loss one winter when Foster had yet another ear infection. He

215

suggested she get a complete work-up with her own doctor, and if that didn't uncover anything, she might find a therapist.

"Mind your own damn business," she'd said, snatching Foster's prescription from his hand.

She told someone at work what the doctor had said.

"My sister's on Prozac," was the reply.

Clearly people had seen something in her that she hadn't.

When had it stopped? Around the time she decided to leave Potter. Knowing she could change her life let her remember what hope felt like.

When she got into her car, she called Mel and told him about the shoplifting woman.

"Do you think you did the right thing?" he asked.

"I wasn't going to ruin her day."

"You mean you felt sorry for her."

"I suppose."

He said he admired her compassion. She said she didn't know why she bothered to tell him anything if he was just going to talk nonsense.

Lavinia said nothing of the shoplifting woman to Patty and Murph. Instead, she modeled her new clothes for them. Murph was enthusiastic. Patty, skeptical.

"You think I'm an idiot, right?" Lavinia asked her.

"Of course not. It's just such a big change for you."

"A big change is just what I need."

Lavinia twirled. Her boots squeaked on the polished wood floor. The jeans made her feel … not exactly dressed up, but special. The last time she'd felt that way she was a young girl, getting a new dress for the holidays.

Does this mean I'm regressing?

For a moment, the idea disturbed her.

Oh, who cares?

She twirled once more.

"You need some tunes to go with those moves," Murph said. He beamed. He'd had a good day, apparently. But then, Murph was pretty sunny. Patty was lucky. A moody man was a huge pain in the ass.

"Let's go out dancing," Murph said.

"I thought you wanted to watch that movie later," Patty said.

"Movie can wait. I'm in the mood for a zingy two-step."

Lavinia watched their silent exchange. She could see Patty not wanting to give in, then yielding. Patty shook her head at him, yet smiled at the same time, and suddenly Lavinia felt very much like an outsider, even an intruder, watching a degree of intimacy that deepened her own loneliness.

They were in luck, Murph said. His buddy's band had a gig over at Louisa's.

"You mean Jimmy Joe's actually working?" Patty asked.

"Working, earning, living the dream."

"Sally must be happy."

Patty explained that Sally was Jimmy Joe's wife. Jimmy Joe gave up a decent job in construction to pursue his musical career. He'd burned a couple of CD's that didn't sell. Sally supported him by working as a nurse. Her devotion was admirable, if a bit misplaced, but that was between them, and who was she to criticize?

"Murph played for a while, too," Patty said. By then, they were sitting three across in Murph's pickup truck, cruising for an empty spot behind the bar.

"Wasn't too good."

"Yes, you were. You were very good."

Again, Lavinia felt on the outside looking in.

It was a Friday night, and the place was packed. Lavinia instantly regretted being there. Crowds were fine when you were full of self-confidence and sass. She had neither. They wove among smoky tables to the only empty one in sight, way in the back by the double doors that led to the kitchen. Cheerful cries of greeting met Murph as he escorted Patty and Lavinia along. Looking around, Lavinia realized with dismay that she was the only woman in the place with a Western-style shirt. She saw many blue jeans that were embroidered, but none with studs. There were a lot of cowboy boots, though, which made her feel a little better.

She sank gratefully into a wooden chair with a rounded back. Her stomach reminded her how little she'd had of the prime rib and mashed potatoes Patty had brought home from the restaurant. If she drank too much, she'd be sorry. Yet she already knew she was heading for a bender.

The first whiskey took the edge off. The second let the music in. The stage was a raised platform on the opposite end from where they sat, yet Jimmy Joe was easy to make out. He was tall and lean, dressed in black. His string tie had a large turquoise clasp, and Lavinia was reminded again of her shopping trip.

"The funniest thing happened today," Lavinia said to Patty, leaning close because of the noise.

"What?"

"Never mind."

Patty had had one drink to Lavinia's two, and her glass still held some wine. Lavinia had assumed she'd prefer whiskey, and thought that at one point that had been her drink of choice, but tastes could change, right? Murph was on his first beer. Lavinia was stupidly proud of herself for out-drinking them, especially when she ordered a third shot from the waitress.

Murph pulled Patty to her feet and led her toward the band where a few other people were two-stepping and spinning like mad. Lavinia had never liked country music much until now. She like jazz and easy listening. Sitting there, she began to lose herself in the pedal steel and Jimmy Joe's luscious tenor voice.

"Say you love me, baby, say it, and we'll call it a day!"

The song filled her with a slippery blend of joy and grief, which she supposed was exactly the point. She closed her eyes and dropped back to a time when the future was like a big shiny jewel waiting for her to grab it.

The waitress dropped off her shot. Lavinia sipped it this time. The river could get going a little too fast if you weren't careful. She closed her eyes again. She swayed gently in her seat.

"Ma'am?"

Some guy was standing at the table, grinning down at her.

"What do you want?" she asked, aware of the very slight slur in her speech.

"Would you care to dance?"

He wasn't bad, though older than she'd have liked in a dance partner. She put him around her age, somewhere in his early fifties. His face was tanned, seamed, and clean-shaven. Lavinia preferred facial hair on a man, especially one who was fairly rugged-looking otherwise. His eyes brought her up short. Their light was sharp. She knew her own eyes often looked like that.

"No. But you can sit down if you want," Lavinia said.

The man looked at the tabletop and the two abandoned drinks.

"They're off tripping the light fantastic," Lavinia said.

"And left you all alone."

"Three people dancing could be a clumsy affair, don't you think?"

"Three-ways can be fun."

"You wanna talk like that, get lost."

He sat.

"My name's Craig Carson. I'm single. I own an appliance company."

"Good for you."

Lavinia sipped her drink. She didn't look at Craig, but at the bar in general, the people smiling, smoking their cigarettes, drinking, one old guy frowning at another old guy, a woman laughing hysterically and slapping her hands on the table, then sudden clapping from everyone when the band stopped to take a break.

Lavinia looked for Patty and Murph. They were up on stage talking to Jimmy Joe.

221

The waitress asked Craig if he wanted the same as he'd been having.

"Sure thing, Darla," he said.

"And what were you having?" Lavinia asked.

"Margarita."

"Yuck. Never could stand tequila."

"Yeah? What do you like then?"

Lavinia lifted her glass.

"I see," Craig said.

"And you're not even wearing glasses!"

For the briefest moment, a look passed over Craig's weather-beaten face that said he'd made a big mistake by joining her. She looked him in the eye until he looked away first.

"Why don't you tell me your name," Craig said.

"Lavinia Dugan Starkhurst."

"Well, howdy-do, Miss Lavinia."

He reached out his hand. She took it. His palm was dry and rough. He lifted her hand to his lips and kissed it.

"Oh, for Christ's sake," Lavinia said and yanked her hand away.

Craig laughed.

"You're a firecracker," he said.

"Ain't that the truth."

"Tell me, Miss Lavinia, what brings you to Louisa's tonight?"

"My sister-in-law and her husband. Ex sister-in-law."

"Divorced?"

"Yup."

"Recent?"

"Nope."

"Been on your own awhile then."

"Got married again."

He glanced at her left hand. She'd removed the heavy-duty diamond when she reached Helena.

"But he died a little over a month ago," she said.

"So, a divorcée and a widow." He looked for the waitress and the drink he was waiting on.

"Two for the price of one."

Again, a nervous laugh. Lavinia hoped she'd put him on the edge of panic.

"Can't image the fella who'd let you go," he said.

"Hubby number one? I let him go."

And then the whole story came rolling out. Married too young. Five kids, including a pair of twins, by the time she was twenty-seven, husband who couldn't hold a job, her having to keep everything together, growing apart, having enough and walking out, accepting a proposal of marriage from the man she worked for who'd lost his first wife years before, his three sons—two of whom boycotted the wedding, the little pricks—the third son hotter than a pistol who had no interest in her even when she made her desires known, getting pretty much everything she wanted except that she was too stupid to even realize it, growing apart for a second time, and then out of the blue the guy gets hit by lightning.

"Which of course *wasn't* out of the blue, on account of it was a stormy day," Lavinia said.

The waitress had deposited Craig's drink during Lavinia's romp down memory lane. He was putting it down quickly.

"You must have a hollow leg," she said.

"But a full heart."

Something moved in her. She looked him in the eye until she was the first to drop her gaze.

Murph and Patty appeared.

"Craig, you old dog, you!" Murph said and slapped Craig on the back.

When they were seated, Murph explained that Craig supplied the appliances for all of his renovation projects.

"Except Finstrom," Craig said.

"That was the homeowner's choice, not mine."

"You come to hear Jimmy Joe?" Patty asked.

"Damn straight. That old boy's got it all going on."

"I see you've met Lavinia."

"She looked mighty lonely sitting here by herself, so I came on over. Now we're getting on like a house afire."

"My ex burned down a house once," Lavinia said.

Three faces turned in her direction.

"Well, the moron he was working with burned it down. It was the house he grew up in. Your old house," Lavinia said to Patty.

"Yes, I remember."

Patty's tone was surprisingly nonchalant, given that she'd put up the money for Potter to buy and fix the property and took a huge loss when it went up in flames.

Craig said he'd get the next round. That would make whiskey number four for Lavinia. She didn't care. Patty and Murph drank their seconds slowly. Their chairs were close together, and Murph's arm was around Patty. Craig and Murph talked about the nursing home reno Murph was doing. Did Murph like commercial? Was there a future in it?

"Long as people do business, I figure," Murph said.

Lavinia was aware that Patty was studying her from across the table. What did that light in her gray eyes convey? Irritation? No. Worry? Never, not Patty. They'd already established that. Concern? Yes, that's what it was. Concern for what?

"Don't worry. I won't embarrass you in front of your friend here," Lavinia said.

The music had started up again, and Patty clearly hadn't heard a word.

Craig put his mouth to her ear and asked again if she wanted to dance. She smelled the liquor on his breath.

"Sure."

If he hadn't been holding her hand, she was sure she'd have veered into one of the closely packed tables. Her boots felt heavy. So did her head.

Jimmy Joe segued into a slow dance. Some boisterous couples left the floor. Those that remained moved toward one another and took up the gently lilting rhythm. Craig's grip on her was strong. She liked it. She wasn't going to fight it. He was much taller than she was, putting her about eye-level with his collar bone. He led, she followed. It was easy, effortless, and necessary. She didn't know how long they were out there on the dance floor. Nor could she make out his words as they leaned and swayed. She didn't remember going back for her purse or explaining to Patty and Murph that Craig would take her home. She didn't remember much of the drive to his place, only that it took a while and the sky was thrown with stars.

She did remember the creak of the bed and the weight of him. She remembered how he split her open the way she'd hadn't been since Potter. She remembered hanging on to his wide shoulders for dear life and biting into his bicep. Then came her tears, his holding her, and his fingers brushing her face.

chapter sixteen

The hour was early, the light rising fast. Waking in a strange bed filled her with the usual uneasy energy until she looked at him, sound asleep beside her. She'd had trouble falling asleep afterward because she was naked. She always needed something other than a sheet on her skin, so she had helped herself to one of his shirts from the back of a cedar-lined closet, where she'd replaced it just a moment ago, after getting dressed.

Not long after, he found her on the back porch, taking in the vista. His place was up on a ridge. Two other homes were visible below. His site was the highest.

"Early riser," he said.

"Force of habit."

"Me, too."

She followed him inside. In the kitchen, she was tempted to take charge and didn't. She sat at the long, wooden table and wondered how often there were other people around it.

"Coffee?" he asked.

"Sure."

She had no headache, and said so.

"You can hold your liquor," he said.

228

"I wasn't holding it last night."

"You sorry about that?"

"No."

He made bacon and eggs. He offered her some. She said she never ate in the morning.

"That's how come you're so skinny," he said.

She watched him eat. After he put his breakfast plate in the sink, she asked him to drive her to Patty and Murph's. She studied the route along the way. His place was south of town. You took one country road, turned east on another, went about four miles, and there you were. Everything seemed so much more straightforward here in the West—people, directions, the land itself, all tawny and rolling. In Dunston, it was hard to know what direction you were facing unless you studied the sun, and given how cloudy it usually was, that was often impossible. As she opened the door of his truck, he asked if he could have her cell phone number. She gave it to him.

Patty and Murph were still upstairs, so Lavinia moved silently through the house. She removed her shirt and studded jeans, showered quickly, and put them back on. She examined her reflection. She looked like someone who'd been sleeping for a long time and was just then waking up. Despite last night's revelry, her eyes were clear. Her face was soft, not drawn in its usual taut lines. She took time with her hair. She

patted it with a towel, combed it, and used the pink blow dryer
Patty had thoughtfully put on the counter the day she arrived.
For years, she'd worn a side part. She pulled the comb straight
down the middle and arranged the hair on either side. This
new axis made her look different. Younger? No. Just like
someone who took things easier, whose life was in balance.
She pulled the hair back on one side and fastened it with a
sterling silver clip. She did the same to the other side. She
leaned in to examine the progress of gray. No new hairs for a
couple of weeks. Maybe that was a sign that time, for the
moment, was giving her a break?

She'd been asked to be at Green's Flower Shop by eight.
A nine-minute drive had her there almost twenty minutes
early. She sat in her car, leaned her head back, and closed her
eyes. It suddenly occurred to her that she hadn't looked at her
cell phone once in almost twelve hours.

The only call was from Mel. Dear, loyal Mel who covered
up loneliness and his own private grief—the one everyone
had—with jokes. She'd never thought of him like that before,
as one with depth, capable of courage and grace.

"I'm just a cardboard figure to you, aren't I?" Chip once
asked. They weren't exactly fighting, just out of sorts with each
other. Or rather, she was miffed at him for some harmless
transgression. Not refolding the newspaper, maybe. Or

putting his linen napkin in the collar of his shirt instead of in his lap. What he meant was that she saw him as two-dimensional, a prop, not really a whole human being.

Did she think everyone was shallow? She never saw her children that way. Sometimes Marta and Maggie seemed shallow with their hunger for material things. They were just spoiled, though. Their creative drives lent each complexity. Timothy and Foster weren't shallow by any means. Both were full of unresolved needs and wants. And Angie with her good heart and plain words might seem shallow, yet was anything but. Angie had had her share of grief, first with being overweight as a teenager, then with school, and lastly in love.

She'd stopped looking for things in other people, so she skimmed over them. Chip understood that, yet went on loving her just the same.

She wasn't going to start a new job with red eyes. She balled her fists and put one on each side of her head. She pressed them against her temples until it hurt. Then she was ready to go.

Sara Johnson was flustered. She was in the middle of a family emergency and couldn't stay.

"My sister's oldest girl ran off with some boy. A bad lot, I tell you," Sara said. Her wild red hair was scarcely contained by her bright blue bandana. Lavinia was glad to note that she was wearing a denim blouse and skirt. She felt less out of place in her outfit, though hers was a lot fancier. She'd changed her shirt at the last minute back at Patty and Murph's. The one she chose was black with embroidered pink roses on the sleeves, which she felt would be appropriate for selling flowers.

"And you're forming a posse to go hunt them down?" Lavinia asked.

"We're going to my sister's house for a prayer meeting."

Lavinia nodded.

Sara said Saturday mornings were usually slow, so she didn't need to worry about a lot of customers until the afternoon. There was a delivery due, though. She'd have to manage that on her own. She led her through a door behind the counter and down a narrow hallway with a dingy wood-paneled room to one side that Sara said was the office. At the end of the hall was another door, metal this time. This was the delivery bay. On the far side was a big door that lifted when you flipped a switch, like an automatic garage you might see in someone's house.

"He'll pull up in the alley and ring the bell. You'll hear it up front. Then you push the button—I'll show you where it is—the door goes up, and he unloads the flowers. Then he buzzes you again, you lower the door, and he brings the slip around into the store for you to sign."

"I think I can handle that."

"Can you work a cash register?"

"No."

Sara showed her how to. Next to it was the price book. Flowers were sold by the stem, half-dozen, or dozen.

"Now, back to the flowers. You'll need to bring them into the cases here," Sara said and pointed to two glass-fronted refrigerators on one wall. "But remember to trim them first."

The front counter was shaped like an L. At the far end was a large sink. The middle portion was where the stems were cut, excess leaves removed, and so on. On the nearest end were several rows of black plastic containers the flowers were to sit in, along with some actual vases if she felt the wire shelves in the refrigerators could use something fancier.

"If someone wants an arrangement, use baby's breath and springs of anything green. It's always a super nice touch. The paper's under here; there's gold and white, or blue and white— I ran out of the red last week. Wrapping a bouquet's easy, just tape down the excess. And don't cut yourself when you tear the sheet off. The blade's wicked."

Lavinia nodded once more.

"Don't worry, I won't be gone long," Sara said.

"Speed praying. Sort of like speed dating?"

"What's speed dating?"

233

"Never mind."

Sara hugged Lavinia warmly and said she was a blessing.

"You don't know the half of it," Lavinia said.

Sara went on her way cheerfully, her silver handbag swinging from her shoulder.

Lavinia went over the place. It was clean and tidy. Pens were neatly placed in a coffee cup next to the stapler, Scotch tape dispenser, and three spools of ribbon—green, yellow, and white. There was a box with little cards people could write their messages on, and cheerful matching envelopes. Some were pre-printed.

It's a boy!

It's a girl!

To the graduate!

Enjoy your retirement!

Lavinia took a blank one and wrote, "Congratulations on getting struck by lightning!" She put the card back in the box, face down.

This side of her was new. She'd been a serious child and young adult, though she had a small streak of irreverence, for want of a better word. She'd expressed the usual adolescent sarcasms but hadn't been good at speaking her mind. Maybe she'd been afraid of some consequence, like ruining her chances of getting what she wanted. She'd never been exactly reverential, just circumspect, until Potter. He opened the floodgates on her emotions, both good and bad. She developed a sense of humor with him, which passed soon enough in the face of life's demands. Chip brought it back to life until the boredom of middle-age set in. But pranks? Never.

She opened one of the refrigerators. It held red roses, yellow roses, white roses, but not pink, which was disappointing because those were her personal favorite. There were carnations, lilies, gladiola, which were too funerary she thought, and a surprising number of daisies. Why would someone buy daisies when they could be grown so easily?

The window boxes in their first house had made a poor home for her planted flowers. They faced north. She asked Potter to remove them and put them in the back where the light was better. She'd had to make the request four or five times before he complied. He was good with tools, which made his growing trouble finding work ironic. Homeowners always needed things repaired. He could have done well.

She planted violets, then primroses, a mix of petunias, and trailing geraniums. Lavinia loved geraniums. Later, she'd had them in large terra cotta pots all around the patio at Chip's, but the deer wandered in and consumed them idly. She had an iron fence installed, which helped but disturbed the open view of his two back acres, so she had it removed. The sunroom was never used, so she made it into a sort of greenhouse. The roof leaked badly one winter, many of her plants were damaged, and she lost interest in gardening.

She helped herself to a bunch of blue iris from the refrigerator, took them to the table, trimmed them with a pair of small clippers, and put them in a green vase. She'd taken eight stems. According to the price book, she owed Sara twelve dollars. She wanted to leave a note saying so, but couldn't find a single piece of paper anywhere. She went back to the office and turned on the light. The desk was covered with bills and receipts, tax statements, even some personal correspondence judging from the handwritten envelope.

"What a slob!"

She sat in the chair. There were three drawers on the right-hand side of the desk. She opened the first: rubber bands, paper clips, pen caps, erasers, a bag of cotton balls, and a box of Band-Aids. Drawer number two: loose change, a box of staples, an unopened pack of pencils, a roll of stamps, a cell phone charger, batteries, and a dried-up kitchen sponge. Drawer number three: a desk calendar from two years before, take-out menus, raffle tickets, the program from someone's christening, a map of Arizona, and beneath that a small red leather journal. Lavinia opened it at the back, assuming she'd find a blank page she could pluck out. The entire journal was filled with line after line of wobbly script, broken sometimes by games of Tic-Tac-Toe done in pencil.

I told her it was God's will and to submit to the punishment. Pain of the flesh reminds us of the pain we cause God. She fought back, and Darnell was harder than usual. Then I prayed to God for instruction.

"I hope he told you to go straight to hell."

Lavinia tossed the journal into the drawer. She didn't put it back at the bottom. She didn't care that it would be obvious someone had been digging around. She'd deny everything if accused.

The bell tinkled out front. Lavinia went to see who'd come in. An old man in a pair of denim overalls and a white T-shirt stood with an expression of profound loss on his tan, wrinkled face. At the sight of Lavinia, he removed his baseball cap. He had a good crop of thick white hair which he attempted to bring under control with a little black comb he took from a side pocket.

"And how may I help you this fine morning?" Lavinia asked.

"Well, I reckon I need flowers."

"Then I reckon you're in the right place."

The man said nothing. His gaze wandered. He seemed wobbly, as if standing took a great effort.

"What's the occasion?" Lavinia asked.

"Well, see, my missus passed."

"I'm sorry to hear that."

"Two days ago. Over at St. Joseph's."

"That's a hospital?"

The old man nodded.

"And today's the service, and they said I should bring flowers."

"Who's 'they?'"

"Folks at the funeral home."

"I see. Well, what did you have in mind?"

The man looked blankly into her eyes.

"What sort of flowers?" Lavinia asked.

"Can't rightly say. Don't know too much about 'em, truth be told."

Lavinia asked him to please wait a moment. She went behind the counter where there was a barstool with arms, probably for those dull afternoons when all the work was done and you could enjoy the book you'd brought. She took the chair over to the old man and invited him to sit down. He motioned for her to.

A gentleman of the old school!

"I'm afraid I won't be able to wait on you if I'm off my feet," Lavinia said. The old man sat. His relief was clear.

Lavinia noticed that his shoes were leather wingtips that had been highly polished. He must have been getting into his best suit when he remembered this errand. Either that, or he'd just plain gone off the rails.

"She liked white ones, I think," the man said.

Clearly a woman who didn't receive many bouquets over the course of a lifetime.

Lavinia pulled out every white flower in both refrigerators. A dozen carnations, a dozen roses, two dozen gladiola stalks, and two dozen lilies. Most of them had long enough stems to be put into a deep vase. She supposed the funeral home would see to that? The old man had no idea. Lavinia had seen a stack of long, narrow cardboard boxes in the office. She returned with seven of them, put them on the counter, trimmed the flowers, wrapped the ends with damp paper towels secured with rubber bands, and loaded them in.

"All set," she said.

The old man stood up and reached for his wallet in his back pocket. Lavinia held up her hand.

"On the house," she said.

"Oh, I couldn't let you do that."

"Already done."

Lavinia calculated that she'd just given away roughly two hundred dollars' worth of flowers.

"Please."

"It's part of our commitment to the community. Once a month we help one of our fellow citizens with a free gift of beauty. We believe that to lift the spirit is the highest calling of man."

Are you for real?

"Oh, well, gosh. I don't know what to say." The old man looked like he was about to weep. With a growing sense of alarm, Lavinia said she'd be glad to drive the flowers to the funeral home for him, if he wanted.

"You've done enough," he said, his voice breaking.

"Don't be silly. It's our pleasure, really."

"Well, I'd sure like to thank you from the bottom of my heart." The old man extended his hand. Lavinia shook it. His grip was weak.

"I best be on my way then," he said, yet stayed right where he was.

"Is there anything else I can do for you, Mr. …?"

"Sanders. Brian Sanders. Didn't properly introduce myself."

"Lavinia Dugan."

There had been one other time when she'd forgotten the name Starkhurst, and it was also in a flower shop, where she'd gone to order the arrangements for Patty and Murph's wedding.

What is it about flowers that gives me amnesia?

The old man dropped his gaze to the tile floor and shifted his weight from one leg to the other.

"There is something you can do for me, if you're willing. Come to Bessie's funeral."

"What, me? I'm a stranger."

"You've shown me a kindness, and Bessie always appreciated kindness."

"Really, I couldn't."

"I sure do wish you'd change your mind."

"When is it?"

"In about half an hour."

Lavinia didn't feel quite right about leaving before Sara got back. She was a responsible person. Someone you could trust, and clearly Sara had trusted her. Then there was the fact that a funeral service would be hard to bear, given how recent Chip's had been. Being surrounded by grief might cause her to break down yet again.

"All right, if you like," Lavinia said.

She fetched her purse from behind the counter and turned the sign on the door from "Come On In to Please Stop By Another Time." Mr. Sanders collected the boxes with some difficulty and ferried them out. Lavinia followed. She had no key, so there was no way to lock the door. She hoped someone didn't come in and trash the place, but that seemed unlikely. From what she could tell, Helena was a pretty quiet place.

Lavinia told Mr. Sanders she'd follow him in her car, which was parked half a block away. His was right in front, an ancient pickup truck with a broken taillight and dented rear fender. Mr. Sanders tossed the flowers into the bed of the truck one box at a time. By the time she pulled up, he was just getting behind the wheel.

As she followed him around the next corner a white van came into view bearing the name Dawson's Nursery. The flower delivery! She'd forgotten all about that. At the stoplight, she rested her head lightly on the steering wheel and wondered if she was losing her marbles.

The car behind her honked. The light had turned green. Lavinia drove forward. She couldn't see the pickup truck anywhere. Why hadn't she asked him for the address of the funeral home, or at least for its name? She passed through two more intersections, looking up each side street as she went. Nothing. She could just go home and pretend today never happened, except that Sara was certain to call her up and ask what the hell she meant by waltzing off shift like that. She'd just not answer. How easy! But what if Sara did her bookkeeping and realized the missing flowers hadn't been paid for. Then what? Lavinia didn't want to be accused of theft. That could make her future plans—whatever the hell they were—a bit problematic. Note to self: pay Sara back for the flowers she gave Mr. Sanders, and then some for the inconvenience caused. Problem solved! Now what about this goddamned service she'd agreed to attend? It couldn't be that hard to find. How many funeral homes were there in the town that had the dear, departed Bessie Sanders on ice?

She turned into a convenience store parking lot and took out her cell phone. Chip had opted for the most expensive data package their carrier offered, way more than Lavinia ever used, though she was glad for it now. Her search yielded three names: Carson, Brinks, and Dodge. No one answered the phone number for Carson.

Just a bunch of stiffs! HA!

Brinks gave a recorded message saying the place was closed until August.

What if you're just dying to get in?

Dodge said yes, the mourners were gathering and the service would be underway shortly. Lavinia hung up and typed their address into her Google Maps function.

Easy peasy!

As she followed Siri's cheerful instructions, Lavinia realized she felt pretty damn cheerful herself.

Because of Craig?

No doubt.

Being loved was a good thing, even if it was only physical. It was both stunning and delightful to discover that she was capable of that much passion. She wondered if he were thinking of her, too, and knew he surely must be.

Because she was free to change her mind about pretty much anything at this point?

Certainly.

What had started as a need to feel free was slowly becoming something more powerful—the ability to choose. And choosing needn't cause anxiety or stress, as long as the consequences were evenly weighed.

Because she was learning the fine art of compassion? This was probably the truest source of her rising hope. She'd long thought herself fair, if on the strict side. Now she also could think herself kind, thanks to Delray, the shoplifting women, and Mr. Sanders.

The building looked like an ordinary storefront, with a white brick façade and a large picture window. A torn awning extended about four feet from the door. On either side was a tall stone planter with wilted ivy. Lavinia's optimism vanished.

She stood, hand poised above the doorknob, turned it, and entered.

She was met by murmuring voices, the stuttering tones of an organ being clumsily played, and the smell of freshly baked cookies. A child shrieked and was angrily hushed. A man in a cheap brown suit approached her. His face was young, but his eyes were old and exhausted looking. He put his hand on Lavinia's arm. Through the fabric of her shirt sleeve she could feel the dampness of his palm. She reclaimed her arm as he gestured to the entrance of a much larger space with rows of wooden benches and an arch at the far end where a coffin in dark wood was stationed. Part of the coffin's lid was open, and the figure of a woman with white hair lay in profile.

Jesus Christ!

Lavinia's heart sped up. She hung back, then saw Mr. Sanders standing in the aisle talking to a tall, skinny woman dressed in a black cowboy shirt and black jeans. Mr. Sanders was still in his overalls. She approached. When he turned to look at her, his face was blank. Then a light of recognition showed in his now red-rimmed eyes.

"Looking pretty darn good," he said, tossing his head in the direction of the altar. It took Lavinia a moment to realize he'd referred to the flowers. Two teenaged girls were stuffing them roughly into a few containers on either side of the coffin.

The woman talking to Mr. Sanders turned to Lavinia and said, "So, you decided to come after all."

"Excuse me?"

"Now, daughter," Mr. Sanders said.

"Must feel strange, doing the right thing."

"Daughter, climb down off your high horse."

"I'm afraid you have me confused with someone else," Lavinia said.

"One thing I never was confused about is you," his daughter said in a fierce whisper.

Lavinia turned and walked down the aisle, out of the room, and into the foyer. The wilted young man who'd ushered her in was there, sitting on a chair. He looked at her.

"Bailing out?" he asked. His voice was high and weak.

"I think I'm in the wrong place."

"She would have been glad you came, even just for a little minute. She talked about you all the time. Even afterward. You know."

"Just who the hell does everyone seem to think I am?"

"Come on, Gladys. It's okay."

Lavinia felt like the stained green carpet was holding her in place.

"You know me?" she asked.

"*Of* you. Everyone does."

"Well, I'm not Gladys. I'm Lavinia."

The man peered at her closely. He seemed to study every square inch of her face. He asked to see her hands. She extended her arms. He took her right one, turned it over, and stared at her palm for a moment. He did the same to the other one.

"She was scarred from a fire she set, then had to stamp out," he said.

"No scars here."

"Nope."

"But I look like her?"

"I'd say the resemblance is mighty darn close."

The man motioned for her to sit in the empty chair next to him. He said his name was Buck, well that was just a nickname really. His Christian name was Bertram. He was Bessie's second cousin twice removed, or maybe it was once removed, he was never sure. Those extended family relationships always confused him. He paused and closed his eyes for a moment. Lavinia wondered what ailed him. He reminded her of someone from another time, before medicine became modern, when people were afflicted with mysterious conditions that slowly wasted them away.

A short, middle-aged woman in an orange pantsuit approached them with the intensity of a small rodent. She walked so quickly Lavinia could hear her pantyhose rasp. Buck opened his eyes at the sound of her. She bent down and said, "I'm so sorry. The director's been detained. It should only be a few more minutes." Buck nodded. The woman went into the hall beyond, where she was heard making her announcement.

Buck cleared his throat. It seemed hard for him to swallow. Lavinia offered to get him a glass of water, but from where she had no idea. He shook his head.

"Anyhow, about Gladys," he said. She was Bessie's special project, a girl she'd found wandering around the streets one day when she came into town to get a tooth pulled. Bessie's own kids were grown by then, and maybe getting on in years had made her that much lonelier; Buck didn't know. He figured old folks needed company a little more than other people did, but that was probably beside the point. Gladys had no one and nowhere to go. They later learned that her husband had kicked her out for getting involved with the man she worked for. He told her not to come back, and to forget about ever seeing their dog again. From what Buck had been led to understand, it had been a particularly nice dog, too, and its loss was especially hard on Gladys and probably contributed to her rotten state.

Bessie brought her home. Brian wasn't too happy, but he adjusted because old Brian was the adjusting type. Gladys was useful around the place. She learned how to muck a barn, milk a cow, corner a sow when the vet was there to give an injection. Bessie seemed younger then, too; she was that happy for the friendship. Trouble was, old Gladys took off one day with Bessie's wedding silver—the only nice thing that poor woman ever owned. Brian reported the loss; the cops found Gladys easily enough over in Spokane where she always talked about going someday. Plus, she was driving an old hand-me-down car of Brian's, a white Chevy sedan he just let her have, and he was able to provide the license plate number. Gladys said Bessie gave her the silver as a thank you for all the work she'd done around the place in the year and a half she lived there. The cops asked Bessie about that directly, and she backed Gladys up. And being the good guy that he was, Brian said he'd made a mistake; he'd forgotten that he'd been right there in the kitchen when Bessie said Gladys could take the silver. So, Gladys got off the hook and was never heard from again. A betrayal is hard on anyone, but on an old heart, it can weigh particularly heavy.

"You said something about a fire," Lavinia said.

"Smoking in bed. She had the downstairs room, and if she hadn't woken up, they'd all have gone up flames."

Buck needed to take a few moments to recover from all his talking. The rodent woman returned, looking at her watch.

249

Lavinia glanced into the hall. Mr. Sanders was up at the coffin with several other people, all staring down at wax figure Bess. Had he invited her because she looked so much like Gladys? Why would he want to be reminded of such a creep?

So he could say, "Look, darling, here she is!"

Lavinia's cell phone buzzed in her purse. She stood and went to the door before answering it. It was Mel.

"Just calling to say hello," he said.

"Can't really talk now. I'm at a funeral."

"Who died?"

"I'll explain later."

She didn't hang up. She just stood, listening to Mel breathe on the other end.

"Mel," she said.

"Yes, love?"

"Did anyone ever take you for someone else?"

"Mistaken identity, you mean?"

"Yes."

"Can't say so. Besides, a face as handsome as mine doesn't come around twice in life, right?"

"Oh, honestly. I'll talk to you later."

For a moment she thought about turning around and saying goodbye to Mr. Sanders, then thought it was better to leave him in the company of his family.

chapter seventeen

Another Sunday rolled around. Lavinia sat with her coffee and recalled Sara's response to being handed a thousand dollars. At the sight of it, she went pale. When it was pressed into her palm, she flushed.

She'd returned to the store shortly after Lavinia had left, and rather than being angry, she was terrified that someone had abducted her.

"Are you kidding?" Lavinia had asked.

Sara said she could come in the next day, if she still wanted to. The gooey look in her eyes said she'd spoken out of pity.

The poor scatterbrained widow.

Lavinia said she clearly wasn't up to committing to a job at this point. She needed more time to process her grief. Sara bent her head and invited Lavinia to pray. Lavinia said she wasn't the praying kind—though if it ever seemed like a good idea, Sara would be the first to know.

Then Lavinia asked if Sara knew the Sanders family, Brian and Bessie. Sara had to think for a moment and then thought she might have, at one time.

"Did you know anything about a woman who came to live with them? Gladys?"

"Not that I recall. Why?"

"Never mind."

Sitting alone now, Lavinia reflected further. She had left Dunston twelve days before. She had to count twice to make sure, because she couldn't believe it had been that short a time. Some milestone had been reached within her, though the precise significance of it was still unclear.

Karen had called the evening before, in tears. The man she'd been seeing had gone cold when she told him she was ready to leave Phil.

"What does he think this is, some game?" she asked, her voice heavy with grief.

Lavinia forced herself to call back, ready to listen, offering no advice unless asked. She was grateful when Karen didn't pick up. This time, she didn't leave a message.

Craig had asked to see her again. She put him off. Until she knew what her next move was, a romantic complication, though surely a marvelous pastime, could also make a mess of things.

"If you're going to stick around longer, why not volunteer somewhere? You might find it very rewarding," Patty said.

Lavinia had done plenty of volunteering in her day. At the kids' school, raising money for the Rotary fund scholarship, addressing envelopes when Chip ran for City Council and won by a huge margin.

Patty wrote something on a piece of paper and pushed it across the table to Lavinia.

"Give her a call tomorrow," she said.

"Who's Lucy Cross?"

"Runs the local United Way office downtown. She was telling me the other day they're trying to place ex-cons with local businesses, sort of give them a leg up. They need help with interviewing skills. You interviewed people when you worked for Chip, right?"

"Sure."

"Should be a cinch, then."

"Dear Patty. I do believe you're trying to turn me into a useful human being."

"Let's not get carried away."

But Lucy Cross's office was locked, so Lavinia tried the Helena Public Association down the hall. There she found an acne-scarred young woman with an air of barely suppressed rage. Lavinia said she would like to volunteer. Was there anything she could do? The woman looked at her for an awkwardly long moment before asking her to sit down.

Yes, she said, there was. Many low-income residents needed help getting to a doctor's appointment, to a court hearing, or somewhere beyond the boundaries of the city bus system. They needed people with cars willing to drive them. Did Lavinia have a car?

"Yes."

What was her interest in helping the needy?

"Nothing really. I mean, we're all needy in our way, I suppose."

At this the woman, Laura Smith according to the sign on her desk, turned bright red.

"Oh, I didn't mean you in particular. I'm sure you're just fine. I mean in the larger sense, we're all sort of screwed," Lavinia said.

Laura Smith cleared her throat. She asked to see Lavinia's driver's license.

"New York State. You're a long way from home," Laura Smith said.

"You got that right."

"You'll need to get fingerprinted."

"Why?"

"To check your driving record."

"Oh, I'm pretty solid behind the wheel."

Laura Smith focused on Lavinia's outfit—the same studded jeans but with a different shirt, this time with pink piping and white buttons carved in the shapes of roses. She told Lavinia where to go for the fingerprinting, when she could pick up her list of people to call upon, and to be sure to bring extra pens because they always got left behind.

"We reimburse your driving expenses, so keep track of the mileage," Laura Smith said.

She gave Lavinia a brochure entitled *Staying Safe On The Job*. It listed things to be aware of when meeting with strangers, like if they seemed agitated, intoxicated, or predatory. One point said, "If someone has a firearm or other weapon, it's best not to let them inside your car."

Good Lord!

Assuming everything came back okay, Lavinia could be assigned her first client that Thursday.

"Sounds like a plan," Lavinia said.

Laura Smith made no comment. The telephone on her desk rang. As she lifted the receiver, Lavinia stood, saluted her, and went on her way.

The clear air of an hour before was now hazy. Looking east Lavinia could see smoke rising beyond the ridge. Its acrid smell claimed her at once. Chip burned the autumn leaves rather than turning them into mulch. The kids always loved watching the flames dance, but if the wind shifted and smoke got in their eyes, there were quick cries of distress. Even after they'd tumbled back into the house, Chip remained outside to watch the pile shrink and smolder.

He loved indoor fires, too. The house had several fireplaces. Lavinia found maintaining them a nuisance. The man who cleaned the chimney always left soot behind, despite his meticulously hung plastic sheets. In Chip's office, the fireplace was marble imported from Italy, creamy white with gray-green veins, always icy to the touch, even with a roaring fire in its mouth. She'd find him standing before it, often with a drink in hand, gazing intently at the flames as if they were a code he needed to break. In warm weather, she used it as a backdrop for some elaborate floral display or a fleshy plant— once an anthurium whose shiny red leaves stood out so beautifully against the pale stone. One year she found a charming brass screen at an antiques fair in the Adirondacks.

Chip didn't care for it, so she moved it to the fireplace in the living room, which was seldom used. There were two others, one in the room Angie had had when she lived there, and one in their master bedroom. Angie had enjoyed hers even during her sullen goth years when she'd be found, all in black, cross-legged before it. "Like a witch with a cauldron," Chip once suggested. The wood in theirs had been lit on nights when Chip was feeling romantic, though they only made love to firelight once that Lavinia could recall.

One summer—no, it had been early fall—they'd gone to Cape Cod. Chip found them a house right on the beach. It was isolated, and slightly grim in terms of all the gray tones both inside and out. Lavinia had been out of sorts, anxious about leaving the children with Alma, though it was only for a couple of days. There was another source of uneasiness, too. Chip wasn't happy with her just then. They'd had the Rotary Club over for a barbeque, and she got into an argument with the Chairman about a ballot measure to raise the minimum wage. He argued that it would unfairly burden small business owners. Lavinia said people were entitled to make ends meet. While she kept her cool, her irritation was plain when she abruptly walked off. The Chairman told Chip he wasn't offended and that he admired Lavinia's spirit, but Chip was embarrassed. In private he told Lavinia that an honest opinion was one thing, good manners another. She was furious. She refused to be lectured to. Things turned steely and cold between them. She relented, but he stayed cool. She suggested a getaway. He made the arrangements.

Being alone forced them to open the door that had been shut between them. The incident at the barbeque wasn't raised. Rather, they stayed on neutral topics—a restaurant

257

they'd passed that looked interesting, the collection of skeins draping one side of a neighbor's house, whether a howling wind made one feel cozy or forlorn. He suggested they build a bonfire on the beach to celebrate their last night there.

The owners of the house had collected wood over the course of the summer, anything that had washed up, and set it on the side porch to dry. They put what could be contained in a very wobbly wheelbarrow that Chip nearly toppled several times going down the wooden walk. At the end of the walk, they emptied the wheelbarrow and carried armful after armful down a set of stairs that finally brought them to the water's edge. The day was dying, the wind on the rise. The screech of seagulls made Lavinia wish she could fly.

Hollow bones, she'd thought, and felt the weight of her own flesh with a sorrow she'd not known before.

Chip had to go back for some rolled-up newspaper and matches. He was gone a long time, long enough for Lavinia to turn away from the sea, look up at the house, and wonder if he'd thrown his things back in his suitcase and driven off. He'd have known she'd make her way home eventually. He often praised her resourcefulness. Was he the type to teach her a lesson? What lesson would there be in his temporarily deserting her? She turned back to face the waves, loving both their endurance and restlessness, and decided either he'd return to the beach, or he wouldn't. Then it occurred to her that something might have happened—he'd had a heart attack or fallen over something and hit his head—and that if she didn't go find out, she might condemn him to a rotten fate. So, she spun around and there he was, ambling along the walk, then descending the stairs carefully, holding the rail with one hand and the rolls of newspaper with the other. From a distance, years were wiped away. His hair was mostly brown, his face unlined, his back straight. It was only as he approached that age found him again. Lavinia hadn't made sense of the transformation and assumed that maybe her grateful heart had given him an aura of youth. It didn't matter.

The fire was lit and took time to gain strength. As it did, brilliant red sparks lifted into the night, drawn heavenward as they burned out. The heat grew, and Lavinia's face, which the wind had numbed, warmed pleasantly. She'd put her hair up that day, though many strands had come loose. Chip unpinned it and helped it fall down her back. He put his arm around her as they watched the fire consume the wood below the darkening vault above. They could have been two people from a hundred years before, or a thousand, or many years in the future. This is what Chip wanted, Lavinia realized, to bring them to an ultimate point where one stood with the other before something much more powerful than either of them. It

259

was his way of saying that no matter what, he would always love her.

In the brief time of Lavinia's daydream, the smoke had thickened. She'd heard what forest fires could do out there in the West, how many acres they could destroy. She was witnessing the start of one, she was sure. No controlled burn would look like that.

She drove to Patty's restaurant, The Dusty Boot, and asked the hostess where she could be found. She was directed to Patty's office. She was going through a stack of papers with a benign expression. She wore a blue silk scarf in her hair that Lavinia found a particularly elegant touch.

"There's a fire up in the mountains," she said.

Patty looked up.

"Typical, this time of year," she said.

"Aren't you worried?"

"If I got antsy over every pine tree that went up in smoke, I wouldn't have time for much else."

"This is a lot more than one tree. It's pretty intense."

"You spend much more time out here, you'll get used to it. We're in high fire season."

"What starts them?"

"Lightning, usually, but there hasn't been any. Probably some bonehead didn't properly smother his camp fire."

Lavinia helped herself to the empty chair across from Patty's desk.

Patty said someone could have started it on purpose, too. Several years back, down in Colorado, there was a woman who worked for the forest service, who wanted to impress her boss with how good she was at spotting early fires. Her need for approval was complicated by the fact that she was in love with the guy. So, she sets a small patch of brush on fire, easy enough to contain, she figures, only she can't contain it, and off it goes. Before you know it, four hundred thousand acres across the whole goddamned state get torched.

"Guess she really impressed him," Lavinia said.

"No kidding."

They sat, listening to the sounds of restaurant life—plates clattering, the kitchen door swooshing open and closed, rapid footsteps along the tile hallways, silenced by the carpet beyond. Lavinia kept wondering if she were smelling smoke, and decided she wasn't.

Yet when she was outside again, the smell was strong, the air still hazy. The smoke had changed color from black to white, which she hoped meant that someone was dousing its source.

By that evening, the news was all about the growing fire in the Helena National Forest. For the time being, no homes were in danger, but the winds were predicted to shift the following day, bringing the fire close to the small town of Bueller. The air had taken on a distinctly yellow tone. Patty said it was turning into a big one, for sure. Murph said they'd seen bigger. Didn't she remember the one three years before? Yes, Patty said, but that was much farther off, in an unpopulated area of the state.

Lavinia asked if the fire would reach Helena itself. Murph said he sure as hell hoped not.

Two days later, Mel called.

"All those helicopters! What's that stuff they're dropping?" he asked.

"Fire retardant?"

"Ah."

He wanted to know if she were scared.

"When have I ever been scared?" she asked.

"True."

She was though, but not of the fire.

Craig had called again. She didn't pick up, though she really wanted to. Patty and Murph knew he'd been in touch, though how, she couldn't say. Maybe they sensed her unease, the electricity in her eyes, the hands that wouldn't stay still and cleaned Patty's already clean kitchen from top to bottom, including inside the cabinets, oven, and refrigerator.

The evacuations began that Thursday, three days after Lavinia first saw smoke. Everyone in Bueller plus the residents in six outlying ranches were brought in. The livestock posed a transportation problem. Anyone with an animal trailer was asked to lend their equipment, pasture, and barn space for the duration. Craig didn't keep animals on his property, though he had at one time. He ended up hosting four horses in his barn and three pregnant cows in the six-acre pasture behind the house. If the fire came close enough, they'd all have to be moved again.

This information was relayed to Lavinia via Murph, who'd taken time from the nursing home job to help out.

"Had to put a bandana over my mouth, it was that thick up there. And we saw flames. They weren't exactly distant, let me tell you," he said. The smell of burning wood was heavy on his plaid shirt.

Lavinia called Craig. She wanted to know how the horses were faring, if the smoke bothered them, if they were agitated.

"They're doing good. But if you want, come on over and take a look for yourself," he said.

"Not until the smoke clears."

"Shouldn't be too long now."

"Good."

Some people were able to stay with family in Helena. The Red Cross was housing others in the gym of the high school.

"I'm heading on over later with some chow from the restaurant," Patty told Lavinia.

"I'll come, too."

Displaced people all have the same look, Lavinia quickly learned. Hollow eyes, still faces, slack hands. They sat on their cots, in folding metal chairs, or on the shiny wood floor itself, their suitcases, bags, paperback books, stuffed animals, and water bottles scattered around, until there was something for them to do. Many used their cell phones. Exhausted voices drifted past. There were worries about pets that had run off, or not being able to reach a neighbor to see if they were all right. One woman corralled one of the volunteers and said she was expecting an important delivery at her home and that she must be allowed to go back and see if it had arrived.

Those who had managed to bring their pets were asked to crate them at one end, behind a partition. The crates had come from the Red Cross. The back and sides of each were solid, and they were arranged in rows so the animals couldn't see each other. Foster had mentioned once how important that was, because animals, usually cats, could get very aggressive if they caught sight of a stranger. Pet food was stacked on one wall next to jugs of water. Meals would be served on the folding table in the cafeteria, and this was where Patty went to work with Ernesto, her head chef from The Dusty Boot. They'd taken over one range and two steam tables in the kitchen. They worked silently, understanding one another through the way they moved. Lavinia joined them. She put a pan of barbecued ribs on the steam table, then a pan of Mexican rice and one of green beans. She carried jugs of lemonade and milk and put one on each table, also a pitcher of ice water. She filled a large coffee maker with water and ground coffee Patty had also been smart enough to bring. Paper plates, napkins, and plastic utensils went on a table outside the cafeteria. She made sure there was a good stack of trays for people to slide over the metal bars as they went along.

People came, ate, shared stories of their escape, spoke angrily about local law enforcement who'd made them go, and swore that the fire wasn't as bad as they said. The next day, though, the smoke was thicker, and people were advised to stay indoors. Finally, on the fifth day, the wind shifted and slowed, and the fire became more and more contained.

Lavinia hadn't admitted how uneasy the whole thing had made her. More than once she'd thought of just leaving, continuing her journey west, and probably would have, if not for the volunteer gig she'd committed to.

Then Laura Smith called to say there'd been a little trouble with Lavinia's fingerprints. Seemed like she'd gotten arrested for drunk driving a few years before.

"Oh, that. What difference does it make now?" Lavinia asked.

"A lot, I'm afraid. Rules are rules."

"To hell with rules."

"An enviable state of affairs, I admit, but in this case impossible."

Lavinia hung up. So much for that. Here she was, trying to move on, to not exactly flee the past but put it behind, and she had to be reminded of some stupid indiscretion that happened, what, eight years ago? Nine?

The kids never knew about it. No one did. Only Chip.

They'd had a fight about Angie, who was in college then, and was recovering from that bad affair with her professor. Lavinia had intervened when she learned who the man was. She'd invited him to lunch on the pretext of hiring him for a project that would help the underprivileged of Dunston. He was a professor of Social Work, so this sounded reasonable. He didn't connect Angie and Lavinia, because they had different last names. They met at a pricey restaurant. Lavinia could see him enjoy the luxury of the place. She was vague about her project. Instead she spoke of a fictional college roommate she'd once had, Claire Maltby, who killed herself after being rejected by her lover. The lover was one of her professors, and wasn't that so sad? Lavinia said it was such a shame that some young women were so vulnerable and that some men were so callous and cruel. Whether he connected the dots or not, she couldn't say. She managed to lay all of this on him before they had a chance to order anything besides drinks, and after only one, he excused himself. She stayed on to have two more to celebrate the sight of his rushing off with some inane excuse—that he'd just remembered he had to bring his dog to the vet! A week later Angie said he'd taken a leave of absence for the rest of the semester.

Lavinia was spectacularly pleased with herself. She shared the whole story with Chip. Chip wasn't pleased. He felt she'd been reckless, not exactly unfair to the professor since he was a cad, after all, but because she'd involved Chip by name in the scheme. She had to, didn't he see that? It was his money she was dangling as a lure. He said since she made the whole thing up anyway, why not invent a husband who didn't actually exist? Someone whose reputation could never be harmed?

Of course, he had a point. She wasn't so pig-headed that she couldn't admit that. But at the time, pumped up by her own cleverness, she wanted praise and compliments, not criticism. The three drinks she had at lunch were quickly joined by several glasses of a good quality California Merlot. Because it was summer, she partook on the patio, gazing crossly into the unevenly trimmed hedge the palsied gardener had done his best with. Chip didn't have the heart to let him go. Rather, he hired a younger man to come in afterward and right the flaws. Then, when first gardener, who'd been with Chip from before the time of his first wife's death, returned, he was instantly reassured that his skills were still intact, because just look! What a fine job he'd done!

And here Chip was, reaming her a new one because she dared to mention his real name to Professor Cop-a-Feel. He stepped out a couple of times to assess her mood, which only made it darker. Finally, he just left her alone.

As the light faded, she killed off the bottle. She was restless. She couldn't bear the thought of being in the house another moment. The kids were with Potter. Alma was at her sister's. She knew Chip hungered for her company, as he always did when the house emptied, not because he was lonely, but because without the distractions and demands of everyone else, he could focus on her and her alone. It gave him great pleasure. Usually she enjoyed it, too. But not now.

She took herself for a drive, realizing the moment she started the car that she was three sheets to the wind. She persisted. She *had* to. The roads were empty, as she knew they would be. The Heights were so quiet that time of day, everyone safely at home, hashing out their own private agonies, a full glass in hand.

She drove fine. Stopped at every stop sign. Followed the curves. Never veered onto the shoulder or across the center line. She even remembered to turn her lights on. So, when the flashing blue and red appeared in her rearview, she was shocked.

The officer who knocked politely on her window was the same one who'd arrested Timothy for shoplifting years before. Burns. Barret. She couldn't make out the name tag. One of her taillights was out. She'd known it was, and had forgotten. She said exactly that. He looked so sad then, smelling the booze on her. He had her step out of the car and breathe into the tube. Her blood alcohol level was almost three times the legal limit. He really hated to do it, but he had to take her downtown. It was the law. She couldn't be let off with a warning.

By the time Chip lumbered through the door of the station, her resentment toward him had turned to immense relief. He paid her bail. She had to do one hundred and twenty hours of community service and attend a substance abuse counseling program. Looking back on that now, she was amazed at how they'd kept it from the kids and from Alma, too. But then, at that point, no one really paid much attention to where she was or how she spent her time except Chip, who did ask how the park cleanup had gone and if the food bank was as nasty as ever.

Had it humbled her? Not really. She made a mistake. No one had been harmed. She never thought it would come back to get her now, so long afterward.

With the prospect of her volunteer activity off the table, Lavinia got herself in gear. Time to figure out her next move.

chapter eighteen

Carefully set out on the polished wooden table were the boxes of dried bouquets, the stuffed bear, the vase, the family photographs, and the thimbles. She added the watercolors, although they were purchased before the trip, not during it. Then she added the fancy Western clothes she bought, and put the cowboy boots by themselves on the floor. At the moment, she was in one of her silk jumpsuits. Craig stood in the doorway of his kitchen and took her in.

"Everything I've collected along the way," Lavinia said.

"Including me?"

He'd just returned from town. He hadn't expected to find her there. She assumed the door would be locked. When the knob turned in her hand, she knew he'd left it open for her, though she hadn't agreed to be there at any particular time, or even to come at all.

"I wouldn't say that," she said.

He put his hand on her shoulder.

"I'm uncollectible?"

"Not at all."

They kissed.

"Are you leaving this here?" he asked.

"No. I was just taking inventory."

He sat on the bench by the window and removed his boots. He held out his hands. She took them.

"You can stay. No strings," he said.

"I know."

"But the road's calling your name."

"Something like that. Besides, it's Tuesday. I left home on a Tuesday. Sort of want to keep the trend going, I guess."

He made her a lunch to take along. Her heart broke watching him slap the bologna down on the bread. She carried her things to her car. He followed with the sandwich in a brown paper bag.

They kissed once more. She could tell from how he held her that he was trying to change her mind. She almost did.

She looked in the rearview mirror only once as she went down the long, dusty drive. He'd already gone back inside.

When she reached the state highway, she called Mel. She put him on speaker. His voice had a rich resonance.

"Were they sorry to see you go?" he asked.

"I was there two weeks, well two weeks and a day, so no."

But they were. Patty's eyes had a glint of regret. Murph, too, looked a little lost.

"And the man you were seeing?"

"What man?"

"The one you stuck around for."

"There isn't anyone, Mel."

"Okay."

Neither spoke for a few seconds. Lavinia followed the highway west, toward the interstate.

"Where to now?" he asked.

"The Pacific."

"Via?"

"Idaho and Washington, obviously."

"I know someone in Pocatello, if you're going that way."

"That's pretty far south."

She asked him to call her family and let them know she was once more in motion. She said her cell signal was about to get iffy, judging from the pass she was about to ascend, or she would do it herself.

The sky gathered in dark, inky knots. Lightening broke. After the first boom of thunder, her heart quickened. Fat, heavy drops of rain hit the windshield slowly at first, then much faster. When they became ice, the noise was alarming. So was trying to see. She pulled onto the shoulder to wait it out. The shoulder was narrow and not level with the main road, and for a moment she thought she might tumble down the steep slope only a few feet away.

That would be a silly way to end things.

No worse than getting struck by lightning.

The hail increased. The noise deadened rational thought. It was as if she *were* the din, random and wild, growing stronger even as energy was spent.

It stopped. The silence rang. The windshield was coated with snow and ice. She turned off the wipers. Then she turned off the engine and stepped out of the car. There was no traffic. Ice crunched under the soles of her ridiculous sandals. The temperature had to have dropped about twenty degrees since she'd left Helena. She could see her breath, yet didn't feel cold. She was exhilarated.

A truck roared past. A car followed, and about a half a minute later another went by. No one stopped to ask if she were all right.

One afternoon, driving through the Heights after dropping the twins at a playdate, she passed a car on the shoulder near a stand of autumn oaks. She assumed it was someone collecting leaves. The car was still there when she passed again an hour later—their time had been cut short because Maggie didn't feel well, though she later confessed to having been bored. Then she needed something from the store, and passed the car a third time. She circled back and pulled in behind it. It was a late-model Buick, so she was surprised to find a young woman behind the wheel, weeping.

She had assumed the driver would be an old person, suddenly taken ill. It took a moment for the driver to see Lavinia standing there, peering at her. Lavinia motioned for her to lower the window. The woman turned the engine on just long enough to activate the button.

"Are you all right?" Lavinia asked.

The woman looked to be in her early twenties. Her blonde hair had come loose from her ponytail. She was wearing a tan raincoat, which made her look older than she was, perhaps intentionally. On one wrist was a leather bracelet inlaid with blue and white beads. She twisted it with her other hand as she stared silently up at Lavinia.

"I saw your car here a while ago, and I hoped no one was sick or hurt. Are you?" Lavinia asked.

The woman shook her head.

"What's your name?"

"Tammy."

"Like that old song."

The woman looked blank.

"From the Fifties. 'Tammy's In Love.'"

At this, Tammy bawled.

So, that's it. Of course.

Lavinia handed her a piece of Kleenex she had in her pocket. Tammy took it and just pressed it into a ball without using it. She dropped the ball on the floor and put both of her hands back on the wheel.

"I know this is none of my business, but I speak from experience when I say that things like this happen, and he probably wasn't worth it," Lavinia said.

A queer light came into the woman's eyes.

"My cat died," she said.

"I'm so sorry!"

"She was a really great cat, too."

Lavinia nodded.

"Had her since I was six."

"What happened?"

"Got hit by a car."

Lavinia had killed a cat once that had dashed across the road on a very dark, wet night. Chip told her to stop so they could get out and see. She didn't want to, but he was firm. It was their duty, he said. It hadn't gone far, just beyond the shoulder. Lavinia was glad it had no collar, because she couldn't bear the idea of having to contact the owner. Then she felt sad, thinking they'd be at home wondering where the cat was, then anxious, and ultimately heartsick when it never returned.

"Maybe you should get another one," she said.

"People say that. But she'd never be the same as Florence."

"Pretty name."

Tammy nodded miserably. Her face calmed, and her shoulders seemed to loosen.

"Did you have a funeral for her?" Lavinia asked.

"They cremated her at the vet's."

"Can you get the ashes?"

"Don't think so."

"You could still have a ceremony. A memorial service. It might help you feel better."

Tammy's expression changed from woe to irritation.

"I'm late," she said, and turned on the engine.

Lavinia stepped back to allow the car room to pull out. Then she went home and thought Tammy could at least have said thank you for her attempted kindness.

It wasn't an attempt. It was genuine because she *felt* kind at the time.

So, kindness was both an action *and* a feeling?

Lavinia realized she was freezing, standing there in the slush. She got back in the Lexus and turned the heat on high.

The road rose toward the pass. It narrowed, and twisted sharply. Lavinia dropped her speed to accommodate the sudden turns. The sky lifted enough to let a few rays of sunlight cut across the evergreens. The beauty was intense. She felt almost drunk with joy, taking it all in, thinking how far she was from home, making her way deeper and deeper into this glorious, unknown place. Past the summit, the descent was much more gradual. A valley below was visible, with a river gracing its floor like a silver ribbon. She dropped for about another fifteen miles and then a sign said she had entered the town of Hamilton, population 1,734. The speed limit was down to thirty-five miles an hour, and Lavinia obeyed it. The downtown area consisted of two blocks of storefronts, most of which seemed to be in good condition. A banner was strung high across the street announcing a rodeo the week before. As a girl, she'd been around horses a lot because of her father's work as a farrier; she even rode for a while, always in the English style. She just might get back up on a horse one of these days, just for the hell of it. What a photo op that would make! The family would appreciate it.

She pulled into one of the angled parking spots so she could take a moment and put on a pair of socks and then her cowboy boots. The thermometer on the dash had been as low as forty-eight degrees on the pass, and now had only climbed to fifty-four. In July! It must be a fluke of the storm. The usual warm weather gear was on display in the window of the drugstore—rubber flip-flops, lawn chairs, a barbeque grill, and a bag of briquettes. She could have been anywhere in the US just then, except for the wall of mountains she'd driven through.

After thinking she'd never pair one of her jumpsuits with her boots, there she was. She looked at her reflection in the window of a burger joint. She twisted one way, then another. She didn't look so bad. She dug around in her backpack for the only sweater she'd brought, made of alpaca and dyed teal, which when combined with the pink of her jumpsuit made her look like an Easter egg. She picked up her purse from the passenger seat of the car, where it had been sitting with the bear, now once again riding shotgun, and walked two doors down into a brightly lit diner with red vinyl booths and a black and white tile floor. She took a stool at the counter. A heavy-set twenty-something girl with spiky blonde hair presented her with a glass of water and a menu. She reminded Lavinia instantly of Angie when she was younger. There was a sullen resentment in her eyes that made Lavinia want to tell her to chill out, life would work out if she gave it half a chance, but those words would sound hollow because they were vague and could mean just about anything.

That was the problem with giving advice—it always sounded too easy. Life didn't change course based on greeting card hype and cheery generalities. You had to dig down to the pivot point, the thing on which everything relied, and nudge it in a new direction. You couldn't do that unless you knew the whole story, or at least the parts of it that mattered.

Lavinia asked for her usual cup of black coffee. The waitress brought it. The hand that lowered it onto the counter had a letter tattooed upside down on each finger except the thumb. All together they spelled "Lola."

"Is that you?" Lavinia asked, nodding to the fingers. The waitress looked at her hand. She seemed surprised by what she saw.

"My ex," she said.

Lavinia nodded. She'd once thought of getting a tattoo on the inside of one wrist, something easy that she wouldn't tire of. A flower, maybe. Or a word that summed everything up.

Mine.

How should the letters be oriented, though? So when she looked at them, they were right-side up? Or upside down for someone else's benefit, the way the waitress had done hers?

The coffee was bitter, as if it had been sitting too long. She pushed it away. When the waitress dropped off the check, Lavinia asked where she'd gotten her tattoo done.

"In The Pink Ink."

"Here in town?"

"End of the block," the waitress said, and tossed her head over her right shoulder.

Lavinia put down a five-dollar bill.

"Be right back with your change," the waitress said.

"Keep it."

The morning hadn't warmed at all, though the sun was bright. The few people who passed her stared hard. She smiled to one and all. Maybe what they said about smiling was true. The more you did it, the lighter you felt. In the corner of her eye, her bright, colorful reflection bobbed cheerfully along in the storefronts. She felt positively sassy by the time she reached the tattoo parlor where she was met by a large, orange cat sprawled on the stone threshold. The cat didn't move as Lavinia stepped over it and opened the door.

The darkness, after the bright sun, took a moment to reckon. Cigarette smoke hung in the air. Lavinia was reminded of the candy store she used to love as a child, because of the glass cases displaying all the rods and metal balls you could install if you were crazy enough. On the walls were images to choose from if you just wanted a tattoo. Swans, peacocks, flying fish, sailboats, all kinds of flowers and plants, wolves, dragons, a snowy peak, a grenade, swords, and racecars were only a few. Most were in red or blue. Lavinia wondered which colors lasted best.

A figure emerged from the back, a short, stocky guy who, as he got closer, was actually a female. Her head was shaved.

Her young face, though unlined, wore a world-weary expression. She had large, red gauges in her ears. A wide leather band was around each wrist. She looked like she could take you down in one, swift blow. She sized Lavinia up, lingering on the legs of her bright pink jumpsuit.

"No, the circus isn't in town," Lavinia said.

The woman chewed her toothpick thoughtfully.

"You here to collect for something?" she asked.

"No. I want a tattoo."

The woman moved the toothpick around in her mouth some more.

"First?" she asked.

"Yes."

"You picked one?"

"A name."

"Everybody chooses a name the first time around."

She showed Lavinia the four fingers of her left hand. Each had a letter inked on the back, spelling Suzi.

"I don't suppose you're Lola," Lavinia said.

"I am."

"Suzi recommended you."

"Super nice of her." The woman's tone was harsh.

Lola ushered Lavinia to a chair. She said she'd go collect her tools and be right back. Did she want a magazine to look at or something? Maybe some coffee? Lavinia's stomach lurched at the idea of coffee. She asked for a glass of water. Lola brought it in a paper cup. When she'd gone off again, Lavinia stared into the water, looking for anything strange floating in it. It looked fine, tasted fresh. She drank all of it.

A child's voice pierced the quiet, full of protest and rage. Something clattered to the floor. The noise stopped. Lola returned, her face hard and tight.

"Yours?" Lavinia asked.

"Suzi's. I been taking care of him for the last month."

"How old?"

"Five."

"No daycare?"

"Not on what I make."

Lola asked Lavinia what color ink she wanted.

"Blue."

What was she going to have inscribed?

"Chip."

"As in chocolate?"

"My husband."

"You're very devoted."

After the fact.

Lola put the tattoo gun together and asked Lavinia how big the letters should be.

"Not very. Maybe one eighth of an inch."

"Facing how?"

Lavinia said she wanted the name right-side up from her viewpoint.

"Block letters or script? I'm not too good at script. If you want, you can write it out, and I can trace it."

"Block. My handwriting's probably no better than yours."

"It'll be seventy-five dollars."

"Fine."

Lola asked if Lavinia were allergic to latex, then pulled on a pair of rubber gloves. She swabbed the inside of Lavinia's wrist with disinfectant. She said not to move suddenly. She placed the buzzing needle on Lavinia's skin. It burned, but not terribly. More than anything, she felt pressure.

Lola concentrated hard on her work. The child cried out again. He trotted out from wherever he'd been and appeared at Lavinia's side. He was blond. His nose ran. His striped shirt was clean, but his blue jeans had grass stains on the knees. He held a plastic toy in one hand. Lavinia recognized it as a Teenage Mutant Ninja Turtle. Lola stopped what she was doing and told the boy if he wanted to stay, fine, but keep back and out of the way. Then she beckoned him with a nod. He brought his cheek within range, and she kissed it quickly. He trotted over to a bench where customers could wait, climbed onto it, knelt, looked out the window, and hummed.

He seemed like a nice little boy. He was certainly well-behaved, despite the earlier wail. Kids weren't supposed to be silent. They just needed to do as they were told. Lola had taught him well.

After Lola inked the '*i*', Lavinia asked her where the restroom was.

"Right back there."

Lavinia stood. The sudden wetness was unmistakable. Her periods had been irregular for the last year and absent altogether for about five months. Of course, she had no tampons or pads with her.

She told Lola the situation. Lola looked at the stain spreading across the jumpsuit's pink silk.

"You're also gonna need a change of clothes," she said.

The little boy turned around, looked at Lavinia, and said, "You have an owie!"

Lola shushed him and said to sit still. She led Lavinia back into the room where the little boy had been watching TV, which was still showing cartoons, and into the bathroom. To Lavinia's surprise, it was spotless. Lola said there was a box of tampons in the cabinet under the sink. As to something she could borrow to wear, she'd be right back. She returned a few minutes later with a pair of worn overalls. Lavinia took them. She removed her sweater, then the soiled jumpsuit, and slid into the overalls, which were huge. She rolled up the legs, then put her sweater back on and pulled up the top of the overalls. She didn't look any worse than she had in the first outfit. She leaned her head out of the bathroom and asked Lola if she had a belt she could use.

"No. But I have an old scarf." She dug through the drawers of a dresser against the wall. The scarf was in the bottom one. It was silver and embroidered with stars. She couldn't see Lola wearing a thing like that. The price tag dangling from a thread said it had been an ill-chosen gift from someone who hadn't figured out that Lola had no use for the trappings of femininity. She handed it to her, and Lavinia tied it around her waist.

"You want to soak that in cold water?" Lola asked, meaning the jumpsuit.

"It's jumped its last jump, I'm afraid."

Lola picked the garment up from the floor. She balled it up, put it under her arm, went back to the front with Lavinia behind her, and stuffed it into a tall plastic trash can under the counter.

"You can keep the overalls," Lola said.

"Are you sure?"

"They're not exactly precious."

"They're a man's, aren't they?"

"Yup."

A tall, fat man. A brute, maybe. Lavinia felt uneasy for a moment, there in his clothes, as if she'd slipped into a callused skin.

Lola went back to work on Lavinia's wrist. The little boy stood by, looking with concern at Lavinia. Lola told him to go get himself a cookie in the back.

"Would you like one, too?" the little boy asked Lavinia.

"What's your name?"

"Jeremy."

"No thank you, Jeremy. But I appreciate the offer."

Jeremy trotted off. Lola lifted her head and looked after him fondly.

Suzi wasn't cut out to be a parent, she said. Wasn't much of a girlfriend, either. Didn't make her a bad person, just not the right partner.

"You get me?" Lola asked. She'd just inked the final letter.

"Yes."

Lavinia looked at her inflamed wrist.

Chip

"Not bad," she said.

"Thanks. Leave the bandage on for a couple of hours."

"I figured."

"Then wash it gently with this and lukewarm water."

Lola gave her a small bottle of antimicrobial soap.

The cramps, which hadn't been present at first, began with sudden strength. Lavinia gritted her teeth. She wondered if sleeping with Craig had made her hormones all wonky. She'd assumed she was sliding gracefully into her change of life.

Guess again!

Lola reminded her of the charge.

Lavinia opened her purse, which she'd hung on the back of the chair, and removed two one hundred dollar bills.

"You kidding me?" Lola asked.

"Do something nice for Jeremy."

"He's been asking for a new firetruck."

"There you go."

"But really, I don't feel right."

"You'll get over it."

Lavinia shook Lola's hand and left.

She drew far fewer stares wearing the coveralls than she had the jumpsuit, even with her flashy belt.

Her pain level told her she wasn't going to get much more driving done that day. She'd never found anything that worked for her menstrual cramps, except being pregnant, and that always came with its own bag of misery. When she reached the car, she looked at her silenced phone. No new messages or missed calls. For a moment, she was gripped by a searing loneliness. She looked at herself in the rearview mirror and told herself to buck up.

After a quick stop at the grocery store for her daily piece of fruit—this one a pear so juicy it spilled down the front of the overalls, on which she'd begun to detect a smell of stale cigarette smoke that she hadn't noticed back in the tattoo parlor—she made her way to the interstate and cruised toward Coeur d'Alene, Idaho.

chapter nineteen

After the modest motels, Lavinia was glad to check into a high-end resort with a killer view of the lake and mountains. The mattress of the king-sized bed was firm, and she dropped into a deep sleep, broken in the early morning by the fact that she'd bled all over the sheets. She got up, stripped the bed, showered, and dressed in a pair of her fancy blue jeans and an embroidered shirt. She stood before the mirror and decided she looked like an idiot. There was a clothing store just off the lobby, and the moment it opened, she'd go in.

She picked up the phone and asked for a pot of coffee. Just a few minutes later, after a discreet knock on the door, it was ferried in by a short, dark-skinned young man in a white jacket and pants. He asked where she wanted it. She indicated the coffee table, which she'd moved over by the window so she could sit and gaze. He offered to pour for her. She let him. His hand was steady. Lavinia didn't think she'd like doing something as simple as pouring coffee into a cup under the close watch of a stranger.

Potter would watch her every move when they were first married. She seemed to possess some light only he could see. That light never dimmed, only became too glaring to look at.

Her children watched her busy hands with awe, even when their touch was abrupt and rough. She wasn't a slapper. She didn't believe in it. But she could grip a thin arm hard enough to bring tears. More than once she'd pinched the tip of a tender, pink ear. Then she would hate herself and soften her tone. She supposed on balance she'd gotten the tricky business of parenthood more or less right.

At the country club back home, one of the waitresses didn't have a left hand. The first time Lavinia had gone there, Chip made sure to explain that she'd been born without it. The arm ended in an odd little fleshy mound. Lavinia didn't understand what difference it made, why the hand was missing. If she'd lost it in an accident, would she have been shown greater sympathy? Lavinia remembered her clearly. She was young, wiry, and moved fast. Her hair was pulled tightly back in a perfectly molded bun. She didn't seem like she needed anyone to feel sorry for her. Her gaze was fierce, her voice firm yet pleasant. That was a girl who could take care of herself.

Lavinia held the coffee cup in her hands, feeling its warmth. She put down the cup and called Mel. He answered on the fourth ring.

"Sorry, I was cleaning out Sandy's cage," he said a bit breathlessly.

"When was the last time you ate at the county club?"

"Monday. Why?"

"Is that girl still there, the one with only one hand?"

"Mara? Yes. Why?"

"I was just thinking of her."

"Lavinia, are you all right?"

"Of course."

"Where are you?"

"At a posh resort in Idaho."

"That's more like it. Stay there awhile. I'll fly out, and we can drive back together."

"Don't be silly."

"Not silly at all. Just itching for a little travel, myself."

She told him about the view from her window, how she was going to pick a couple of new outfits for herself, and about the tattoo.

Mel didn't say anything. Lavinia understood that he was disappointed in her somehow, that clinging to Chip's name had cast a shadow over a possible future of theirs.

He's really serious!

"I'm sorry," she said.

"Why? You can do what you want. It's your skin, after all."

He said he'd done as she'd asked and contacted the children and Alma to say she was on the road again. They all wished her well.

"They've stopped calling," Lavinia said.

"Isn't that what you wanted?"

"Yes."

"Well, then."

She said sometimes she was lonely. She hadn't expected that. In fact, she hadn't felt it at all until quite recently, and as she said this, she recalled her sense of being on the outside looking in at Patty and Murph's, which she understood now was a shade of loneliness, too. That part she didn't mention.

"When you get lonely enough, you'll come home," Mel said.

"You sound as if you want me to learn my lesson."

"No, dear, that's not what I'm saying at all."

The coffee had grown cold. The wind came up, and a sailboat on the lake leaned hard. She said she needed to get going, that she'd check in again soon.

She was cross with herself for having called. Why couldn't she cut the damn cord?

Because a pretty big one already got cut.

She looked at her healing wrist. The blue ink was becoming something closer to azure rather than navy. Lola had said it would probably do that. Lavinia didn't mind.

Got myself a real blue-chip stock!

She laughed aloud, then headed downstairs.

She bought a pair of tailored pants, a silk blouse, and a linen jacket. Also, a red knit dress that made her look both elegant and commanding, though for whose benefit she'd wear it she had no idea. The woman in the store was delighted by the amount Lavinia spent.

A placard by the concierge desk advertised a lake cruise that afternoon for guests of the resort. Drinks and appetizers were included in the price. Why not put her new clothes to good use? She asked the man behind the counter if there were still enough room for her. There was. Maybe being out on the water would ease her cramps, which were as vicious as ever.

When she was young, her period never kept her in bed. She had high school friends who carried on as if they were in hard labor. She powered through everything. That's how she was. Her own daughters suffered and made the most of it. She waited on them when they were off their feet. She was that way, too.

"Might be chilly, out on the water," the man behind the desk said. His tone was kind, almost deferential.

Aside from the teal sweater, Lavinia had nothing heavy to put on. Back she went to the high-end clothing store, bags in hand from a few minutes earlier, and asked for something warm to wear.

The woman showed her a stack of shawls made of light-weight wool bordered with silk.

Lavinia dropped her bags and took one in sky blue. She wrapped it around herself, covering her head, and stood before the full-length mirror.

"Can you see me as a granny?" she asked.

The woman didn't reply.

"Or a Muslim? I don't see why they have to cover their hair. What's wrong with hair, for God's sake?"

The woman asked if Lavinia would like to try another one.

"No, this is fine. It's lovely. I'd even say delicious."

The fabric was so soothing! So light and cozy on her skin.

She paid, added the shawl to one of her bags, and left.

At 5 p.m. sharp, Lavinia teetered up the gangway onto the yacht, where a young woman in a white uniform offered a hand to steady her. She admired Lavinia's red dress, blue shawl, and particularly the bangle on her right arm, bought just an hour before from a jewelry store down the block from the resort. It was eighteen karat gold, studded with small sapphires, which had been Chip's birthstone. Lavinia's wrist felt heavy because of it. The other was still sore.

Another young woman in a short dress appeared with a tray of glasses, and offered one to Lavinia.

"Domestic or French?" she asked. The woman didn't know what she meant.

"Either is fine," Lavinia said, and took a glass. She'd never cared much for champagne, but it had its uses—like now, to put her in a non-road-trip mood, to make her forget she was a recent widow, to make her forget everything bad in her life.

What, besides losing Chip?

You know who I'm talking about.

There were probably about twenty other people on board, most of them old, a few middle-aged, and several younger children who raced around making a huge racket Lavinia instantly hated. A female's sharp voice summoned them, and they headed off in the opposite direction. She saw some empty deck chairs near the stern and approached them, wanting to sit and look at the water while she had her drink.

What would Potter think if he could see her now? She'd been such a hostile mess at that stupid dinner. Maybe he and Mary Beth had had words about it.

Your ex needs to learn some manners, Potter! You heard what she said about Nina and her son!

"Is this seat taken?"

The man asking had a thick head of white hair. His face was tanned and lined. His eyes were canny, perhaps a little wary. His blue blazer and pressed gray slacks said he was comfortable in a business meeting, at the country club, anywhere there was money in the air. Lavinia gestured to the vacant chair beside her. He sat, grunting softly as he went down.

He said nothing for a while. Lavinia was glad. She was enjoying the water and the distant mountains. A young man in a white uniform came by with a tray of hors d'oeuvres and offered them to Lavinia and the man beside her. She shook her head. The man took two crackers mounded with what looked like smoked salmon and cream cheese.

As he ate, crumbs fell down the front of his jacket. He brushed them away.

"I'm Ted," he said when he'd finished the last swallow.

"Lavinia."

"Is that a family name?"

"My aunt. Or great-aunt. I don't really know. Didn't listen much to that part of things when I was growing up."

And what part is that?

"It's a nice tradition, naming children after the dead," he said.

Lavinia sipped her champagne. It had warmed considerably under the heat of her hand. The flavor wasn't as bright.

"You didn't care for any?" Lavinia asked, meaning a glass for himself.

"Doctor says it's a bad idea at my age."

"You look in the prime to me."

"You're awfully kind."

The boat turned abruptly. Its horn sounded. Lavinia started, spilling her champagne on her lap.

"Must have been another boat in the way. Careless, really. Oh, permit me," Ted said and removed the handkerchief from the breast pocket of his jacket. He dabbed gently at the fabric of her dress. She pushed his hand away.

"Let me get you another," he said. He took her almost-empty glass, got awkwardly to his feet, and went off with a lopsided gait, as if one of his hips was bad. Lavinia wondered if she should find another chair on the other side of the boat where he wouldn't find her right away, and felt like a bratty girl at a high school dance. She'd wait for him to return, have her drink, and enjoy herself, goddamn it!

Her phone buzzed inside her purse. She'd intended to leave it behind in her room, then forgot.

Ignore it!

"Hello?"

"Well, hello there."

"How are you, Craig?" she asked.

"Lonely."

"Go into town."

"Been. Same old town. Same old faces."

"And you're looking for something new."

"Nope. Just looking for you."

Two seagulls were drifting high up against the far shore. Their cries were clear and urgent.

"Where are you?" Craig asked.

"Sailing around Lake Coeur d'Alene."

"Why don't you turn yourself around and sail on back here?"

"Not enough water along the way?"

Craig laughed, then fell silent.

The gulls changed direction and drifted back the way they came. One lifted Lavinia out of her chair, over the deck, past the railing, and into the cool air above the water.

"Well, I shouldn't have bothered you," Craig said.

"You're not bothering me. I'm glad you called."

"I admire a woman who can fib so nicely." He wasn't mad, she could tell.

"No fib. I *am* glad."

The connection failed. Lavinia hoped he didn't think she hung up on him.

Ted returned, bearing two glasses of champagne.

Lavinia asked what made him decide to overrule his medical advice. He smiled, showing an expensive set of dentures.

She took both glasses so he could drop himself clumsily back into his chair. He took his, touched the rim to hers, and drank. She drank, too.

"Lovely day," she said. The wind was rising and notably cooler than only a few minutes before.

"First time to our corner of the world?"

"Yes. Do you live here, then?"

"Spokane. We come over every chance we get."

"It's quite a lovely spot."

Ted had more of his drink. He seemed to love it.

Former boozer, for sure.

People wandered by, slightly hunched against the breeze. The roaring children were with them, red-cheeked and random. Lavinia was aware of Ted watching her from the corner of his eye. She gave him her warmest smile.

He asked what brought her to the lake. She said she was on an extended road trip. She'd just gotten out of jail and needed to discover the world again. It was amazing how much could change in just eighteen months, especially clothing ads, but they were always in flux, weren't they? Given the constant hunger of the fashion industry.

"Jail?"

"I'm sorry. I shouldn't have brought that up."

"You don't look like someone who could commit a crime." He leaned toward her, his voice low, though it didn't need to be. There was no one else around.

Lavinia dropped her gaze and sighed. She hadn't meant to do it, really, but she had no choice. He was a brute. He'd hit her before. She was sure he was going to again, so she hit him first. With a baseball bat. His bat. The one he practiced with every Saturday, trying to relive his glory days in the major leagues, though of course that had been years before. That she got him from behind was the tipping point, criminal charge-wise. And that she never reported any of the previous assaults. Alleged assaults.

"Is that his name?" Ted asked, nodding at Lavinia's wrist.

Lavinia nodded miserably.

"And you tried to scratch it off. You poor dear."

The ache in her hands was sudden, unmistakable, and disastrous. She took a deep breath as her eyes welled. Ted passed her his champagne-dampened handkerchief.

"Sometimes it's better just to let it out," he said.

Lavinia held the handkerchief without using it.

She emptied her glass. The bubbles raced down her throat. She wanted to go with them.

"Did you go back to him? When you got out?" Ted asked.

Lavinia shook her head.

"Very brave."

"He left me."

"Ah."

"He said I was a monster."

"You're no monster."

Lavinia tossed the balled-up handkerchief into Ted's lap. She wanted to get up and walk around a little but found she had no will to rise.

A voice on the loud speaker said they would reach the end of the lake soon, then make their way back to the resort in another forty-five minutes. Lavinia wished she'd thought about how long she'd be trapped. Her cramps became vicious, and she hoped to hell she wouldn't spring a leak.

"Look at the water. It's very calming, don't you think?" Ted asked.

"Yes."

"I don't suppose you've ever been on an ocean crossing?"

"No."

"Only cruise ships take to the open sea anymore, but back in the day, before jet travel, that's how you got anywhere."

Lavinia put her empty glass on the deck beside her chair. The alcohol sat badly. It hadn't done its job.

Ted's father had been an English professor at Yale. Romantic poets. Had Lavinia ever read Shelley?

"Afraid not."

"No matter."

Professors had the life, really. Every seven years they got to take time off just to study. They went to England when Ted was ten—that was in 1953, not that he should give his age away so easily. They sailed on the SS *America* outbound and on the SS *United States* coming back, though he supposed those names probably didn't mean much to Lavinia.

"No."

They travelled second class. Their room had two sets of bunk beds with netting you attached at night so the pitching of the vessel wouldn't land you on the floor. His younger brother wanted the top bunk at first, then complained, so Ted switched. Then the bottom bunk wasn't good enough either. Their father, never a patient man, boxed the brother's ears, which settled the matter.

The crossing took five days. Could she imagine what it was like to stand at the rail, four stories above the surface of the Atlantic Ocean, and see nothing but water and sky for that entire time? And at night, only the black void below and the starry vault above?

Lavinia closed her eyes. She hadn't expected the imagery to be so stirring.

The weather got rough, Ted said. Eight-foot swells. The passengers were advised to stay in their cabins, and when they emerged, to hold the heavy velvet ropes attached to the walls. The tables in the dining room were bolted to the floor, but the chairs tended to slip unless someone was sitting in them. Many people became seasick. Others reveled in the chaos and took up residence in the bar. A day and a half later, the rain stopped, but the sea remained restless. The surface was cut with bobbing whitecaps as far as the eye could see, and the ship continued its slow rise and fall with the remaining swell. He stood at the stern, looking at the churning wake, and thought if he fell, he'd die, because by the time someone was alerted, the freezing water would have easily claimed him.

"That's quite a story," Lavinia said. She had to stand up and couldn't.

Ted said nothing. He was still looking down at that remembered broken sea.

"Ted!" A woman's sharp voice brought his head up with a snap.

"Martha, my dear, where have you been?"

The woman was obviously the wife from the way she glared at Lavinia. She was short and compact. She wore a tailored navy pantsuit with a pair of bright white running shoes. Her hair was dyed deep red, like the coat of an Irish Setter. She looked worn out, except for the fire in her brown eyes, as she peered over her half-moon bifocal lenses. She reminded Lavinia of Angie's third grade teacher. A harsh, critical woman who thought Angie should see a therapist.

"Dear, I'd like you to meet Lavinia …"

"Dugan."

"How do you do?"

Martha had not extended her hand. Nor had Lavinia.

Ted rose to his feet with difficulty.

"We're meeting some friends for drinks after we dock. Won't you join us?" Ted asked her.

"I'm afraid not."

"Oh, but you must!"

"I couldn't possibly."

"We're coming in," Martha said, peering into the distance.

"Not for a little bit yet," Ted said.

She took Ted roughly by the arm and guided him away.

Lavinia sat alone until the boat docked. When she stood, the blood rushed but didn't leak. She went back to her quiet, pretty room, cleaned up, collapsed in the same chair she'd had coffee in that morning, flipped the switch to bring the gas fireplace to life, then thought about tomorrow and driving west once more.

chapter twenty

Before she left the next morning, Lavinia bought a handful of postcards and sat in the elegantly appointed lobby to fill them out. On each she wrote the same thing: *Having a wonderful time, wish you were here.* Then she couldn't remember anyone's address. She seldom mailed anything, which was probably why. Unless she was starting to lose it. Her tall tale to Ted on the boat the day before was a frontier she shouldn't have crossed. There were so many different reasons to lie—to cover your ass, to spare someone's feelings, to make a stupid problem go away, but this? Lying for the hell of it? Just to garner sympathy? That bordered on nuts. She couldn't do anything about it now, though.

When she finished the postcards—eight in all, including Karen's—she called Alma.

"What the hell took you so long?" she asked when Alma picked up on the eighth ring.

"Yard guy's here."

"You're getting the grass cut?"

"And the hedges trimmed. And the roses fertilized. And the weeds yanked."

"I was going to do that when I got home."

307

"Well, no one seems to know when that will be, so I thought I'd better get on it."

"Dear Alma."

Ted and Martha marched across the lobby, trailed by a young man pushing their luggage on a shiny silver cart. They wouldn't see her unless they turned around for some reason. They didn't.

"You'll be getting a batch of postcards I'll need you to forward to everyone," Lavinia said.

"Postcards? Whatever for?"

"Because I'm a sweetheart."

"Uh, huh. Well, whatever. Where's your address book?"

"The study?"

"Okie dokie."

Lavinia had her eye on Ted and Martha, whose car had just pulled up in the circular drive by the entrance. The valet hopped out and held open the passenger door so Martha could slide her fat ass onto the seat.

Alma wanted to know where she could find Lavinia's checkbook. Was that in the study, too?

"Go and look for yourself," Lavinia said. She told Alma she had to get going. She had a long drive ahead of her.

"You gonna make it all the way to the Pacific?"

"If you stop gabbing at me so I can get in the car, yes."

"Dear Lavinia."

Afterward, Lavinia gave the postcards to the desk clerk; told him to look up her home address, which she'd given when she checked in; mail them there; and add the postage to her bill.

"Shall I just put them in a large envelope?" he asked. Lavinia studied his name tag.

"Sure, Darren. That sounds like a great idea."

While she waited for her car to be brought up, she thought about how some people couldn't figure anything out for themselves. Good problem solvers were in short supply. Chip liked that she could think for herself. That was why he hired her, promoted her, and asked her to be his wife. He'd offered her the kind of partnership she'd wanted with Potter and never got. You needed two adults in a marriage, not one adult and one child, not one responsible person and one self-indulgent sot.

Take it easy.

She slid two twenty-dollar bills into the valet's hand, got in the car, and headed for the highway.

Two hours later she was well into Washington State and starving. The drive so far had been across high prairies dressed in tall grasses that swayed in the wind. The sky was enormous. She took the exit for Moses Lake and found herself on a treeless street with a diner. In the distance, the Columbia River cut through dry, rocky banks. The sun was strong. She removed her shawl, which she'd developed a fondness for. There, in her wrinkled linen suit, she was again out of place among the denim everyone else was wearing.

Can't spend all my damn time trying to fit in!

But that wasn't the problem, was it? Not knowing who she was—what she needed from life—remained elusive.

A bell tinkled as she opened the door. The place was dark and full of cigarette smoke, more like a bar than a place to get breakfast. She sat in the first booth, facing the street and a group of young children being corralled down the sidewalk by two tightly smiling young women.

She looked at the sticky plastic menu the waitress had dropped off. A teenage boy came through the door and sat down roughly in the booth across from her, flushed and breathing hard. He held up his hand to ask for her silence. He hunched low in his seat. On the street outside, two men ran down the sidewalk. After a moment, they walked briskly back the other way and stopped to peer in the window of the diner. They moved on out of sight.

"They're gone," Lavinia said.

His hair was short and badly cut, as if he'd done it himself. He smelled strongly of sweat, and Lavinia was taken back to the teenage years of her two boys, particularly Timothy who never liked bathing and had to be bullied to do so.

"You better not be a bank robber or something. I don't have time for that," she said.

He stared at her. His eyes held a sharp blend of fear and rage, like an injured animal.

The waitress returned. She looked at the boy.

"I told you before not to come in here," she said.

"He's with me," Lavinia said.

"Well okay then."

When she'd gone, the boy muttered, "Bitch."

Lavinia grabbed his arm and squeezed it hard. His muscles tensed beneath her grip. Just before he yanked free, she said, "None of that talk, you hear?"

He leaned back in his seat.

"You're free to go, you know. I'm fine with having a nice, peaceful breakfast by myself. Which is what I was sitting here doing when you bolted in. What the hell's it all about, anyway?"

"Them's my uncles."

"You mean 'They're.' Why are they chasing you?"

He glared.

"Have it your way," she said.

Lavinia raised her hand to signal the waitress.

"Two coffees, sourdough toast and scrambled eggs for me, and how about a number three for Mr. Charm and Grace over here?"

The waitress made her notes, gave the boy a look of disgust, and left.

"Number three don't have no bacon. I like bacon," he said.

"Do you now? It clogs the arteries."

"I don't like pancakes."

Lavinia leaned forward with her elbows on the table and held his gaze.

"But I ain't had 'em in a while, so I'm sure I'll like 'em now."

"Good."

The coffee arrived. The boy stared into his cup.

"Can't I get a milkshake or something?" he asked.

"How old are you?"

"Sixteen. Why?"

"There's an age limit on milkshakes. But, we'll overlook that for the moment. What flavor?"

The boy shrugged.

Lavinia summoned the waitress once more, asked for a vanilla milkshake, and apologized for the add-on to the order.

"No skin off my nose," the waitress said.

The boy fidgeted. Lavinia told him to sit still. She drank her coffee. Her cell phone buzzed. She looked at the screen. The number of the hotel in Coeur d'Alene was displayed. She declined the call and saw that there was a message from Mel, one from Angie, and another from Timothy. She dialed Angie's number at work. It went into her voicemail. Next, she tried Timothy at home. His roommate Sam answered. No, everything was fine, she said. She had no idea why everyone was calling her all of a sudden, unless it was because she hadn't checked in for a while.

"I wrote some postcards," Lavinia said, and realized how lame that sounded. The boy had been watching her closely ever since she'd removed her phone.

"Oh? That's nice!" Sam said.

Lavinia said she'd let her go now, but please tell Timothy and Angie that she'd been in touch.

"Sure thing. Where are you, anyway?"

"Moses Lake, Washington."

"Never heard of it."

"Me neither, until this morning."

The food arrived. Lavinia stared at it with distaste. Her hunger had vanished when the boy came racing into the diner. She knew if she didn't force a few mouthfuls down, she'd regret it soon. The eggs were creamy and luscious. The toast was perfectly crisp. The order included hash browns, which she sampled. They were made of cut up red potatoes, sautéed green peppers and onions, and were delicious.

The boy poured a huge amount of syrup over his pancakes.

"What's your name, anyway?" Lavinia asked him.

"Chuck."

"Don't talk with your mouth full, Chuck."

He chewed a long time and swallowed.

Lavinia put down her folk and pushed her plate away.

"That's short for Charles, isn't it?" she asked.

"Yup."

"Anyone ever call you Chip?"

"Nope. Call my uncle that, though."

"His name is Charles, too?"

"Yup."

Lavinia shook her head, then put her face in her hands. The sounds of the restaurant were now enhanced. The waitress's heavy stride, the tinkling bell over the front door, wordless voices that reminded her of warm honey, the clatter of silverware, ice being scooped into a glass.

"Lady?"

She lowered her hands and opened her eyes. Chuck shoveled in another large portion of pancakes. The open-mouthed chewing continued.

"I'm fine."

"You don't look too good."

"Because your table manners are atrocious."

Chuck put down his fork. His face reddened.

The waitress asked if she could take Lavinia's plate. Lavinia handed it to her.

"You're still eating, I suppose," the waitress asked Chuck. He nodded.

When they were alone again, Lavinia said, "Why were your uncles chasing you?"

"I dunno."

"Cut the crap."

He brought his head up sharply.

"Maybe women don't talk like that around here?" she said.

"I figure plenty of 'em do, just not where I live."

"And where's that?"

"Bakerton ranch. Five miles that way," he tossed his head to the right.

"Finish up. I'll give you a lift."

Chuck regarded her with suspicion.

315

"I buy you breakfast, but you don't trust me to get you home safely?" she asked.

He sucked down the milkshake as fast as he could, then belched.

"You're disgusting. But for some reason, I don't seem to mind as much as I should."

Lavinia put a fifty-dollar bill on the table. Chuck stared at it.

"Don't even think about it," she said.

They stood up. Chuck was only about her height. He was wearing bell-bottomed blue jeans, the kind that were in fashion about forty years earlier. Lavinia admired them. They looked like they'd fit her. She asked Chuck if he had a change of clothes in his backpack. He asked why. She said she'd give him twenty bucks for the jeans. They could do the swap in a gas station, rather than spend any more time in the diner, using their restrooms.

She directed him to her car. He appraised it coolly. She opened the passenger door. The bear was in there, in his customary spot. She tossed it into the back seat.

"Sorry," she said.

Chuck got in with a soft grunt.

There were two gas stations at the edge of town. She chose the one on her side of the street. She realized she couldn't wear the jeans with the top of her linen suit, so once they were parked, she dug out a T-shirt from the bottom of her backpack. Her clothes would need to be laundered again soon. She looked down at her sandals. She wanted a good pair of sneakers and thought she could probably find a place to buy some. Then it struck her that this entire road trip had been a strange sartorial tale. She'd never paid so much attention to what she was wearing before in her life, except when she first started at Chip's manufactured home company. In those days, she was all about power suits, though the one she'd worn when he declared his love for her had been lavender silk, her only one that wasn't brown, black, or gray.

She sent Chuck into the men's room. He reappeared wearing a pair of track shorts that revealed sparsely haired white legs. He'd taken off his jacket and was in an oversized button-down denim shirt with cut off sleeves. His arms were wimpy. His heavy lace-up boots were much more prominent now that the bellbottoms were gone. Lavinia asked him if they were steel-toed. He said they were. He worked part-time for one of his uncles, stacking bags of feed. He flushed when he said this.

"One of the uncles chasing you down the street?" she asked.

"Yup."

"Because …?"

"I borrowed ten bucks from him, and he wanted it back."

"Especially because he didn't actually lend it to you, right?"

Chuck said nothing. He handed her the pants.

"Why was the other one after you?" she asked.

"On account-a he runs better, I guess."

In the ladies' room, she changed her tampon. Her period was already waning. The pants were a pain to button up. She'd naturally assumed they'd have a zipper. Even so, they fit perfectly. That she'd had five kids and still had the hips of a teenage boy filled her with sudden glee until she faced the mirror and saw that she was too damn thin. Her ribs were visible under the skin of her chest. The pits below her eyes had deepened. It was her hands that really made her look hard. Her nails were uneven and too short, as if she'd been scrubbing something that just wouldn't come clean. She had no idea how they'd gotten that way. She'd never been a nail biter.

She bent down to dig through the backpack one more time. It took a few moments of scrambling to find the bottle of perfume she'd taken from Patty's. It had been at the back of her dresser, which suggested she seldom used it. The first spray said it was expensive and would obviously be missed. How could she have been so stupid? All the years Patty had disliked her, then slowly came around and was kind and sympathetic about Chip, and now all that would be undone by one impulsive moment! Unless Patty just overlooked it and figured that Lavinia was running through her days half-cocked. Which she clearly was.

Chuck stared at her as she emerged.

"You missed a button," he said.

She turned around and struggled with the one she'd overlooked.

Then, as she drew near, his nose wrinkled.

"Yikes," he said.

"Stop that. Can't a girl smell pretty?"

"You stink worse than a cattle vaccine."

"At least you know I'm healthy."

They got back in the car. Chuck told her which way to go. Soon they were out in the open country, off the interstate, driving through sagebrush. Then the road became dirt. When Lavinia looked in the rearview, she saw plumes of yellow dust.

"There!" Chuck pointed to a turn at the last minute. Lavinia jerked the wheel. The car skidded, but she controlled it.

"A little more warning next time?"

"No more turns. It's right up yonder."

Yonder?

The house was bigger than Lavinia had expected, and it looked fairly new, too. It was essentially a larger version of a log cabin with a wrap-around porch. One outbuilding had to be a barn, another had a roof but no walls—a shed, really. Lavinia asked what that was used for.

"Used to be where the blacksmith set up. Now a fella comes out from town when one of the mares throws a shoe," he said.

"You have only mares?"

"Nope. Plentya geldings, too. The mares just got more hoof trouble."

"My father shoed horses."

"Get out."

"It's true."

Lavinia had developed a stabbing pain above her eye. She removed twenty dollars from her purse and handed it to Chuck. He put it in the pocket of his shorts. He stared out the window, his hand on the door handle. He rubbed his chin. He sighed. Beads of sweat broke out on his forehead, although the air conditioning had been off for only a few moments.

"Well," Lavinia said.

"Where you heading to, anyhow?"

"The coast."

"What for?"

"Because."

"Take me with you."

She could see he was serious from the urgent despair in his eyes.

"That's a bad plan."

"I won't be no trouble."

"You already are."

She instantly regretted saying that. He was pulling himself together, trying not to cry. He looked then like he was about ten years old.

"I'm sure it's not that bad, whatever you're running away from," she said.

"You don't know shit."

"Probably true. But I still can't take you along. Now, out you get."

Chuck shook his head, then grabbed her arm so hard she squawked. He had a friend in Portland. He could stay there. He had about two hundred dollars saved. He'd get a job. His family wouldn't come after him. They hated him. And he hated them. He had to go, and if she didn't take him, he'd find another way.

Lavinia looked up at the house, expecting the door to open and some sturdy ranch woman to stand there and look angrily down at them. There was no one. She was exhausted, and said so.

"I can drive," Chuck said.

"Show me your license."

"Don't have one."

"Learner's permit?"

"Nope. But I know how."

Lavinia started the car and drove them back the way they came until they found the highway.

"What makes you think they won't call the police?" she asked, furious with herself for not having thought of this before.

"'Cause they kicked me out once before. I didn't have nowhere to go, so I had to go back."

"Why did they kick you out?"

"That's my business."

She told Chuck not to talk to her for a while, because she had to do some hard thinking about why the hell she'd agreed to this. Mel, when she told him, would be patient, yet patronizing.

I know you have a big heart, Lavinia, but you took an unnecessary risk with your own safety. Young people can be very unpredictable.

Two hours later the high desert gave way to dense forests and a sharp rise to another mountain pass. The descent on the far side was through even thicker stands of evergreens, with waterfalls slithering from high rocks down into the trees. She'd never seen such country. She asked Chuck what he thought.

"Pretty enough, I guess."

Despite the natural glory, Lavinia knew she couldn't get all the way to the coast on the energy she had. They'd stop early. They came to Issaquah, a prosperous-looking place with a sign that said Seattle was only another thirty miles west.

The motel was nicer than most, with a large lobby and big windows that looked out on rolling hills covered with large houses.

"All that Microsoft money," Lavinia told Chuck as they registered. The desk clerk looked at Chuck with suspicion and told Lavinia he couldn't have his own room unless he was eighteen.

"Funny you should mention that. Today's his birthday!"

Lavinia took both keys. They found their rooms, one across from the other. The hall was wide and bright and made Lavinia's head hurt more. Hers was bigger because of the king-sized bed. Chuck looked stunned at the space in his. He dropped his backpack on the floor and stood in front of the window, staring at the late afternoon light. She said she wanted to lie down for a while. She understood if he was gone when she woke up. It might be faster to hitch a ride at this point, though she didn't recommend it. As she said this, she took out three hundred more dollars and said he could buy a bus ticket to Portland if he didn't want to wait. Chuck stared at the money with the same dazed expression he'd worn since leaving Moses Lake. When he didn't take it, she left it on the dresser and went to her own room.

It was dark when she awoke. She was hungry. Her headache had abated. She got to her feet and drank two glasses of water in the bathroom. Her skin felt soft and elastic. Maybe it was the greater humidity there, that much nearer the sea? She changed into a different T-shirt, brushed her hair until her arm was sore, plucked her eyebrows, and applied eyeliner. Her phone showed no new calls. She hoped everyone would be glad to get her postcard in a few days. Where would she be then? Still at the coast? On her way back? Or settling down someplace else?

It wasn't a serious consideration, but there it was. The idea of a brand-new town and a brand-new name, not Starkhurst or Dugan, but all the way back to the beginning when she was just herself, a woman on her own, Lavinia Fields. Then what? Back into sales? Some charitable work to keep her from going crazy with boredom? And what about when she got lonely, which she would before too long?

Craig.

She'd lived with an unreliable young man and a reliable old man; how about a man who was solid, but with a wild streak? It had been there when he twirled her on the dance floor, in the furious way he made love, and in those sudden embraces the morning after. There was cruelty in him, too. The line of his mouth when she'd said she was leaving suggested a man whose words might cut if he felt freer to speak them.

"Nope," she announced to the empty room.

There was no answer when she knocked on Chuck's door. Then there was noise within—crying, sobbing, muted by the heavy door but unmistakable. Her knock was harder the second time. She called his name. The sobbing stopped; the door opened. Chuck's face was red and damp. His breathing was ragged.

Lavinia pushed her way inside. He'd been lying on the bed, but not in it. The contents of his backpack were strewn across the floor. Several bloody balled-up wads of toilet paper were on the bathroom counter. The toilet seat had a smear of blood, as well.

"Lady, do you got a Kotex on you?" Chuck asked.

No wonder you have to run!

"Tampons. I'll be right back."

She returned and put a handful on the bed next to him. He took one and went into the bathroom. He was in there so long that Lavinia thought she should knock and ask what the hell was going on. Water ran in the sink. The toilet flushed, and he came out.

Lavinia helped herself to the easy chair by the window. Chuck sat back down on the bed. They didn't look at each other.

"What the hell's wrong with being a girl, anyhow?" she asked.

"Everything."

"You may be right about that."

Chuck flung himself on his back and stared at the ceiling. Lavinia said she better have the rest of it.

It started when he was about three or four. A sense of knowing something was wrong with you, that you weren't what you were supposed to be. It was more than being a tomboy. Every girl that lived on a ranch was a tomboy. It was not wanting to wear a dress to church or be quiet when the men were talking. It was being a stranger in your own body— as if your body had betrayed you.

One day he made the mistake of saying he wanted to be a boy. He didn't think anyone would take him seriously. No one ever really listened to him. His mother told his father, and the shit hit the fan. Lectures about God's plan and not going against His laws or the laws of nature, since all of nature was God's creation, too. So, he wore dresses to school and felt like a freak. Boys were free. They did what they wanted. They acted badly and were admired for having spirit. When he acted badly, when any of the girls did, they were condemned for being unladylike and bossy, and were told they would grow up into the kind of woman no man would ever want to marry.

"Jesus Christ, it sounds like the goddamn 1950s!" Lavinia said.

"So, what's it like where you're from?"

Lavinia said it was a college town, three hours from New York City. She talked about the gorges, the lake, the ice skating in the winter, shoveling snow, summer thunderstorms. She stopped.

"You got transgender people there?"

Lavinia said yes, she assumed so. She didn't really know any, but she didn't pay much attention to that kind of thing. What people wanted to be, what they did with themselves, or who they had sex with—it had never mattered all that much.

"So, what does?"

"Being reliable."

Chuck sighed and closed his eyes.

"What's your given name?" Lavinia asked.

"Charlene."

"Let's stick with Chuck. What say we go eat? We'll get an early start in the morning. We'll go straight to Portland and get you together with your friend."

Chuck sat up and looked at Lavinia. She couldn't stand the tears in his eyes.

chapter twenty-one

The bungalow was at the end of the block and looked out over a ravine where rushing water could be heard when traffic was light. It was Sunday, and the neighborhood was quiet.

She'd assumed that being among teenagers again would strain her nerves. The opposite was true. Their collective urgency put her at ease. She was grateful not to think of herself, grateful to feel quite unexpectedly at home.

They were an odd lot, all transgender or gay, none with any sort of summer job, living, it seemed, on what they collected panhandling. The neighbors had complained about the condition of the overgrown yard where several empty beer cans had taken up residence, so an all-out effort was made that afternoon to clean up.

Lavinia sat on the porch, on a wobbly kitchen stool, and watched them.

Soo Lin was sixteen, obese, long-haired, and born a boy. Her dream was to undergo surgery to become the female God had intended her to be, for along with her dislike of her given gender was a deep Christian faith that brightened her black eyes and softened her voice whenever she spoke of the Almighty.

So, God made a mistake? Is that it?

Lavinia held her tongue.

Franny was also sixteen, tall, and even thinner than Lavinia, with a shaved head and a tattoo behind her right ear that said "la femme." Lavinia didn't know if these words were a celebration of the female sex or simply to identify the bearer as a member. Franny was a lesbian. Her girlfriend, Cara, had just gone back home to her parents.

"Couldn't hack the hand-to-mouth thing, I guess," Franny said with no trace of grief. Lavinia decided she was a practical soul who could take things as they came.

That left Rooster, Chuck's friend, formerly Rhonda. Rooster also came from Moses Lake. She was the oldest at seventeen, with a yellow mohawk Lavinia found unfortunate. Cultivating one's personal style—one's brand—was fine. But deliberate ugliness? Never.

The rent was paid by Soo Lin's older brother, a computer coder living in Los Angeles. Their parents had forbidden him to have anything to do with her. They'd emigrated from China at a time when people were being persecuted for individual expression. Their fear for their son's (daughter's) welfare had ended in a schism neither side would mend. The brother, however, refused to let his brother (sister) live on the street.

There were three bedrooms. Soo Lin and Franny shared one, Chuck and Rooster shared the other—everyone sleeping on the floor on mattresses, under thin, filthy sheets. The third room had a couch. This was generously offered to Lavinia for the kindness she'd shown Chuck.

She went on watching them collect their cans. Franny went around back and reappeared with a pathetic hand mower and started pushing it around the dead yard. Lavinia left her stool, took the handle from Franny, and said, "For God's sake, just let me do that!"

She made quick work of it. She told Franny to go find a rake. Franny searched the detached one-car garage and said they didn't have one.

When the cans had been stowed—after taking a while to find the box of yard waste bags— Lavinia told everyone to come inside and gather around the tiny kitchen table. There were only three chairs, so Chuck stood along with Lavinia, who patted her wrists with cool water.

"You people need to get organized," she said.

"We are," Rooster said. The gel in her peaks glistened.

"This place is a dump, and you're going to clean it up."

"It's fine," said Chuck.

"Take pride in how you live."

"You sound like my mother," Soo Lin said.

"Your mother was right."

Everyone avoided making eye contact with her. The kitchen was stuffy because the small window over the sink had been painted shut. Rooster lit a cigarette. Lavinia coughed. Rooster blew smoke in her direction. Lavinia said nothing. She pointed at Franny and Chuck and said, "Clean out that refrigerator. It stinks enough to gag a maggot." Then to Soo Lin and Rooster she said, "We're going shopping."

"Fuck that," Rooster said.

"Hey," Chuck said.

"She's not the boss of me."

"Look, dumb shit, we're talking free groceries here." Chuck got up and struggled into a pair of ancient yellow rubber gloves Lavinia had found in the bathroom. Yesterday, when she took stock of the garage, she'd also come across a bottle of bleach on a wooden table at the back under a window hung delicately with spider webs. There were no sponges anywhere—not in the kitchen drawers; or on top of the cabinets where in a former life she'd left more than one behind after a hard bout of lonely scrubbing, only to find it again when she went up there to hide Potter's booze; nor even under the sink, where sponges, in her experience, tended to randomly collect—so he used paper towels, which he tore into smaller pieces. The house had plenty of paper towels. Also, toilet paper.

Rooster got to her feet and ambled out the back door where a weather-beaten picnic table stood below a huge cedar. She sat down and continued smoking her cigarette.

"Don't worry about her. She gets like that," Soo Lin said.

Franny went on sitting, as if the chore with the lawn mower had exhausted her.

Lavinia and Soo Lin got in the car. Lavinia told Soo Lin to navigate. Soo Lin said to turn left at the bottom of the hill. She'd done a poor job of shaving that morning, and her upper lip had a line of soft black hairs. She'd badly applied pink lipstick. Lavinia used her thumb to wipe off the greasy smear below her nose. Soo Lin drew back at her touch. Lavinia motioned for her to pull down the visor and use the mirror on its back side. Soo Lin looked at herself with such scrutiny that Lavinia's heart ached.

She asked how they'd all met.

"At a rally for the LGBT community," Soo Lin said.

"How long have you been in Portland?"

"Almost a year."

"And Franny?"

"She was born here."

"Where are her parents?"

"Beaverton. It's a suburb."

"And you'll be going back to school in September?"

Soo Lin shook her head. They'd all quit.

"What? You're drop outs? You'll never get ahead that way. You have to get your GED, then think about college."

"College costs money."

Which brought Lavinia to the next question—what were they living on, besides the generosity of Soo Lin's brother?

"Food bank, mostly."

To choose poverty was the luxury of having grown up with money. Chuck's ranch had looked pretty prosperous. The thick gold ring on Soo Lin's middle finger spoke of family assets, too. They were playing at life without understanding its seriousness.

Maybe that wasn't fair, though. Each of those four young people had been driven out or felt they had no choice but to go. There was nothing easy about that.

The car in front of her braked suddenly. A squirrel sped madly to safety.

When they reached the grocery store, Lavinia told Soo Lin to go in and buy everything they would need for a week. Soo Lin looked blank.

"Can you cook?" Lavinia asked.

"Some."

"Well, all right then. Go get started. I'll be along in a minute."

Soo Lin waddled across the parking lot, her sandals flapping audibly as she went.

Lavinia locked the car and went to a bench by a second entrance to the store. She called Karen, who answered on the first ring.

"Lavinia, thank God. I got a new phone, and my contacts list didn't transfer, so I lost your number," she said.

"Angie has it."

"Oh, I didn't think of that."

"Listen. I need to ask Phil something."

"What?"

"About dealing with stubborn teenagers who aren't your own."

"You'll have to call him yourself. I moved out."

"Oh, right, of course you did. You were going to. I guess I forgot."

"You forgot?" Karen's voice had gone up a few notes. Lavinia apologized. She said she'd found herself in a strange situation, a very unexpected one, in fact, and was unusually distracted.

"You're always distracted," Karen said. Her tone, though tense, wasn't particularly mean. There was traffic noise in the background on her end. Lavinia asked where she was. On the balcony of her new apartment, she said, gazing down at the traffic on Route 13.

"And your friend, the other man, where's he?"

"Good question. I haven't heard from him for four days."

Which was exactly how long it had been since she moved out. She knew the score. She'd been dumped.

"I'd hunt him down and kick his ass if I were you."

Karen laughed, and went on laughing until Lavinia wondered if she'd come unglued.

A young guy on a skateboard rolled across the parking lot, causing an old woman pushing a cart to stop abruptly. When he reached the end, he came back the other way, faster, lifting off over the speed bumps, landing loudly, all the while controlling the board with the angle of his body. He sailed one way, then another in a long S-shape, making cars have to stop and slow to avoid hitting him. He was oblivious.

Lavinia couldn't decide if he were brave or a complete idiot. Sometimes the two were one and the same. Before Chip died, she wouldn't have had the guts to take off across country on her own, yet her courage had been tinged with idiocy. She looked at her still-healing wrist. She no longer was confident that she would be glad to look down and see his name inscribed there every day for the rest of her life.

"It's a fine line," she said.

"What is?" Karen asked.

"Between being tough enough to do something you never dreamed of doing before and being stupid."

"You're saying I shouldn't have left, that I should go back."

"No, no, not at all."

The skateboarder raced toward the overhang where Lavinia sat, grateful for its shade, and stopped short just in front of her. He got off the board and asked if he could bum a cigarette. Lavinia shook her head. Then he asked for spare change.

"Beat it," she said.

He gave her the finger and sped off.

"Who the hell was that?" Karen asked. Lavinia explained, then said she had to go, someone was waiting for her inside the store. Karen asked what store. Lavinia said it wasn't important and that she would be sure to call her later tonight, knowing she wouldn't.

Soo Lin had filled her grocery cart with boxes of cereal, cookies, crackers, and ice cream. There were also two gallons of milk, chocolate syrup, strawberry syrup, plastic cups, paper plates, and a bottle of lavender-scented shampoo. In the part where a small child sits were two boxes of Kotex pads.

"Oh, give me that," Lavinia said. She took control of the cart, went through the whole store with Soo Lin in tow, and added eggs, butter, cheese, bread, apples, bananas, peanut butter, two pounds of ground beef although Soo Lin said they were all vegetarian, four packages of sponges, and a manicure kit. At the checkout, the total came to over two hundred dollars.

"Why are you doing this?" Soo Lin asked her.

"Because I'm your fairy godmother."

Soo Lin was in the process of putting her credit card away when Lavinia caught sight of it.

"I thought you were broke," Lavinia said.

"They are. I'm not."

"Then next time it's on you."

As they put bag after bag into Lavinia's trunk, she became aware that the daylight was unusually bright. That and a familiar pain behind her eyes told her she was running a low-grade fever. She'd planned to get to the coast no later than tomorrow. She didn't like the idea of driving sick, but she could probably manage it.

By early afternoon, she was flat on her back on her assigned couch, teeth chattering, muttering orders for aspirin, water, and a thermometer. Only water was on hand. Could any of them drive? Rooster had a license. Lavinia told her where the car keys were and said to take Soo Lin along for the use of her credit card. They were gone a long time, it seemed, though each said it was less than half an hour. The aspirin caused her to break out in a sweat. She then demanded that her sheets be washed, her clothes, too. Could one of them dig through her things and find her nightgown?

As the summer twilight slowly fell, Lavinia wondered if she'd been stupid. What would keep them from running off with her car, her wallet, and her hefty diamond buried deep down in Foster's old backpack? She couldn't stop them. She couldn't even make a call because her phone was dead.

She slept in bits. Chip paid her a visit; so did Potter and Angie. Alma told her to take it easy, even though everything was still up in the air. Sandy made so much noise with her mindless cawing that Lavinia begged Chuck to take her from the room.

Franny's aunt was a public health nurse, and she was summoned on Lavinia's behalf the next morning. Her hands were cold. Lavinia didn't like them on her neck and throat, pulling down her lower eyelids. The stethoscope was icy on her back and chest.

"Lungs are clear," a voice said. "She needs to get more calories on board. She's underweight and malnourished."

The voices went on for a little longer. They spoke of going to the zoo.

"We've got chicken and cream of mushroom," one said.

"Great. And push the fluids. Gatorade, if you have it."

"Is she going to be all right?"

"As long as there's no secondary infection."

Then there were more hands; spoons in her mouth; hot liquid; being helped to the toilet and back to the couch; cold water dabbed on her face.

"Potter."

"Did she say water?"

"Give her some."

Lavinia pushed the hand away.

That day and the next passed the same way. Feeling freezing alternated with being soaked in sweat. There were bright circles behind her closed eyelids. Everything hurt. When her mind cleared, she thought of Chip standing on the green, looking at the sky as the storm closed down on him. She worried about the house and what to do with it. She couldn't go on living there. She knew that now. Then her thoughts grew random and wild again. On the night of the third day, she woke up drenched, calm, and clear-headed. It was over.

In the morning, she sat up and looked for her phone on the table at the end of the couch. It wasn't there. Someone had put it on the windowsill. It was as dead as ever. Where the hell was the charger? Bending over to look through the small backpack made her feel weak and wobbly, but she persisted. When she found it, she plugged the phone in and made her way slowly to the kitchen, where she stood with one hand on the door jamb and watched Rooster wash dishes.

"Hi," Lavinia said.

Rooster turned.

"You shouldn't be up," she said.

"Fever's gone."

"Still. You need one more day at least."

Lavinia sat down at the table.

"I don't suppose anyone around here drinks coffee," she said.

"All we got is instant."

"It'll do."

Rooster turned on the stove under the tea kettle. She put a spoonful of tiny brown pellets into a coffee mug decorated with a picture of Mount Hood.

"Chuck and Franny are washing your car. They borrowed the neighbor's hose. At least, I think they asked. They might not have."

"That's awfully nice of them. They really don't need to."

"They're probably bored."

"Oh. Who moved my phone, by the way?" she asked.

"Chuck, I think."

"Why?"

"He was looking at it."

"What for?"

"To find a number he could call, in case you got worse."

"He wouldn't have known who to try."

"Anyone would have been a start. Besides, it was dead."

"Yeah, it ran out of juice. I just plugged it in."

Rooster lit herself a cigarette and put Lavinia's coffee in front of her. She asked if she were hungry.

"You're really a nice person, in your way, aren't you?" Lavinia asked.

Rooster shrugged.

"It's just too bad …"

"That I look like a freak?"

"No!"

"It's what you meant."

Lavinia sipped her coffee. It was surprisingly good. Rooster had added sugar, though Lavinia hadn't asked for it. She loved it. She'd take it that way from now on.

"Is the way a person looks so important?" Rooster asked. Sweat was slick on her neck and chest.

"Sometimes."

Rooster's expression was smug, pitying.

"You think so, too, or you wouldn't do your hair like that," Lavinia said.

Rooster smoked her cigarette. Lavinia couldn't quite read her then. She was dragged down by a wave of exhaustion and hunger. Her condition must have been obvious because Rooster said, "I'm making you some food."

Her skill breaking eggs one-handed said she was no stranger in the kitchen. She volunteered that she'd grown up in one, at her grandparent's place.

"Cowboys eat a lot, three times a day like clockwork, and they're not patient when their stomachs are empty."

"But ranch life didn't suit you any more than it suited Chuck," Lavinia said. She was already half-way through the pile of buttery scrambled eggs Rooster had served along with two English muffins. Rooster sat opposite her, examining the gold flecks in the dingy Formica surface of the table.

"I'm pretty sure it was harder for him," Rooster said.

"How?"

Rooster looked at Lavinia with her icy blue eyes. She took another cigarette from the pack on the table, then put it back.

She scratched her chin. Soo Lin thumped loudly up the basement stairs with a basket of clean laundry in her arms. She put it on the floor and peered at Lavinia.

"You're better," she said. Her smile was warm and charming. Lavinia extended her hand, and Soo Lin took it. After a moment, Lavinia felt awkward and let go. She wasn't sure why she'd reached out. Habit, maybe, particularly when she felt motherly. Did she, though?

Soon she needed to lie down again and rest. When she woke, the light was dimmer, and the room had cooled a little. She got up briefly to use the bathroom. Soo Lin brought a pile of folded clothes into the room and put them next to Lavinia's backpack. She asked what Lavinia wanted for dinner. Lavinia had no idea.

Chuck and Franny stopped by. They said her car was nice and clean, even on the inside because they'd gotten on a roll. They'd been careful not to mess up her stuff—those old flowers in the plastic box, the thimbles (at least that's what they looked like from the outside), and that vase. Franny liked it because you could see it was done by an amateur. The bear had been brought inside the first day of Lavinia's illness and was at the opposite end of the couch, listing calmly to one side. Chuck picked it up and put it in Lavinia's out-stretched hand.

A little while later she got off the couch, feeling close to strong. She took a long shower, and saw that the stall had been cleaned. Afterward, she wiped the steam from the mirror. It gave back dark circles below her eyes, and pale skin. But she felt well. That was all that mattered. Back in her room, she counted the money in her wallet. It was all there. She put forty dollars in the pocket of her blue jeans—Chuck's again because they were way more comfortable than the ones she'd bought in Helena—got into a tank top, and went into the living room. Chuck and Franny were playing a game of cards. Rooster was in back, at the picnic table, reading. Lavinia asked her to come in for a moment. Soo Lin was outside talking on her cell phone in Chinese. Her left hand jabbed at the air every now and then. She paced as she spoke.

"Order a pizza," Lavinia told the group. "On me."

"You done enough," Chuck said.

"You're the ones who've done enough. Thank you so much for taking care of me."

"No problemo."

Such sentiment!

"Besides, it's my last night," she said.

"Really? Are you going to the coast?" Chuck asked.

"Yes."

Franny and Chuck exchanged an excited look.

"Alone," Lavinia said.

Faces fell.

Lavinia gave Chuck the money and told him to get whatever toppings they wanted. Rooster, Franny, and Chuck debated which were best.

She thought about tomorrow, arriving at the ocean, standing there, hearing it. It was high summer, so it made sense to reserve ahead. She went and got her phone. She turned it on, and found she couldn't access Google. She typed in Mel's number as a test. That didn't work, either.

Goddamn it!

She'd have to drive into town, find a store, and get them to tell her what was wrong with it.

Soo Lin gave her directions, found on her own phone when her call finally came to an end. It hadn't gone well, apparently. Lavinia wondered if the brother were threatening to cut her off. Or if the parents had gotten even uglier about the whole situation.

It's not your problem! Go fix your phone!

The sweaty young man at the phone store explained, in a cheerful, almost bouncy tone, that she'd let her service lapse.

"That's impossible!"

He turned his computer monitor around to show her the billing history on the account. She'd missed two bills, which were no doubt sitting in the growing stack on Chip's desk.

"They would have sent you several text messages about it," the man said.

"Oh, is that what those were? I figured it was some promotion or an offer to upgrade, so I ignored them."

"Gotcha."

He told her how much to pay to reinstate the account and make the phone operable. Lavinia gave him her card.

"Will it take long?" she asked.

"It's processing right now. Turn it off, and turn it on again."

She did. There were several voicemails. She went outside to listen to them in the car.

Mel's was anxious.

"No one knows where you are! Are you all right?"

She'd talked to Sam back at the diner where she'd picked up Chuck, and that was what, six days ago? Of course, she'd called Karen the day she got sick, but she wouldn't have contacted anyone else.

Alma's said she got the postcards but couldn't find the address book, at least it wasn't where Lavinia said it was, and

347

she wasn't about to turn the house upside down, thank you very much.

Angie was stoic. She understood that Lavinia really needed to put distance between herself and home. That said, it would relieve everyone a lot if she'd take the time to check in.

Patty was a little put out that the others had been calling her to find out where the hell she was, and though she'd been tempted to suggest that she was possibly with Craig, she didn't.

Marta was going after the theater guy full force now; he had another thing coming if he thought he was going to avoid *her*. Oh, and Angie had asked if she'd heard from her. It seemed no one had.

Maggie apologized that she wouldn't be able to pay her back for a little while longer, because she lost the barista job after only two days—and no, it hadn't been her fault. By the way, where was she, exactly?

Timothy didn't know why everyone was so flipped out; she was a grown woman after all, and if anything truly awful had happened, they would have heard.

Foster had gotten a pet from work, a black and white mutt whose owner was too old to care for it any longer. He was working on a name—it had been called Do-Do for years, so maybe it would never answer to anything else, but in his experience with dogs, they were fairly flexible creatures.

Karen caught her boyfriend, well ex-boyfriend, in a bar with another woman, which pissed her off to no end, but it didn't mean she was about to waltz back to Phil, because that boat had already sailed. Oh, and Lily was taking it all pretty well, despite still having morning sickness up to her eyeballs, the poor thing.

Craig understood if she didn't want to talk to him for a while, but he did want her to know he didn't usually make it a habit to try to track anyone down, particularly a woman.

And then, "I got to admit I'm worried. I know you've been unhappy, probably for a long time, and a lot of that is no doubt still my fault. I never figured you'd just up and cut us all off like that, but I understand, at least I'm trying to. When you surface, you don't have to let me know, just tell one of the kids; they'll pass it along." A long pause followed. "So, I hope you're having fun out there, wherever you are. That's about it for now. I love you."

Lavinia put her head on the steering wheel.

Loved her how? As a friend? As the mother of his children?

Knock it off.

349

She called Angie, explained about the unpaid bill, and told her to tell everyone she was okay, alive and well. No, she didn't know when she'd be home yet. She had to wait and see. Oh, and one last thing. Would she mind buying a bottle of Shalimar and sending it to Aunt Patty? She'd explain later. She said nothing of being sick, figuring she'd worried everyone enough already.

chapter twenty-two

Walking barefoot in the sand wasn't as great as everyone said it was. For one thing, it was very difficult to get any sort of traction when it was dry. Where it was wet and compacted, walking was easier, but then you had to rinse it off unless you didn't mind tracking it across the carpet. She was in a nice ocean-front room, with Haystack rock to the right, where a large flock of seagulls swooped and dove, crying out some private message to their fellows. Not long after she checked in, one had perched for a little while on the metal railing of her porch, surprising her with its size. She'd never seen one up close before. The town of Cannon Beach itself wasn't much, but it was amusing enough with its galleries and taverns. Lavinia had been through all the galleries but only one tavern in the two days she'd been there.

The day she arrived marked exactly one month since she'd left Dunston. Sometimes, she'd felt more alive during those thirty-one days than she ever had. Other times, none of it seemed real, until her eye fell on her tattoo or Chuck's blue jeans folded in her backpack or the thimbles lined up on the dresser next to the television set she didn't turn on, preferring the novels she'd bought at the dingy yet dignified bookstore in town.

The first story involved three children who vie for the mother's affection, which is given in large part to her second husband. The mother is a widow. The second husband is a widower, and they commit to forging a fierce and binding love.

But after a sudden prolonged illness, the husband strays, as if the weakness in his body clarified his true desire. He wants not his recent bride, but her young housekeeper, a sweet, dull-witted girl. This revelation occurs, somewhat conveniently, in a moonlit garden.

The mother accuses her children of not showing him enough acceptance and respect. The children are all young adults at that point, and don't care for their mother's criticism. They're not afraid of her anymore, only disappointed, except for the middle child, the only boy, whose heart remains tender.

The second is again about a woman cast adrift by a reversal of fortune. She's never been married, in love only once with a man she works for, a driven, ambitious soul who ignores her increasingly desperate gestures and pleas. His business fails; she's out of a job, homeless, loveless, driven further and further into despair. She decides to throw herself off a bridge, and when she gets to the tallest point of the span, someone is already there, contemplating his own end. She talks him out of it, and together they walk back to safety.

In the evening, with the setting sun bearing through the sliding glass door, Lavinia pulled the blind until the light eased, and then sat, wine glass in hand, and watched it drop into the sea. She focused on the horizon until sky and water became one, then sat on while the stars came out.

On her third night, some kids lit a bonfire on the beach. She joined them. She recognized a couple of them from the hotel, freed from their parents for the evening. One had smuggled a six-pack of beer. Another had a joint. They talked about an absent friend and the trouble she'd gotten into during the school year. Lavinia refused the offer of beer and a drag of the joint, preferring just to sit dreamily with their voices in her ear, the flames warming her skin, the sound of the surf before her, its white foam pulling and pushing so leisurely in the moonlight. She leaned back and gazed upward.

You know I truly loved you, right?

"You're not from around here," one of the boys said to her.

"No."

"Where, then?"

"Upstate New York."

"Long way."

"Yes."

353

"Vacation?"

"More like a scavenger hunt."

After a while the group disbanded, and Lavinia returned to her room.

She woke in the early morning to take stock of the fact that it was now the month of August. And another Sunday. These were simple truths. Another was that it was time to go home. But not by car. She'd sell it and buy herself a plane ticket.

And then? Once she'd walked back through the door of that big, empty house?

Begin again.

THE END

about the author

Anne Leigh Parrish is the author of five previously published books: *Women Within*, a novel (Black Rose Writing, 2017); *By the Wayside*, stories (Unsolicited Press, 2017); *What Is Found, What Is Lost*, a novel (She Writes Press, 2014); *Our Love Could Light The World*, stories (She Writes Press, 2013); and *All The Roads That Lead From Home*, stories (Press 53, 2011). Her short stories have been published widely in literary venues. Her essays have appeared in *Book Riot, Writer's Digest,* and *Women Writers, Women's Books.*

about the press

Unsolicited Press is a small publishing house operated by dedicated volunteers with extensive backgrounds in the publishing industry. You can read more books from Unsolicited Press – check out their catalog at www.unsolicitedpress.com

CPSIA information can be obtained
at www.ICGtesting.com
Printed in the USA
LVHW090543030519
616432LV00001BA/130/P